THE
LAST TIME
WE SAY
GOODBYE

ALSO BY CYNTHIA HAND

UNEARTHLY

HALLOWED

BOUNDLESS

RADIANT: AN UNEARTHLY NOVELLA
(available as an ebook only)

THE LAST TIME

WE SAY

GOODBYE

CYNTHIA HAND

HARPER TEEN

An Imprint of HarperCollinsPublishers

HarperTeen is an imprint of HarperCollins Publishers.
The Last Time We Say Goodbye
Copyright © 2015 by Cynthia Hand

Library of Congress Cataloging-in-Publication Data
Hand, Cynthia, 1978- author.
The last time we say goodbye / Cynthia Hand. — First edition.
pages cm
Summary: After her younger brother, Tyler, commits suicide, Lex struggles to work through her
grief in the face of a family that has fallen apart, the sudden distance between her and her friends, and
memories of Tyler that still feel all too real.
ISBN 978-0-06-231847-3 (hardcover)
[1. Grief—Fiction. 2. Family problems—Fiction. 3. Suicide—Fiction.] I. Title.
PZ7.H1917Las 2015   2014038645
[Fic]—dc23   CIP
                                                                                         AC

Typography by Ellice M. Lee
15 16 17 18   PC/RRDH   10 9 8 7 6 5 4 3
❖
First Edition

FOR JEFF.

Because this is the only way I know to reach for you.

Help your brother's boat across,

        and your own will reach the shore.

—Hindu proverb

5 February

First I'd like to state for the record that the whole notion of writing this down was not my idea. It was Dave's. My therapist's. He thinks I'm having trouble expressing my feelings, which is why he suggested I write in a journal—to get it out, he said, like in the old days when physicians used to bleed their patients in order to drain the mysterious poisons. Which almost always ended up killing them in spite of the doctors' good intentions, I might point out.

Our conversation went something like this:

He wanted me to start taking antidepressants.

I told him to stick it where the sun don't shine.

So we were at a bit of an impasse.

"Let's take a new approach," he said finally, and reached behind him and produced a small black book. He held it out to me. I took it, thumbed it open, then looked up at him, confused.

The book was blank.

"I thought you might try writing, as an alternative," he said.

"That's a moleskin notebook," he elaborated when all I did was stare at him. "Hemingway used to write in those."

"An alternative to what?" I asked. "To Xanax?"

"I want you to try it for a week," he said. "Writing, I mean."

I tried to hand the journal back to him. "I'm not a writer."

"I've found that you can be quite eloquent, Alexis, when you choose to be."

"Why? What's the point?"

"You need an outlet," he said. "You're keeping everything inside, and it's not good for you."

Nice, I thought. Next he'd be telling me to eat my vegetables and take my vitamins and be sure to get 8 uninterrupted hours of sleep every night.

"Right. And you would be reading it?" I asked, because there's not even a remote possibility that I'm going to be doing that. Talking about my unexpectedly tragic life for an hour every week is bad enough. No way I'm going to pour my thoughts out into a book so that he can take it home and scrutinize my grammar.

"No," Dave answered. "But hopefully you might feel comfortable enough someday to talk with me about what you've written."

Not likely, I thought, but what I said was, "Okay. But don't expect Hemingway."

I don't know why I agreed to it. I try to be a good little patient, I guess.

Dave looked supremely pleased with himself. "I don't want you to be Hemingway. Hemingway was an ass. I want you to write whatever

2

strikes you. Your daily life. Your thoughts. Your feelings."

I don't have feelings, I wanted to tell him, but instead I nodded, because he seemed so expectant, like the status of my mental health entirely depended on my cooperation with writing in the stupid journal.

But then he said, "And I think for this to be truly effective, you should also write about Tyler."

Which made all the muscles in my jaw involuntarily tighten.

"I can't," I managed to get out from between my teeth.

"Don't write about the end," Dave said. "Try to write about a time when he was happy. When you were happy, together."

I shook my head. "I can't remember." And this is true. Even after almost 7 weeks, a mere 47 days of not interacting with my brother every day, not hurling peas at him across the kitchen table, not seeing him in the halls at school and acting, as any dutiful older sister would, for the sake of appearances, like he bugged me, Ty's image has grown hazy in my mind. I can't visualize the Ty that isn't dead. My brain gravitates toward the end. The body. The coffin. The grave.

I can't even begin to pull up happy.

"Focus on the firsts and the lasts," Dave instructed. "It will help you remember. For example: About twenty years ago I owned an '83 Mustang. I put a lot of work into that car, and I loved it more than I should probably admit, but now, all these years later, I can't fully picture it. But if I think about the firsts and the lasts with the Mustang, I could tell you about the first time I drove it, or the last time I took it on a long road trip, or the first time I spent an hour in the backseat with the woman who would become my wife, and then I see it so clearly." He cleared his throat. "It's those key moments that burn bright in our minds."

3

This is not a car, I thought. This is my brother.

Plus I thought Dave might have just been telling me about having sex with his wife. Which was the last thing I wanted to picture.

"So that's your official assignment," he said, sitting back as if that settled it. "Write about the last time you remember Tyler being happy."

Which brings me to now.

Writing in a journal about how I don't want to be writing in a journal.

I'm aware of the irony.

Seriously, though, I'm not a writer. I got a 720 on the writing section of the SAT, which is decent enough, but nobody ever pays any attention to that score next to my perfect 800 in math. I've never kept a diary. Dad got me one for my 13th birthday, a pink one with a horse on it. It ended up on the back of my bookshelf with a copy of the <u>NIV Teen Study Bible</u> and the <u>Seventeen Ultimate Guide to Beauty</u> and all the other stuff that was supposed to prepare me for life from ages 13 to 19—as if I could ever be prepared for that. Which is all still there, 5 years later, gathering dust.

That's not me. I was born with numbers on the brain. I think in equations. What I would do, if I could really put this pen to paper and produce something useful, is take my memories, these fleeting, painful moments of my life, and find some way to add and subtract and divide them, insert variables and move them, try to isolate them, to discover their elusive meanings, to translate them from possibilities to certainties.

I would try to solve myself. Find out where it all went wrong. How I got here, from A to B, A being the Alexis Riggs who was so sure of herself, who was smart and solid and laughed a lot and cried occasionally and didn't fail at the most important things.

To this.

But instead, the blank page yawns at me. The pen feels unnatural in my hand. It's so much weightier than pencil. Permanent. There are no erasers, in life.

I would cross out everything and start again.

1.

MOM IS CRYING AGAIN THIS MORNING. She does this thing lately where it's like a faucet gets turned on inside her at random times. We'll be grocery shopping or driving or watching TV, and I'll glance over and she'll be silently weeping, like she's not even aware she's doing it—no sobbing or wailing or sniffling, just a river of tears flowing down her face.

So. This morning. Mom cooks breakfast, just like she's done nearly every single morning of my life. She scrapes the scrambled eggs onto my plate, butters the toast, pours me a glass of orange juice, and sets it all on the kitchen table.

Crying the entire time.

When she does the waterworks thing, I try to act like nothing is out of the ordinary, like it's perfectly normal for your mother to be weeping over your breakfast. Like it doesn't get to me. So I say something chipper like, "This looks great, Mom. I'm starved," and start pushing the burned food around my plate in a way that I hope will convince her I'm eating.

If this was before, if Ty were here, he'd make her laugh. He'd blow bubbles in his chocolate milk. He'd make a face out of his bacon and eggs, and pretend to talk with it, and scream like he was in the middle of a slasher film as he slowly ate one of the eyes.

Ty knew how to fix things. I don't.

Mom sits down across from me, tears dripping off her chin, and folds her hands in her lap. I stop fake-eating and bow my head, because even though I quit believing in God awhile ago, I don't want to complicate things by confessing my budding atheism to my mother. Not now. She has enough to deal with.

But instead of praying she wipes her wet face with her napkin and looks up at me with shining eyes, her eyelashes stuck damply together. She takes a deep breath, the kind of breath you take when you're about to say something important. And she smiles.

I can't remember the last time I saw her smile.

"Mom?" I say. "Are you okay?"

And that's when she says it. The crazy thing. The thing I don't know how to handle.

She says:

"I think your brother is still in the house."

She goes on to explain that last night she woke from a dead sleep for no reason. She got up for a glass of wine and a Valium. To help her get back to sleep, she says. She was standing at the kitchen sink when, out of the blue, she smelled my brother's cologne. All around her, she says.

Like he was standing next to her, she says.

It's distinctive, that cologne. Ty purchased it for himself two Christmases ago in like a half-gallon bottle from Walmart, this giant radioactive-sludge-green container of Brut—"the essence of man," the box had bragged. Whenever my brother wore that stuff, which was pretty often, that smell would fill the room. It was like a cloud floating six feet ahead of him as he walked down the hall at school. And it's not that it smelled bad, exactly, but it forced you into this weird takeover of the senses. *SMELL ME,* it demanded. *Don't I smell manly? HERE I COME.*

I swallow a bite of eggs and try to think of something helpful to say.

"I'm pretty sure that bottle gives off some kind of spontaneous emissions," I tell her finally. "And the house is drafty."

There you go, Mom. Perfectly logical explanation.

"No, Lexie," she says, shaking her head, the remains of the strange smile still lingering at the corners of her mouth. "He's here. I can feel it."

The thing is, she doesn't look crazy. She looks hopeful. Like the past seven weeks have all been a bad dream. Like she hasn't lost him. Like he isn't dead.

This is going to be a problem, I think.

2.

I RIDE THE BUS TO SCHOOL. I know it's a bold statement to make as a senior, especially one who owns a car, but in the age-old paradox of choosing between time and money, I'll choose money every time. I live in the sleepy little town of Raymond, Nebraska (population 179), but I attend school in the sprawling metropolis of Lincoln (population 258,379). The high school is 12.4 miles away from my house. That's 24.8 miles round trip. My crappy old Kia Rio (which I not-so-affectionately refer to as "the Lemon") gets approximately 29 miles to the gallon, and gas in this neck of Nebraska costs an average of $3.59 per gallon. So driving to school would cost me $3.07 a day. There are 179 days of school this year, which adds up to a whopping $549.53, all so I can have an extra 58 minutes of my day.

It's a no-brainer. I have college to pay for next year. I have serious savings, a plan. Part of that plan involves taking the school bus.

I actually liked the bus. Before, I mean. When I used to be

able to put in my earbuds and crank up the Bach and watch the sun come up over the white, empty cornfields and the clichéd sun-beaten farmhouses tucked back from the road. The windmills outside turning. Cows huddling together for warmth. Birds—gray-slated junco and chickadees and the occasional bright flashes of cardinals—slipping effortlessly through the winter air. It was quiet and cozy and nice.

But since Ty died, I feel like everybody on the bus is watching me, some people out of sympathy, sure, ready to rush over with a tissue at a moment's notice, but others like I've become something dangerous. Like I have the bad gene in my blood, like my sad life is something that could be transmitted through casual contact. Like a disease.

Yeah, well, screw them.

Of course, being angry is pointless. Unproductive. They don't understand yet. That they are all waiting for that one phone call that will change everything. That every one of them will feel like me eventually. Because someone they love will die. It's one of life's cruel certainties.

So with that in mind I try to ignore them, turn up my music, and read. And I don't look up until we've gone the twelve miles to school.

This week I'm rereading *A Beautiful Mind*, which is a biography of the mathematician John Nash. There was a movie, which had entirely too little math, in my opinion, but was otherwise okay. The book is great stuff. I like thinking about how Nash saw our behavior as mathematical. That was his genius, even if he did go crazy and start to see imaginary people: he understood the connections between numbers and the physical world, between our actions and the invisible equations that govern them.

Take my mother, for instance, and her announcement that my brother is still with us. She's trying to restructure our universe so that Ty doesn't disappear. Like the way a fish will thrash its body on the sand when it's beached, an involuntary reaction, a survival mechanism, in hopes that it might rock its way back into the water.

Mom is trying to find her way back to the water. It makes sense, if I look at it from that angle.

Not that it's healthy. Not that I know what to do about it.

I don't for a second believe that Ty is still in our house. He's gone. The minute the life left him, the minute the neurons in his brain quit firing, he stopped being my brother. He became a collection of dead cells. And is now, thanks to the miracles of the modern embalming process, well on his way to becoming a coffin full of green goo.

I will never see him again.

The thought brings back the hole in my chest. This keeps happening, every few days since the funeral. It feels like a giant gaping cavity opens up between my third and fourth ribs on the left side, an empty space that reveals the vinyl bus seat behind my shoulder blades. It hurts, and my whole body tightens with the pain, my jaw locking and my fists clenching and my breath freezing in my lungs. I always feel like I could die, when it happens. Like I *am* dying. Then, as suddenly as it comes on, the hole fills in again. I can breathe. I try to swallow, but my mouth has gone bone dry.

The hole is Ty, I think.

The hole is something like grief.

School is largely uneventful. I float through on autopilot, lost in thoughts of John Nash and beached fish and the logistics of how currents of air could have carried the scent of my brother's cologne from where it sits all dusty by the sink in the basement bathroom through the den, up the stairs, to the kitchen to utterly confuse my mother.

Then I hit what used to be the best class of the day: sixth period, Honors Calculus Lab. I like to call it Nerd Central, the highest concentration of the smartest people in the school you'll ever be likely to find in a given place.

My home sweet home.

The point of this class is to give the students time to study and do their calculus homework. But because we are nerds, we all finish our homework in the first ten minutes of class. Then we spend the rest of the hour playing cards: poker, war, hearts, rummy, whatever strikes our fancy.

Our teacher, the brilliant and mathtastic Miss Mahoney, sits at her desk at the front of the room and pretends that we're doing serious scholarly work. Because it's kind of her free period, too, since the school budget cutbacks eliminated her prep hour.

She has a thing for cat videos on YouTube.

We've all got our weaknesses.

So there we are, playing a rousing game of five-card draw.

I'm killing it. I have three aces. Which is a lovely math problem all on its own—the probability of getting three aces in one hand is 94/54,145 or (if you want to talk odds) 575 to 1, which is pretty freaking unlikely, when you think about it.

Jill is sitting on my left, twirling a lock of her bright red hair around her finger. I think she means the hair twirling to look like some kind of tell, as if she has an amazing hand, but it probably means just the opposite. Eleanor is sitting on my right, and she has a lousy hand, which I know because she just comes out and says, "I have a lousy hand," and folds. That's El—she says what she thinks, no filter.

Which brings us to Steven, who is sitting across from me with a very good hand. How do I know? He's trying to be all stone-faced, which he fails at in every way. It's one of the things I used to like so much about Steven—his inability to hide his feelings. You can reliably see what's going on in his head through those big brown eyes of his. Which at the moment are definitely happy about the cards he's been dealt.

So yeah, he has a good hand, but three aces good? Probably not.

"I'll see your bet, and raise you fifty Skittles." I count and push the candy into the center of the table.

The players suck in a collective breath—that's a lot of candy.

Steven looks at me dubiously.

"Well?" I say, a challenge, and I think, *Just because we broke up doesn't mean I have to go easy on you. Just because something bad happened doesn't mean you have to go easy on me.*

But before he can respond, Miss Mahoney calls my name.

"Alexis, can I talk to you for a minute?"

Singling me out. That can't be good.

I put my cards facedown on the table and make my reluctant way over to her desk. She's chewing on her bottom lip, another ominous sign.

"What's up?" I chirp.

"I wanted to talk to you about this."

She pushes a piece of paper across her desk toward me.

Last week's midterm.

Worth 25 percent of my total grade.

Upon which, next to my name, is scrawled a big red *71%*.

I push my glasses up on my nose and scan the innocuous piece of paper, aghast. Apparently I got the answers to three whole problems outright wrong, and she gave me only partial credit on a fourth problem. Out of ten.

71 percent.

Practically a D.

I swallow. I don't know what to say.

"I know this stuff," I say hoarsely after a few excruciating seconds, looking it over yet again, seeing my own glaring errors so plainly it feels like some kind of cruel practical joke.

There goes my 4.0, I think. Boom.

"I'm sorry," Miss Mahoney says quietly, as if everybody in the room isn't already straining to hear this conversation. "I can let you retake it on Friday, if you think that would help."

It takes me a few seconds to understand. What she is sorry for.

Why she's offering me a do-over when she never gives do-overs. Your grade is a fact, she always says. You must learn to deal with the facts.

I straighten.

"No. I'll take it." I grab the edge of the paper and pull it toward me, pick it up, fold it in half to hide the grade. "I'll do better on the final."

She nods. "I'm so sorry, Lex," she says again.

My chin lifts. "For what?" I ask, like I don't know. "You didn't bomb the test. I did."

"I know things have been hard since Tyler . . ."

And she pauses.

God, I hate that pause, while the person speaking searches for the most watered-down way to say *died*, like calling it by another name is going to make it any less awful: terms like *laid to rest*, like death's some kind of nap; *passed* or *departed*, like it's a vacation; *expired*, which is supposed to be more technical but really sounds like the deceased is a carton of milk, a date stamped on them, after which they become—well, sour milk.

"Killed himself," I fill in for Miss Mahoney.

At least I'm determined to be straight about it. My brother killed himself. In our garage. With a hunting rifle. This makes it sound like the most morbid game of Clue ever, but there it is.

The facts.

We must learn to deal with the facts.

"I'm fine," I tell her. Then, again: "I'll do better on the final."

She stares up at me, her eyes full of that terrible pity.

15

"Is there anything else?" I ask.

"No, that's—that's all, Alexis," she says. "Thank you."

I go back to the poker table. I can feel the stares of the other students on me, my friends, my classmates, most of whom I've known since at least sixth grade and have done Math Club or the Science Olympiad Team or Physics Bowl with over the past four years. All now thinking I must be so cold and clinical, to say it like that. Like I don't care. Like I clearly didn't love my brother if I can just rattle off the fact that he's dead so easily.

I sit down, slip the offending test into my backpack, and try to face my friends. Which is turning out to be kind of impossible.

Jill's eyes are shining with tears. I can't look at her, or I know she'll start full-out sobbing. Which could set off every girl in the room, except possibly El. Because hysterical girly crying, unlike suicide, is definitely contagious.

I could go, I think. I could simply walk out, down the hall, out of the school, into the frigid 21-degree afternoon and a twelve-mile walk home. Freezing to death might be preferable to this. Miss Mahoney would let me go. I wouldn't get in trouble.

But it's because I wouldn't get in trouble that I can't leave.

I can't have special treatment, not for this.

So I pick up my cards and try and totally fail to smile and say, as casually as I can manage, "Now, let's see, where were we?"

Ah, yes. Three aces.

"Lex . . . ," says El. "What grade did you—"

I point at Steven. "I believe you were going to call."

He shakes his head. "I fold." This time what's written all over his face is that he has more that he wants to say. A lot more. But he doesn't know if that's his job anymore, to try to comfort me. He doesn't know how to comfort me. So he folds.

I glance at El. She doesn't meet my eyes, but shrugs one shoulder and stares at her fingernails like she's bored. "I had the crap hand, remember?"

"Beaker?" I prompt.

Jill nods and takes a shaky breath and pushes most of her remaining Skittles to the center of the table. "I'm in," she says.

She has nothing. A pair of queens.

I put my cards down, aces up. So hooray, I win all the candy. But it feels like I've lost something so much more important.

3.

IT'S LATER THAT NIGHT WHEN IT HAPPENS.

It's a typical night, post-Ty. I'm in the downstairs den in my pj's, lounging in Dad's abandoned recliner. Mom is upstairs on the living room sofa, still wearing her work scrubs, reading *When Bad Things Happen to Good People*. She's highlighting every few lines, the way she does with these kinds of books that people keep giving us, like every single thing the author says is aimed directly at her. But at least she's not crying. She's not going on about ghosts. She's functional.

So I've left her studying and have spent the better part of the past few hours crunching slightly burned microwaved kettle corn and fast-forwarding through commercials on the DVR, watching *Bones*. I plan to watch reruns of season two until I get too tired to follow the plot, thus too tired to run through today's little calculus debacle over and over in my head.

The evening has pretty much been one gnarly corpse after another.

I'm trying to immunize myself to the sight of the dead. To think of us, of all the living creatures under the sun, as meat. Sour milk. Green goo. Whatever. Something that, inevitably, will rot. I don't know why, but it helps me to see death as inescapable and unavoidable and certain.

Yeah, it's messed up, I realize. But you do what you have to do.

And so it happens that at exactly 10:11, just as I am finishing up episode seventeen, I smell my brother's cologne.

Strong.

SMELL ME, it says. *HERE I COME.*

I don't have time to process this. If I could stop and process it, I would rationalize that the bottle of cologne is much closer to where I'm sitting (in the basement, only approximately fifteen feet from the basement bathroom) than it was to Mom when she smelled it upstairs last night. It would be easy to explain away.

But I don't have time to process. Because right then I glance away from the television for a split second, to check the time on my phone, and when I look up . . .

There he is.

Standing by the door to his room in his favorite jeans and a white T-shirt.

Ty.

I don't think.

I yelp and throw my phone at him.

He vanishes before it reaches him, like a bolt of lightning

flashing across the sky, his image there and then gone. My phone strikes the wall hard with a sickening crunch.

"Lexie?" calls my mother from upstairs, her voice muffled by the layers of wood and carpet between us. "What was that?"

I can't catch my breath.

Ty.

"Lex?" Mom calls again.

"I'm fine," I call. "Everything's fine. . . ." I make myself get up and go over and collect my phone. My hands are shaking as I try to assess the damage, and not just because I saw Ty. Because I've broken my phone.

Because there's something on my phone I don't ever want to lose. That I can't lose. I can't.

I push the power button and stare at the cracked black screen. My own fractured reflection stares back. I look completely freaked out.

The screen flashes.

It goes on. Reboots.

I close my eyes for a few seconds. Please, I think. Please.

Miraculously, aside from the cracked screen, the phone seems fine. I scroll through the messages, back and back, through the hundreds of concerned texts that have piled up over the past six weeks, the *so sorry to hear*s and *I'm praying for you and your family*s and *let us know if*s, to a text dated December 20.

The night Ty died.

It's still there.

My vision blurs so I can't see the words, but I don't need to see them anymore. I don't know why, really, the idea of losing this text put me in such a panic. I will never lose this text. It will be stamped in my brain for the rest of my life.

I let myself breathe. It takes me two or three good deep breaths before I can even attempt to get my head around what just happened.

Tyler.

Ty. The word is like a heartbeat.

I stare at the spot where he was standing. "Ty," I whisper.

But the room is empty.

My brother's not here.

9 February

This is pointless.

~~The last time I saw Ty~~

~~No.~~

~~It wasn't real.~~

~~The last time I saw Ty happy~~

Okay, so Ty never seemed that unhappy, really, not the kind of unhappy you need to be to

He was getting better

He'd been okay. He'd been——

Sure he was sad sometimes. Aren't we all sad sometimes?

He had his reasons for what he did:

Dad

Megan

that girl Ashley

his stupid shallow jock friends

Mom

me

the way it must have felt like nobody was ever there for him

the general suckiness of life

But then again, life bites for most of us. And we don't all exit this world via a bullet to the chest.

I should get this over with.

The last time I saw Ty happy, really and truly happy, was the night of the homecoming dance. October 11th. He'd asked a girl and she'd said yes. He was picking her up at 8. The first part I remember with him being happy was probably around 7:15, when he appeared behind me in the bathroom mirror just as I was finishing up my makeup.

He said I looked nice.

I made a face at him, because I hate makeup. I hate wearing my contacts. I hate the whole high school dance scene, really, the drama of it all, the uncomfortable dresses and the cheesy pictures and the lame punch everybody stands around sipping so they don't have to talk. I get claustrophobic around large groups of people—it's something about how stuffy the air becomes with so many bodies pressing in around you. I have to have my own space. I need to breathe.

But Steven made the argument that dances are rites of passage, and even though they are kind of torture, they are a necessary evil.

"We go so we'll have proof that we were once young," he said.

Really I think he just wanted to see me in a dress.

Anyway, Ty said I looked nice.

"Uh-huh. What do you want?" I asked, suspicious.

"I need your help," he said. "It's important, Lex, and I can't do it without you. Please."

Our eyes met in the mirror. We had the same eyes (Dad's), hazel with a circle of gold around the pupil. We had the same nose (Mom's), with the same slight bump at the bridge. We had the same brown, curly hair that always looked good on Ty with the help of a lot of product, and wild on me, because I don't care to mess with it. Whenever I looked at my brother, I was struck by how he was like a slightly improved copy of myself, in the looks department, anyway.

His expression was so serious that I instantly caved.

"Okay, sure," I said. "What is it?"

He held up a pair of Mom's tweezers. "I need you to fix my unibrow."

I pushed him away. "Yuck! No way! I am not responsible for anything hygiene-related."

"Please!" he begged.

"Do it yourself!"

"I tried. I can't. I don't know how!"

"They have salons for that kind of thing, don't they?"

"It's too late for that. I have to pick her up in less than an hour. Come on, Lex. I look like Bert from _Sesame Street_. You have to help me."

Then he turned on the puppy-dog eyes. I ended up heating the little

pot of wax I use to do my own eyebrows—I'd look like Bert, too, if I
left it up to nature, and while I might not be super concerned about my
appearance most of the time, there was an incident in 9th grade when
Jamie Bigelow called me a hairy cavewoman, and thereafter I started to
pluck and shave and generally torture myself in the name of femininity.

Ty sat on the bathroom counter while I spread the wax carefully
between his eyes. I pressed the cloth down and smoothed it in the direc-
tion of the hair growth. Ty gripped the edge of the counter, hard, and
took a deep breath.

"I trust you," I remember he said. "Don't make me look like a
freak."

"You already look like a freak," I said, but he knew I was joking.
"Okay, I'm going to count to three. . . ."

But I didn't count. I just ripped off the strip.

Ty fell backward off the counter, howling, clutching at his face.

"Ow!" he screamed. "You crazy bitch!"

I was shocked. Ty didn't swear. Neither of us did. When we were
kids, Mom was always giving us a hard time for the way we instinctively
dressed down swear words: heck, crap, dang, a-hole, butt, freaking, and
so on. If it means the same thing, Mom used to scold, why say it at all?
I guess that lecture affected us, because Ty and I couldn't seem to swear
with the proper conviction. Coming from us, bad words sounded stilted
and unnatural.

So, wow. Crazy bitch. I'd never been called a bitch before. I found
I didn't like it.

"A-hole!" I shot back in a kind of knee-jerk reaction. "Imbecilic
butthead!"

"Sadistic harpy shrew!"

"Blubbering manchild!" I retorted.

"Gleeful hair snatcher!"

"Dick!" I yelled awkwardly.

Then we were laughing. Hard. We laughed and laughed, the clutch-your-sides type of laughing where you end up almost crying. We laughed until it hurt. Then we both sighed, and Ty rubbed his face, and we went back to the mirror to inspect my work.

Which didn't look good.

Because the hair was gone—that much was true—but now there was a hot pink stripe of angry skin between Ty's eyebrows. It looked like he'd been attacked by a neon highlighter.

"Uh-oh," I snickered.

"Lex . . . ," he said, "what did you do to me?"

I told him it would be better tomorrow.

He gave me a look.

Then he told me how he really liked this girl he was taking to the dance—Ashley, he said her name was—and he wanted to impress her, and I had just basically ruined his life.

"Hold on, don't get your undies in a wad." I got out a cotton ball to apply the soothing oil that comes with the wax.

The soothing oil, unfortunately, did not live up to its name. We waited 10 minutes post-oil, and his face still looked like someone had branded him between the eyes with a hot iron.

We tried icing it. We tried lotion. We tried hemorrhoid cream, which was one of my more ingenious ideas, but at the end of all that his face was, if anything, pinker.

"Lex," he said. "I think I have to strangle you now."

He was only half kidding.

"There's only one thing left to do," I said gravely.

I held up my bottle of foundation.

He didn't fight it. He stood still while I painted on a layer of Clinique Stay-Matte Oil-Free foundation carefully between his brows. It was a shade too light for his skin, but better than the pink. I also had to cover a large portion of his forehead, so it would blend in.

"Well, now I feel totally emasculated," he said when I was finished.

"Shut up or I'll get out the lipstick," I teased, and then he ran away, downstairs to apply his cologne and finish getting ready. A few minutes later Mom came home from work, and before we left she made Ty and me stand together by the front door for a picture.

"Look at my two beautiful children," I remember she said. Ty slung his arm around me, and I leaned my head into his shoulder, and we smiled. The camera flashed. Mom turned away to dig something out of her purse, and Ty suddenly kissed my cheek, the gross, slobbery razz sort of kiss, which made me pull away and punch him in the shoulder.

"Get out of here, brat," I said, wiping at my cheek.

Mom handed him her car keys.

"Midnight," she said.

"Aye, aye, Captain," he answered.

She squinted up into his face. "Are you wearing . . . makeup?"

He shrugged like he had no idea what she was talking about.

"Well, you look nice," she said after a minute.

He did. His suit fit him perfectly, and he was dashing in it. Of course I didn't say that, because I was his sister and that would have been weird. But he looked, I thought then, like he was finally comfortable in his own skin. Relaxed. Ready to be himself.

"Be a gentleman," Mom said.

"Yes, ma'am." He smiled and saluted her, and then he was gone. She turned to me with parental nostalgia written all over her face.

"My babies are growing up," she sighed.

I rolled my eyes, and then Steven was knocking at the door, come to whisk me off, to prove that yes, once upon a time, we were young.

I can't recall a lot of the dance, but I do remember that when we arrived in the commons, which was set up with silver streamers and blue and white helium balloons and strobe lights, Steven took my hand and twirled me in a circle so that he could take in my dress. I was wearing a sleeveless belted A-line that came to my knee, black lace over green satin, that I'd splurged $79 for at Macy's.

"You look like Euler's equation," he murmured as he looked me up and down.

Nerd translation: Euler's equation is said to be the most perfect formula ever written. Simple but elegant. Beautiful.

"Thank you," I said, blushing, and I tried to think of a similar compliment, maybe general relativity or Callan-Symanzik, but instead I went with, "You look hot. Seriously."

Steven smiled. He's a good-looking guy, with brown eyes and golden-brown hair and straight, orthodontically enhanced white teeth, but the people around us don't usually see that. They see how excited he gets about physics class. They see the calculator in his *back pocket. They see his glasses.*

He raised my hand to his lips and kissed it. "Come, my lady," he said, "let us dance."

We bobbed awkwardly on the dance floor for a while, and soon Beaker and Eleanor came over with their dates, and we quietly poked fun at the girly girls with their poufy hair in their poufy dresses. Then we hypocritically admired one another's dresses, and got our pictures taken for the sake of posterity, and danced some more.

And then there's this part I remember so clearly. I was dancing with Steven to a slow song, and I let my head drop onto his chest, where I could feel his heart beating. The song was Christina Perri's "A Thousand Years." We'd laughed at how cheesy it was, how over-the-top sentimental, and made a couple of <u>Twilight</u> jokes, but then we'd fallen right into dancing. It's a good song for dancing. Steven had his hands at the small of my back, his face in the crook of my shoulder, his breath heating my skin, and I had this moment of sudden euphoria. We're right together, I thought. We fit.

It felt like Euler's equation.

I lifted my head, and he lifted his. Our eyes met. Our legs brushed as we swayed slowly back and forth.

"Darling, don't be afraid, I have loved you for a thousand years," crooned Christina Perri. "I'll love you for a thousand more."

Wait, I thought. Hold on.

I had this whole big life ahead of me, college and a career and adulthood, and this was no time to be "falling in love" with anyone. We were too young for that. Hormones, I could understand. Dating and messing around and finding out what it was to kiss and be kissed, all of that made sense. But this—the way I felt in Steven's arms right then—it felt like more than hormones.

It felt like so much more.

I tightened my arms around Steven's neck and lowered my head again. His heart, when I laid my cheek against his chest, was beating fast.

So was mine.

Randomly I glanced over and saw Ty about 10 feet away, dancing with a girl—Ashley, I assumed. I didn't see her face, just the back of her pale pink gown sweeping the floor and her golden hair tumbling in deliberate waves down her shoulders. But I saw Ty clearly. His eyes were closed, his fingers spread against her hip as he moved with her. He wasn't smiling, but there was a quiet contentment on his face. A stillness.

He looked as happy as I'd ever seen him.

Then, as if he could sense me watching, he opened his eyes, spotted me. Grinned.

Bitch, he mouthed.

I grinned back, then pointed to the space between my eyebrows. Are you wearing makeup? I mouthed.

He subtly gave me the finger.

I laughed out loud, which made Steven pull back and ask, "What's so funny?"

"Nothing," I said, trying to contain my giggles. "My brother's a goofball."

Steven turned and gave Ty the what's-up-bro nod, which Ty returned.

Guys and their codes.

"I like your brother," Steven said.

"He likes you." I smiled because it was true—Ty thoroughly approved of Steven as my boyfriend. "That guy's all right," he told me once. "He gets you." And back then it was true. Steven did get me.

The violins swelled to their final crescendo and then faded. We stopped dancing and looked at each other.

"What now?" Steven asked me.

"Now we drink the lame punch," I quipped, and away we went.

I don't remember the rest of the dance. It's lost along with all the other insignificant passing seconds of my life. Me. Steven. Ty. Ticking away. I didn't know to savor that moment on the dance floor, to understand how beautiful and rare it was, how fragile, how ephemeral, when Ty was happy. When we were all happy, and we were together, and we were safe.

I didn't know.

I didn't know.

4.

DAVE'S OFFICE IS LOCATED in one of those nondescript commercial centers downtown—you know the type of place I mean, where you walk the halls reading the names of lawyers and accountants and realtors on the identical plaques outside their identical doors, until you reach the nameplate that reads DAVID HARRINGTON, MFT, NEW HOPE FAMILY COUNSELING.

That first time I went, about a month ago, I trudged into Dave's office expecting the same gray walls and berber carpet from the hall, but then the door opened to this funky waiting area cluttered with fish tanks, an assortment of lava lamps, a coffee table collection of those wiggly dashboard hula dancers, a wall displaying Dave's impressive collection of vintage Tabasco sauce bottles, and, best of all, the most massive accumulation of comics (like the kind printed in the funnies section of the newspaper) I've ever come across. I sat for ten minutes flipping through an old collection of classic *Peanuts*. Charlie Brown trying to kick the football. Lucy yanking it out from under him. Charlie's rage. And I laughed at poor Charlie, and it felt weird to laugh, because Ty had been dead for two weeks then.

That's when Dave came out of his office. I expected, after the waiting area, for him to be a hippie or some kind of eccentric weirdo, but there he was in his plaid shirt and wrinkle-free khakis, his perfectly groomed beard and graying blond hair cut short and combed carefully into position using a little too much gel. He stuck out his hand to me.

"Lexie, I assume," he said. "I'm Dave."

I must have looked surprised, because then he said, "Sorry. Do you prefer to be called Alexis? When I met with your mother she called you Lexie."

"You talked to my mom? In person?"

"Yes, briefly," he answered. "She wanted to fill me in on the situation."

I couldn't imagine my mom in this place, sitting there with her legs crossed next to the hula dancers and the wall of hot sauce, waiting to go in and tell this man about her dead son and her sad daughter.

"Well," Dave said, gesturing inside his office where the big plaid couch and the box of tissues waited. "Come on in."

I hesitated. "Look, maybe this isn't such a good—"

"I'm basically here to listen, Alexis," he said then. "If you want to talk. Give it a try."

Dave's a nice enough guy. I haven't figured out yet what he's really good for, aside from being a misguided way for my mom to feel like she's doing something for me during this time of need. Like life is not going to absolutely suck right now no matter what. But whatever. My brother's dead. I'm not talking much, and not hanging out with my friends, and not being the normal chipper Lex they all expect.

So clearly I should go to therapy.

This afternoon I sit in Dave's office for a full thirty minutes before I can think of anything productive to say. So far he's been okay with that—letting me talk when I'm ready—but today I can tell that there's something on his mind, some little walnut of my psyche he is eager to crack.

There's something on my mind, too, but I don't tell him.

I want to. The past few days have been pretty hard-core inside my head. I keep thinking that I must be crazy. Something inside this fragile brain of mine must have snapped under all the emotional strain. I've officially lost my grip on reality.

Because Ty is dead.

He's gone. He's never coming back.

What I saw the other night *had to have been* a hallucination or part of a mental breakdown or a waking dream.

It felt real.

But it couldn't have been real.

Anyway, the smart thing to do would be to tell Dave about it. After all, he's paid to listen to me. Rationally speaking he's the perfect person to talk to—impartial, unemotional, practical. This is what therapy is supposed to be good for: to air out your crazy. To get better. To deal.

But what can I say? *Um, yes, I saw the ghost of my dead brother in my basement four nights ago.*

To which Dave will say: *Oh, that's very interesting, Alexis; let's get you some nice pills.*

So Dave asks me how I am and I say I'm fine. Which I am not. He asks me how my week was and I say it was okay. Which it, very definitely, was not.

Then it's quiet while Dave pins me with those kind blue eyes of his and I use the toe of my sneaker to fiddle with the edge of the rug.

Dave finally says: "I hope you're not still upset about last week."

I stare at him blankly for a few seconds before I remember. Oh. Last week.

Right. We had a bit of a disagreement last week.

Because I told him about the hole in my chest. About how I feel like I'm going to die while it's happening. How I'm terrified that these moments will come more and more often, and they'll last longer and longer, until all I feel is the hole, and then maybe it will swallow me up for good.

I thought that was brave of me to confess. I was attempting to open up to him. I was trying to do what you're supposed to do.

What I wanted Dave to tell me was that the hole is horrible, yes, absolutely, but that it's normal, and that it will get better, not worse, and that I'm not going to die, at least not for a long, long time. It will hurt for a while, but I'm going to live.

35

And then I would try to believe him.

But what he said was, "There's a medication we can get you for that."

Then he went on about SSRIs and the wonders of Xanax or maybe starting with Valium, which is nicely non-habit-forming, and I stared at him mutely until he was finished waxing poetically about drugs. Then he said, "What do you think?"

I said, "You want to put me on antidepressants?"

He said that antidepressants with traditional therapy made a very effective combination.

I said, "Do you think I'm depressed?"

He coughed. "I think you've been through something really hard, and medication might make it a little easier."

"I see. Have you ever read the book *Brave New World*?" I asked.

He blinked a few times. "No. I don't think so."

"It's about this society in the future where they have a drug called soma that makes everybody feel happy," I explained. "It's supposed to fix everything. You're not content at work? No problem. You take soma, and nothing bothers you. Your mom dies? Take some soma, and everything will feel hunky-dory."

"Alexis," Dave said. "I'm trying to help you. What you're talking about with this hole sounds like a classic description of a panic attack—"

"But here's the thing," I pushed on. "That futuristic society where everybody is drugged to be happy, all the time, no matter what happens, it's horrible—monstrous, even—it's like the end of humanity. Because we are supposed to feel things, Dave. My brother died, and I'm supposed to feel it."

I stopped myself, suddenly out of breath. I wanted to say more. I wanted to scream about how Ty had taken antidepressants too, had been taking them for more than two years up until his death, and a fat lot of good it did him. I wanted to tell Dave my ironic little secret: that I know I'm supposed to feel this pain for my brother—sorrow, grief, whatever you want to call it—that I even *want* to feel it, but I don't. Outside of those moments with the hole, I don't feel anything at all.

I don't need drugs to numb the pain.

"I understand," Dave said.

"God, when did therapists become pushers?" I said, still worked up.

Dave smiled, like he thought my insult was humorous, and then went straight to placating me. "All right, Alexis, all right. No drugs." And that's when he suggested the diary thing.

Writing as an alternative to Xanax.

"I wrote in the journal this week," I report to him now.

He looks uncharacteristically surprised. "What did you write about?"

I shrug. "Stuff."

He waits for me to say more, and when I don't, he just comes out and says, "Okay. This week I'd like to talk about your friends."

"I don't have friends right now" is what slips out.

He raises his eyebrows. "You don't have friends?"

Whoops. "I mean, yes, I have friends, but . . ."

"Have they stopped being your friends?" he asks. "Sometimes

people don't know how to respond to something like—"

"No," I backpedal. "No, they're great. It's just that . . . I think I stopped being theirs."

Dave makes a thoughtful little noise like this is a therapist's gold mine. "Why?"

I take a minute to think about it. Well, in Jill's case it's because she was suffocating me with sympathy. When Ty first died, she was there every time I turned around, her eyes worried and bloodshot with crying. "Are you okay?" she'd ask, over and over and over.

No, moron, I'd think. I am not okay. My brother's dead.

But I'd suck it up and say, "Yeah, I'm okay," which after a few days gave way to a weak nod, and then she'd say something like "Let me know if you need anything" or "I'm here if you want to talk." Which, after a while, I figured out was what she really wanted me to do. She wanted me to talk about Ty. About his death. About my feelings about his death. And suddenly I got the distinct feeling that she wanted me to cry, so that she could be my shoulder to cry on. She wanted me to break down so that she could build me back up, so she could be my stellar bestie who got me through the worst.

I know I'm probably being unfair. I love Beaker. I do. I've known her since sixth grade, when we were the nerdiest nerds in the gifted and talented class. We've had a hundred sleepovers and many a long, serious conversation into the wee hours of the morning about the meaning of life and the likelihood of aliens on other planets and the stupidity of boys. But this thing with Ty isn't just another serious conversation. It's my whole wrecked, messed-up life. It's me.

She can't fix me.

I was getting sick of watching her try. So I just, like, backed away slowly.

I say all of this to Dave, and he nods. "What about your other friends? Your boyfriend?"

"We broke up a few weeks ago," I say. New topic: "I also have this friend Eleanor, but it's simpler with her, in a way. She's been avoiding me, while trying to seem like she's not avoiding me, of course. I don't think she's looked me in the eye since it happened. But that's okay. I get it. Like you said, some people don't know how to respond."

"So you don't have any friends right now?"

"Well, I see my old friends at school, eat lunch with them, and we have classes together. But I don't really feel like doing anything extracurricular, and I need to be home for my mom. So I guess, no. I don't. Not at the moment."

"That's sad, Lex," he says.

That's my middle name these days. Alexis Sad Riggs.

"You don't have to go through this by yourself," Dave says. "Try to let people in. That's the only way they can help you."

I can't be helped, I think. There is no magic spell that will bring Ty back. There's nothing anybody can do.

"I'll work on that," I say, and go back to fiddling with the rug.

It's quiet again. I can literally hear the clock in his office ticking. Four minutes of therapy left to go.

Three minutes.

Two.

"So do you have anything else you want to talk about?" Dave asks.

Last chance, I think. Tell him about seeing Ty.

"No," I say. "I'm good."

Which has to be like Lie #17 in this session alone.

Then I stand up, even though I still have ninety-six seconds left, and walk away from therapy as fast as I can go.

I have dinner with Dad at Olive Garden. We normally have dinner together on Tuesday nights, after my regular Tuesday session with Dave. Because Megan has yoga on Tuesdays. Dinner with Dad is always a quiet affair because he has even less to say than I do. He doesn't have the most exciting job in the world—he's an accountant—and he knows I don't want to hear about Megan or the house he lives in with her or how they pass their time, so there's not much left to discuss. It was easier when Ty was with us (although Ty hated the Dad dinners and was always finding last-minute excuses not to show), because at least then we could talk about sports.

Now we're down to one safe topic of conversation.

"How's school?" Dad asks.

"I got a seventy-one on my calculus midterm," I blurt out.

I don't know why I tell him. It's embarrassing, especially with my dad, who's obviously a bit of a numbers guy himself. I can't look at him when I say it. I'm sure my face is bright red, but I keep picking at the salad like everything is fine.

Dad puts down his breadstick. "That sounds serious."

"It is serious," I agree. "My grade's down to at least an A-minus. Which means I'm not going to be valedictorian."

"Can you retake it?" he asks.

"No." Lie #18.

"I see." He clears his throat, then goes back to eating the breadstick.

"I'm sorry, Dad," I say after a minute. And I am. I hate disappointing him, even after everything. I care what he thinks.

"It's not important," he says, but he doesn't mean it. Dad's always going on about how hard you have to work to be the best, to excel at everything, to reach for the very top—the best grades, the best education, the best job—so that you can live up to your potential, he always says, which is where I read *so that you don't end up an accountant in Nebraska with a divorce and two (wait, make that one now) kids when you could have been so much more.*

We eat. Dad drinks two glasses of red wine, even though he hates wine. Then he pressures me into ordering dessert.

"How's your mother?" he asks as I disassemble a piece of tiramisu.

I could tell him about the crying thing. But he doesn't want to hear that. He doesn't want to know that she cries all the time and that she doesn't get out of bed unless she has to be at work or church and that she sleeps with Ty's old stuffed monkey clutched to her chest. He doesn't want to hear that she thinks Ty is still in the

41

house, and I don't even know what he'd do if I told him what I saw in the basement.

He wants me to say that Mom's okay.

So I say, "She's all right"—Lie #19—and Dad pays the check. We put on our coats and wander out into the cold night air, and he hugs me stiffly, and then, as usual, we go our separate ways.

5.

THE HOUSE IS DARK WHEN I GET HOME. Mom must have already gone to bed, which isn't so unusual, even at eight o'clock at night. She sleeps so she doesn't have to be awake, so she will be conscious of what's happened as little as possible.

I wish I could sleep like that.

I spend an hour doing homework. Then I reach that time when normally I would go downstairs to watch TV.

This is a dilemma. I haven't ventured into the basement in four days, not even to do laundry. I haven't watched TV. I haven't brought it up with Mom that maybe the cologne thing wasn't so ridiculous after all.

Yes, I'm aware that I'm a total coward.

I take out the journal Dave gave me. For a few seconds I actually consider writing in it again, scribbling down a long confession about everything I haven't said out loud. About the ghost. About the text. About Steven. About Ty. About me. But I can't make myself do it.

So I stick the moleskin notebook under my mattress as a tribute to clichés and curl up on my bed for a while, reading *A Beautiful Mind*, which I can't get into. Then I try *Contact* by Carl Sagan, which is my favorite novel ever, but my eyes move across the page without finding meaning in the words. I keep thinking about the look on Ty's face when I threw the phone at him: startled and offended and a little sad. I'd never thrown anything at him before. We weren't like that. We always got along.

Suddenly I'm furious. I think, So what, I'm never going to go into the basement again? I'm going to tiptoe around my own house until I leave for college? I'm going to be scared of what, a figment of my imagination? What am I, like ten years old? Afraid of the dark?

Get over yourself, Lex, I tell myself. Grow a pair.

So I jump up. I march straight down into the basement and stand for a few minutes glaring at that spot where Ty appeared the other night, at the small dent in the wall that is of course still there from where I chucked my phone at him. I make myself stand there for a full five minutes.

I don't see anything weird. I don't smell anything weird. I just feel stupid.

His bedroom door is open.

I go to the doorway. The moon is shining through the window. I haven't been in Ty's room since we went in to get the clothes he was buried in, but it looks the same as I remember. His desk is cluttered with books and school stuff. Clothes on the floor. Shoes. A partially deflated basketball. A dusty old model airplane dangling from the ceiling that he and Dad built together when he was eleven. Pictures of his friends taped to the walls. Posters of bands and movies he liked and NBA players.

As I step inside, his scent envelops me—not just his cologne but that slightly goatlike aroma he had, and his deodorant, which smells faintly minty. Pencil shavings. Dirty socks. Wood glue.

Ty.

I swallow. It's like he's still here, not in a ghostlike way, but like it never happened. If I stay here, if I close my eyes, I can imagine that Ty is just out somewhere and that he'll be back.

I wish I could cry. That would be the appropriate thing to do at this moment: to remember my brother and cry.

But I can't.

I turn to go out, and that's when I see someone sleeping in his bed. The covers are lumped up around a figure on its side, back to me.

My heart starts to pound. I know it's not Ty, I know it can't be, but in that moment I want it to be. I want to see him again even if it means I'm crazy. Maybe that's why I couldn't tell Dave, or why I can't write it down, because then they'll very definitely make me take the pills and what happened the other night with the phone won't happen again, and I'll never see Ty, not ever, for as long as I live, and I don't believe in an afterlife so I won't get to see him then, either.

I know this isn't the best reasoning.

But I still think it.

I creep around to the other side of the bed. I touch the shoulder of the person lying there, and find it warm, moving slightly with each breath.

Breathing. Alive.

It's not him, I think as I take the edge of the covers and start to pull them back. It's not him.

And I'm right. It's not.

It's my mother. She's sleeping, wearing a faded red Led Zeppelin T-shirt, an old one of Ty's. Lines of mascara are dried like tattoo ink down her cheeks, etched into the wrinkles near her eyes, marking the pillowcase.

She looks old. Small. Worn out. I draw the covers back over her, then sit on the bed and watch her for a while, her breathing, the movements of her eyes behind her eyelids. What would she dream about in Ty's bed, surrounded by his stuff and his smell?

I want to wake her up, to take her out of here, because it's not okay, her being here. It's not healthy. But I let her sleep. Because, at least for the moment, she doesn't seem to be in pain.

Sometimes I wonder if she wishes it was me who died instead of Ty, her snarky daughter instead of her socially acceptable son. I know she loves me. But if she could choose?

But that's Ty's fault.

He left her a note. As suicide notes go, it was short and to the point. It said:

Sorry Mom but I was below empty.

He didn't write a note to Dad. Or to any of his friends. Or to me. He just left those seven little words on a yellow Post-it, stuck to his bedroom mirror. His only explanation.

It's still there. The police took it down for a while, as evidence, but they came back and returned it to exactly where he'd left it. They'd taken a picture of the room so they would know where. So far neither of us has had the guts to take it down.

I stand up and cross to the mirror.

Sorry Mom but I was below empty.

I reach out.

My fingers have just brushed the edge of the paper when I see Ty in the reflection of the mirror.

He's standing right behind me.

Ty.

Again, I don't think about it. I don't stop to contemplate what a rational person might do in this situation. I don't calmly investigate.

I run.

I jerk away from the mirror, away from him, away, up the stairs, out the door, and before I know what's happened I'm outside on the street, my shoes crunching the frozen snow as I run and run and run.

This is not happening is the thought that cycles through my brain. This is not happening.

I get three blocks before I stop, to the edge of a park where Ty and I used to spend every summer afternoon when we were kids. I hunch over, panting, finally feeling the biting cold. I wasn't wearing a coat when I bolted out of my house, just a T-shirt and jeans, and the winter air against my bare arms is sharp and distantly painful.

The moon is bright over my head. The park has a frozen quality to it, the swings hanging perfectly still. Deserted. A car moves along the street, slowing as it passes me. I wipe my nose, straighten, and try to take a full breath. I don't know what I'm doing.

Ty. In the house. In his room.

This is not happening, I think.

A shudder passes through me that has nothing to do with the cold.

I feel a kind of resignation as I walk back. The front door is half open, waiting for me. I shuffle zombielike down to Ty's bedroom, where my mother is still sleeping.

Ty is not in the mirror.

I notice immediately that the top right-hand drawer of his desk is open. I can't remember if it was open before, but now it strikes me as odd, out of place. Was Mom up rummaging around while I was gone? Or was it like that earlier? Or was it someone else?

This is not happening, I think. But it is.

I kneel next to the bed and gently shake Mom by the shoulder. She gives a weak cry as she opens her eyes. It takes her a few seconds before she focuses on my face.

"Oh, Lexie," she says. "Is everything all right?"

She glances around. I watch her expression change as she registers where she is. Ty's room. Ty is gone. Ty is dead.

Grief floods her face.

"I came down to wake him that morning," she says. "He was right here. He seemed all right."

"I know."

"I should have sensed that something was wrong that day. I'm his mother. I should have been able to tell."

I never know what to say to this. She has her blame game and I have mine, the difference being that I actually have something to feel guilty about.

"It's cold down here," I tell her as I help her sit up. "Let's get you upstairs."

Later, after I've got her tucked away in her own bed and she's sleeping again, I slink back to the basement to investigate the open drawer. It's empty, except for a single item. A sealed envelope.

A letter.

My heart jumps, thinking that he might have written it to me. I didn't answer the text, so he wrote down what he wanted to say. His reasons. His accusations, maybe. His last words.

The idea fills me with relief and terror.

I turn the envelope over with unsteady hands, and that's when I see the name scrawled in Ty's terrible handwriting across the paper.

For Ashley, it reads.

12 February

The first time my brother tried to kill himself, almost 2 years ago now, was the day my parents' divorce was finalized. I don't know if he meant it as a kind of grand statement or what. I wasn't there for him that night, either; I was at a movie with Beaker. I can't even remember which movie. I only know I wasn't present when he marched up to the kitchen sink with a family-sized bottle of Advil and proceeded to gulp down pill after pill after pill. He did it practically under our mother's nose as she sat with her back to him at the kitchen table, alternately studying for her nursing board exams, making her slow way through a giant stack of note cards labeled with dosages and parts of the human body and the definitions of different medical terminology, and studying the Bible, trying to come to peace with where it said that divorce was okay so long as there was adultery involved.

At 42, Mom was the oldest student in her class at nursing school, but she was the best. She was focused, driven, determined to make a new life for herself post-Dad. She didn't even look up when her 14-year-old son took 63 tiny maroon tablets of pain reliever, said good night to her, then went downstairs to his bedroom and went to sleep.

He was disappointed when he woke up the next morning. He emerged from the basement with an expression I'll never forget: a kind of resigned, puzzled frustration that he hadn't simply floated away during the night.

"I'm not going to school today," he announced as we sat down to breakfast. "I don't feel good."

My mother, ever the nurse even before she qualified to be one, felt his forehead. It was cool. She asked him some questions: Sore throat? Headache? Stomach pains? He shook his head and looked up at her, shrugged his thin, birdlike shoulders, and told her what he'd done.

At the hospital the most they could really do was put him in a room for observation. It was too late to pump his stomach. I sat in the corner and watched TV with him as the nurses came and went, checking his vitals, changing the saline in the IV. Every now and then Mom burst in, tearful, in agony over the choice she was being forced to make about whether or not to stay with us all day or do her clinical rounds in the hospital, her final week of requirements for her nursing degree. Without which she couldn't graduate.

"I'm okay," Ty told her, and even smiled at her to prove his point, his face wan under the fluorescent hospital lights, his lips colorless as he formed the word <u>go</u>.

"I'll be back," she promised again and again before dashing off.

I didn't know what to say to him that day. I slumped in the uncomfortable plastic chair and tried to think of some big-sisterly advice that would draw him back from the edge. But I was 16 then—what did I know? I had my own problems, my own private miseries, and if I'd been honest I would have admitted that the idea of checking out had crossed my mind a few times in the past gruesome year, between my dad leaving us for the cliché he'd met at the office, who was exactly half his age, and my mom going back to school, the house suddenly empty of adults in a way that felt implicitly wrong.

But I never had a real plan to end my life. I was too afraid of dying. Of the blackness. Of ceasing to exist.

"It was stupid," he ended up saying to me that day when the silence grew thick between us.

I was relieved to hear him say it.

"Yes, it was. Totally moronic," I agreed, and then we went back to watching World's Wildest Police Videos on the TV that perched near the ceiling. The nurses came and went. My mother came and went. And we both wondered (but not out loud) whether our father was going to show up at all.

In the end, he did. He was wearing a golf shirt, I remember. He'd come to take us home, since the hospital had decided to release Ty, and Mom still had 3 more hours of her clinicals. Dad also didn't seem to know what to say as he drove us back to the house. He drummed his fingers on the steering wheel, checked the rearview mirror, met my eyes, looked away, then cleared his throat.

"Tyler—" he said as we pulled into the driveway.

"Come home," Ty interrupted. "Please, Dad. Come home. Please."

My breath lodged itself in my chest. Ty never said things like that. He was angry with Dad; that was how he dealt. He'd always maintained that he hated Dad, that he was glad Dad was gone, that he didn't miss him.

"Please," he said again.

And what about me? I thought. Did I want Dad to come home? Could we pretend that this past humiliating year had never happened, that he wasn't a liar and a cheater and an all-around pathetic excuse for a human being, that everything hadn't been turned upside down? Could we go back to the way things were before? Did I want to go back?

Dad cleared his throat again.

I waited for him to say, I can't. Or I'm sorry, son. Or something about how life is hard, but that doesn't mean we give up.

But he didn't say anything.

And he didn't stay. Even though the doctor had said that Ty needed to be under strict surveillance for the next 24 hours, Dad didn't even get out of the car. He just looked at me and said, "Call me if you need anything," and I kind of nodded, and my eyes burned with furious tears that I didn't let fall, and I turned away and walked Ty up the steps into the house.

Later, when Ty was sleeping, I went from room to room gathering anything that might be dangerous. Razor blades. Pills, although we'd already established that this wasn't an effective method of offing your-self. Rope. Then I unlocked the closet in the back of Dad's office and stared at the line of 3 hunting rifles in their cases. I checked to make sure none of them was loaded, and then I went to the shelf and swept every single bullet into a box with the rest of the stuff. I sealed the box with duct tape, labeled it ROMANCE NOVELS, and hid it in the back corner of my closet under a pile of half-naked Barbie dolls I still had lying around. After that was done I went to check on Ty, listened to him breathe, and tried to convince myself that he was going to be all right. Then I tiptoed back upstairs and sat at the kitchen table and finally allowed myself to cry.

I could cry back then.

I loved Ty. I loved him and I had almost lost him. So I cried. Tears were still a part of my anatomy.

They called him lucky, that time. His body was able to metabolize the Advil. His liver was damaged, but would probably heal. Lucky, they kept saying at the hospital as they took his statement and ran the tests on him and acted in general like the whole thing was a stunt, like he'd tried some harebrained move on his bicycle. You're so lucky. Lucky, lucky you.

Lucky was the last word my brother would pick to describe himself. But in the end he nodded and told them they were right. So they would let him go.

The Advil thing was a "cry for help," they said, so they required him to see a therapist, who got my brother started on antidepressants and tried to get him to talk about his "pain" every week for the next year or so, at 60 bucks a pop, which our insurance didn't cover but Mom convinced my dad to pay. And for 2 whole years, nothing much happened. Mom became a licensed nurse. Dad married the cliché. I got an 800 on the math section of the SATs and everybody began talking about what college I would go to. Ty joined the basketball team. He started lifting weights, and his body filled out. His arms grew strong and muscled. He wore a letterman's jacket when he swaggered through the halls at school. Girls liked him. People in general liked him. He was popular in a way that I never could have dreamed of being. And it was easy to forget that he'd ever been sad enough to down a bottle of pills.

We only talked about it once, after that day at the hospital. It was about 2 weeks later, and we were at Denny's, waiting for Dad to show up for breakfast. Dad was late. I was looking at Ty, really looking at him, and his eyes seemed glazed over, like he was staring out at his life through a pane of glass.

"Are you okay?" I asked him.

He glanced at me, startled. "I'm hungry. I wish Dad would get here already."

"That's not what I mean," I said. "Are you okay?"

His ears went red. "Oh, that. I told you, that was stupid. I'm fine. Really. I won't do that again."

"Okay. But I want you to promise me, if you ever feel like that again, like you want to—"

"I won't—" he said.

"But if you do, you have to tell me. Call me, text me, wake me up at three a.m., I don't care. I want to know about it. I'm here for you."

He didn't meet my eyes, but he nodded. "All right."

"Promise," I said.

"I promise."

"Good," I said, but I worried that he was just telling me what he knew I wanted to hear.

In the end, I shouldn't have concerned myself with whether he'd keep his promise.

I should have thought about whether I'd keep mine.

6.

ASHLEY DAVENPORT, according to the yearbook, is a cheer-leader. She's a sophomore. She has long blond hair, or at least I think she does—it's hard to tell from the 1-by-1.5-inch black-and-white photo on page 173.

She could be the one.

There are 1,879 students at my high school, and nineteen of them are named Ashley: about 1 percent. Over the past two days I've already checked off Ashley Adams, who's practically married to her boyfriend (so clearly not the droid I'm looking for), Ashley Chapple, who's a senior and I know her and no way she dated Ty, and Ashley Chavez, whose raven's-wing-black hair doesn't match my memory of the girl Ty took to homecoming.

So now I'm to the *D*s, and Ashley Davenport. Blond. Sopho-more. Cheerleader.

Ashley Davenport is today's objective.

Also: it's Valentine's Day. Which sucks.

Last year on the dreaded V-Day I discovered a white paper daisy slipped between the upper slats of my locker when I arrived at school. It was paper, but I still stood there holding its green wire stem between my fingers, smiling stupidly, before I bent my head to smell the petals. It smelled like books, a heady mix of paper and ink and glue, a sweet knowledge.

There was no note on the flower. No card. No name.

A mystery.

We weren't dating yet—we didn't officially start dating until June—but I knew the flower was from Steven. He never confessed to leaving it there for me, but I knew. Because of something I'd said once when we were wandering around in a grocery store together that year, trying to find a last-minute gift for Mrs. Seidel, our chemistry teacher, who was in the hospital with cancer. "I don't get the point, really," I'd said as we contemplated the plastic-wrapped roses. "Why give a girl something that's supposed to represent love that's only going to wilt and die in a matter of hours?"

Steven laughed and said that was a pretty pessimistic way to view life, and I shrugged.

Then he said, "All the best things are like that, though, Lex, the most beautiful things. Part of the beauty comes from the fact that they're short-lived." He picked up a bouquet of deep-red roses, held it out to me. "These will never be as beautiful as they are at this moment, so we have to enjoy them now."

I stared at him. He scratched the back of his neck, a little red-faced, then gave me a sheepish grin. "Just call me a romantic," he said.

I wanted to say that there were some things in this world, some rare things, that were beautiful and stayed that way. But instead I took the bouquet out of his hand. "Okay. Flowers it is," I said, and we laughed and bought the roses for Mrs. Seidel.

Then, just a few weeks later, the paper daisy. A flower that would never die. I still have it, pinned to the edge of my corkboard above my desk at home.

Today when I go to my locker, there's no flower waiting. I knew there wouldn't be. I get out my books for first period and slam my locker closed. I tell myself that it was never going to work, Steven and me, and it was for the best to cut it off when I did. Still, I can't help but look for him in the flux of incoming students in the hallway. So many of them are smiling, wearing red and pink and lugging boxes of candies to their oh-so-significant others, and finally I see Steven, walking with his head down, his backpack slung over one shoulder. He glances up. He sees me. He lifts his hand in a faint wave.

I look away. I don't have time for this, I tell myself. I have a task to accomplish here. An objective. So I turn and wander toward the section of sophomore lockers, scrutinizing the blond girls.

One of them is Ashley Davenport, I'm pretty sure.

I just don't know which one.

I spot a group of Ty's old friends, the jock squad, off in a corner laughing at something. They always seem to be laughing, like they're at a frat party already. I look at their faces and try to summon names, but I don't know Ty's high school friends the way I knew his friends from middle school, and I'm not good with names, so all I get is: the guy with the fauxhawk; the kid with the multiple gold medals sewn to his letterman's jacket; Tall Guy from the basketball team; Grayson, although I don't know if this is his first or last name; and a guy who's a swimmer or wrestler or something that makes his body ridiculously triangle-shaped.

One of them, Tall Guy, looks up and notices me staring. This is the part where I should go over and ask them, *Hey, do you know an Ashley? The girl Ty took to homecoming? What's her last name? Is it Davenport?*

But as I stand there looking at them, suddenly I'm thinking, There should be a space. Where Ty used to stand with them. But there isn't. They're arranged in a half circle with the requisite twelve inches between them, guy spacing, and there's no room for anyone else. The space where Ty used to be, they've closed it in.

Which makes the freaking grief hole open up in my chest. I wait for it to pass, but it doesn't, not for what feels like much longer than the normal thirty seconds. As usual I start to feel like there's something physically wrong with my body—I can't breathe, my heart is beating too fast, I can't breathe I can't *breathe*. And Tall Guy has definitely said something about me to Triangle Man, because the members of the jock squad are all looking at me now with the same slightly wary expressions.

Then somebody jostles me from behind, hard enough to knock one of my books to the floor, and all of a sudden my lungs work again.

"Hey," I gasp to no one in particular. "Watch where you're

59

going." Stiffly I bend to retrieve the book, but someone grabs it before I can.

"I got it," he says.

I inhale and exhale a couple of times to prove to myself that I can do it, then look up. "Oh, hi, Damian," I say.

My book rescuer is Damian Whittaker: sophomore, one of those skin-and-bones types who hasn't grown into himself yet, all baggy shirt and greasy hair falling in his eyes and acne dotting his chin. He's a shy kid, inconspicuous, the kind who keeps to himself and doesn't seem to be interested in anything or anyone. A loner, according to the school's social strata.

But these days Damian is trying to be my friend.

He and Ty were best buds a couple years back, the summer my dad took off for Megan's house. Damian and this other boy, Patrick, and Ty were like the three musketeers that year. They spent every available afternoon playing Halo and Guitar Hero and lounging around in our old playhouse listening to Led Zeppelin and the Doors. They thought they were being so classic and cool. But that was a long time ago. Damian hasn't darkened our doorstep since Ty started high school and sports and vying for Mr. Popularity. But Damian always makes an effort to smile and say hello when he sees me. As if he were my friend, instead of my brother's. Which means that lately he's been popping up all around school and trying to engage me in conversation.

It's kind of sweet, even if it's the last thing I want.

And it is—the last thing I want. When I see Damian, all I can think about is how I'm never going to see Ty. When Damian tells me about a movie he saw last weekend, I think, Ty will never see that movie. He'll never play that new video game that Damian loves. He'll never pass his sophomore year. And Damian will.

And it will not seem fair.

"Oh, the horror," Damian says to me now.

"What?"

His smile is timid as he hands me back my book. "*Heart of Darkness*," he says.

"What?" I ask again.

"You're reading *Heart of Darkness*. There's this famous line at the end. 'Oh, the horror.'"

I feel stupid, which is not a normal state of being for me. "Oh, right. Yes. The horror."

"I liked that book," he says.

I'm about a quarter of the way through *HoD*, an assignment for AP English, but so far it's exactly the kind of book I hate, where the story seems simple enough, interesting, but then I get to class and the teacher starts going on and on about the hidden meanings, the metaphors, the significance of the color yellow. All this meaning that the author was trying to say to the reader, like a message written in a secret language.

Not my cup of tea.

I don't know what to say to Damian. He looks expectant, like he and I are about to have a thought-provoking literary discussion of Joseph Conrad.

"I—uh, I haven't finished reading it yet," I say.

His smile drops. "Oh. Spoiler alert. Sorry."

I'm so tired of the word *sorry*.

"Hey, do you know Ashley Davenport?" I blurt out, because I've just remembered what I am doing in sophomore land. "She's a cheerleader?"

Damian's eyes, which are a watery shade of gray, are instantly remote. "Yeah," he mumbles. "I know her. Why?"

"Do you know where I can find her?"

He shrugs. "She's in my biology class."

"Which biology class?" I ask.

"Mr. Slater's."

"When?"

He glances up at the digital clock on the wall over our heads, which reads 6:56 a.m. "In like four minutes."

"Thanks," I say quickly, already moving away from him. "I should—I have to get something out of my locker. Before the bell rings."

"Okay," he says simply, and smiles again. "See you around, Lex."

"Bye." I make a beeline back toward my locker. To get the letter. To get down to the science wing and back to AP English in less than four minutes.

I'm suddenly so freaked out by the prospect of finding the real Ashley (and then what am I going to do, huh?) that when I get back to my locker, I almost miss it.

The flower.

A rose, this time, stuck in the locker slats. It's still made from plain white paper, but more intricately built than last year. There are words written on it in faint pencil, a single sentence that I have to turn the flower around to read across the petals.

I love you as the plant that never blooms but carries in itself the light of hidden flowers.

I close my eyes. Heat rushes to my face. Crap. What red-blooded girl wouldn't go weak in the knees at that?

Oh, Steven, I think. What are you doing?

And now I have approximately two minutes. I should throw the rose away. I don't know if Steven's watching, but I should get rid of it in case he is. That would show him that it's over, because he clearly doesn't think it's really over if he could give me this flower.

I walk to the trash at the end of the hall. My hand trembles moronically as I hold the flower over the gaping gray mouth of the trash can. There's a half-eaten breakfast burrito in there, some random papers and flyers—*Try out for the school play! Gator Girls basketball team bake sale, this Saturday!*—an assortment of empty soda cans, a broken pencil.

Do it, I think.

Let go.

The bell rings. I sigh and walk back to my locker, where I tuck the paper rose into my backpack, into a side pocket, where it won't be crushed by all my other baggage. I grab the letter for Ashley and slip it into the front pocket of my five-subject notebook, not that I'm planning to give it to her right now if she turns out to be the right one—I can't think that far ahead—but because, for some illogical reason, I want to have the letter with me. Then I speed-walk to Mr. Slater's classroom. If I remember correctly, that's room 121B.

I arrive at 121B with a good minute to spare before the tardy bell rings, but before I can get a look inside I'm run down by a red-head in a cheerleader uniform. She's in such a mad rush to get to the classroom before the second bell rings that she smacks right into me. Our books and papers go all over the carpet in front of the door.

"I'm sorry," she says as we're both on our knees sorting out which stuff is whose. "I am so sorry."

The bell rings.

"Ashley," I hear Mr. Slater's voice boom out from inside the classroom. "You're tardy. Again."

She gives me a smile. "Sorry, Mr. S. Be right there," she calls back.

"Ashley Davenport?" I ask.

She looks startled. "Yes. You're . . . Ty's sister, right?"

My fame as the-girl-whose-brother-died has spread far and wide.

I look Ashley over. She's a cheerleader, all right, and a sopho-more, and pretty, with large royal blue eyes and skin so pale it has a translucent quality, so clear I can see a faint blue vein branching out under the surface of her temple and disappearing into her hairline. But the hair's all wrong. It's too short, pulled back into a tight pony-tail that ends in a nub that barely brushes the back of her neck. And it's the color of a coil of copper. Red.

She's not the girl with the long blond hair I saw Ty dancing with that night.

Wrong Ashley.

I let out the breath I was holding. "That's me," I say to answer her previous question. I hand over her biology notebook and straighten up.

"Is this . . . mine?" she asks, and I see she's got the envelope from Ty, frowning now because there's her name written right on it.

I snatch it out of her hand. "No. It's mine." And with no more explanation, I'm on my feet, heading off at a half jog because I'm late, too. For English. For Ty.

For everything. I'm too late.

7.

STEVEN IS IN MY ENGLISH CLASS. Of course he is—
Steven and Eleanor and Beaker are in all my honors classes. There
was a time when that was a good thing, a great thing, even. But not
today. I'm five minutes late, but the desk I usually sit at, the one on
the far right between Steven and Beaker and in front of El, is still
empty. Waiting for me. Steven looks up and smiles, and I feel my
face heating again, thinking about the rose.

Crap.

Mrs. Blackburn stops talking and stares at me from her perch
at the edge of her desk, puzzled by my highly unusual tardiness.

"Sorry," I mumble, and then I slink to the back of the classroom
and find a seat on the left. I can't deal with my friends right now.

Especially Steven.

Mrs. Blackburn continues the lecture she was giving. She's
starting us on an exercise in etymology, she says—the study of the

origin of words. She shows us a website where you can type in any word and it will spit out the word's roots: its definition, where and how that word originated, and how the usage of the word changed over time. In conjunction with our *Heart of Darkness* reading she demonstrates how the website works using the word *heart* (which goes back to the Old Norse *hjarta*) and the word *darkness* (Old English *deorcnysse*) and takes us back through the history of each word.

"So, class," Mrs. Blackburn says when she's done with the general history lesson about the birth of the English language. "What are some other words that you associate with *Heart of Darkness*, so far?"

I raise my hand, which surprises her because I'm not typically so quick to volunteer in this setting (not my cup of tea, remember), then suggest the word *horror*, which the website tells us comes from early fourteenth-century French.

Oh la horreur.

Mrs. Blackburn looks pleased that I have apparently already finished the book and know the significance of the word.

Thank you, Damian.

Then she sends us off on the class laptops to look up our own set of words. "Research a word that's been on your mind," she instructs.

I stare at the blank screen for a long time before I actually type in a word that's on my mind.

GHOST (*noun*):
Origin: before 900; Middle English *goost* (noun), Old
    English gāst; cognate with German Geist spirit

1. The soul of a dead person, a disembodied spirit imagined, usually as a vague, shadowy or evanescent form, as wandering among or haunting living persons.
2. A mere shadow or semblance; a trace.
3. A remote possibility.

As in: there's not even a *ghost* of a chance that what I saw— what I've been seeing, I guess is a more accurate description, as it's happened two times now—is real. It seems real, in the moment. It feels real. But it is not real.

Ghosts do not exist. I am a rational person. I know this.

Which leads me to:

HALLUCINATION (*noun*):
Origin: 1640–50; < Latin hallūcinātiōn- (stem of (h) allūcinātiō) a wandering of the mind.
1. False or distorted perception of objects or events with a compelling sense of their reality, usually resulting from a mental disorder (????) or drug (no, pretty squeaky clean, drugs-wise; I don't even like to take painkillers). The objects or events so perceived. (See also: delusion.)

A lapse of sanity.

A break.

This seems like a far more likely explanation.

I open my notebook and stare at the edge of the Ashley letter peeking out of the front pocket, the way the ink is slightly smeared on the letter *y*. Ty was a lefty; he always had this smudge on the side of his hand at the end of the school day from dragging his hand through everything he wrote.

For Ashley. Not *to* Ashley, but *for* her.

FOR (*preposition*):

Origin: before 900. From the Proto-Germanic fura. Old
    Saxon furi. Middle Dutch voor.

1. With the object or purpose of
2. Intended to belong to, or to be used in connection with
3. Suiting the purposes or needs of
4. In order to obtain, gain, or acquire
5. Used to express a wish, as of something to be
    experienced or obtained

For has too many meanings.

"All right, class," Mrs. Blackburn says abruptly. "That's enough time, I think, to ponder the significance of a word. Let's share."

I can't share this. *Ghost. Hallucination. For.* Hello, class, I'm a crazy person.

I sit quietly panicking while Mrs. Blackburn begins to wander between the rows of desks, occasionally stopping and gathering a word from a student: *baseball* from Rob Milton, *beautiful* from Jen Petterson, *book* from Alice Keisig—we're a terribly original bunch, and apparently stuck on the *B*s. "What I hope that you're coming to understand as you study etymology is that a word is not simply a word," Mrs. Blackburn says with that teacherly touch of drama, like this is life-changing stuff she's giving us here. She's that kind of teacher—the type who inflates everything, calls us by our last names instead of our first so that our conversations sound more formal, stresses the importance of each book we read, each essay we write, like it's the most important thing for us to know before we head out into the big bad world.

We will become cultured intellectuals if it kills her.

She continues: "Each word has a specific history, a context, a slow evolution of meaning. Most of the words we use today come from a clash of cultures: Norman against Saxon, Latin versus Germanic, smooth against guttural." She stops next to Eleanor. "Give me a word, Miss Green."

"*Brave*," El says. Which is of course a word that El would come up with. El once caught a guy trying to steal the license plate off the back of her car on the street outside her house and ended up chasing him through the neighborhood with a baseball bat yelling like an Amazonian warrior queen. El is fearless.

"French, am I right?" queries Mrs. Blackburn.

"Yes."

"And what do you like about this word, *brave*?"

"I like that it's derived from a verb," El answers. "Brave isn't something you are. It's something you do. It comes from action. I appreciate that."

"Excellent," Mrs. Blackburn says, moving on. She turns around and heads back up the row. "Mr. Blake," she says. "A word."

Steven clears his throat. His face goes slightly pink, but his voice doesn't waver when he answers. "I picked *love*."

Mrs. Blackburn widens her eyes and smiles. "Love? So that's what's on the young man's mind."

"It's Valentine's Day," he explains with a hint of a smile. "So I'm thinking about it, yes." His gaze touches mine and then moves quickly away.

"*Love* as a verb or a noun?"

"A verb," he says.

I love you as the plant that never blooms but carries in itself the light of hidden flowers.

Crap.

Mrs. Blackburn nods. "And where does the word *love* come from?"

"Old English," he reads off his laptop. "*Lufian*. To cherish, show delight in, approve. Which comes from the Old High German *lubon*, which meant something like joy."

"Something like joy," Mrs. Blackburn repeats like she's reciting a poem. "Wonderful. How about you, Miss Riggs?"

I'm startled, and I'm not ready. Why would she call on me? I'm at the other side of the freaking room. Is my association with Steven that ingrained in everyone around us? "What?" I ask, like maybe I didn't hear her correctly.

"What's your word?"

"Oh. Mine's not very good," I say.

She waits.

I sigh. My eye falls on a word on my screen. "Delusion," I say as my fingers type it in. See the seat of my pants, and see me flying by

71

it. "From the Latin, *delusio*, it means 'a belief that, though false, has been surrendered to and accepted by the whole mind as a truth.'"

"Interesting," Mrs. Blackburn says thoughtfully. "What made you pick *delusion*?"

"Well, we were talking about love, right? Love is a classic example of a delusion."

Mrs. Blackburn chuckles. "Oh. I see. Not a romantic then, are you?"

"No," I say flatly. "I don't believe in romantic love."

"Why not?" she asks.

Here we go. "Because what we associate with the idea of love is purely chemical. It can be broken down into scientifically proven phases: it starts with a dose of testosterone and estrogen, what we would think of as 'lust,' followed by the goofy 'lovesick' phase, which is a combination of adrenaline, dopamine, and a drop in serotonin levels—which, by the way, makes our brains behave exactly like the brains of crack addicts—and ends up, if we make it through phases one and two, with 'attachment,' where the body produces oxytocin and vasopressin, which basically make us want to cuddle excessively. It's science. That's all."

"Hmm," says Mrs. Blackburn. "That's quite the speech, Alexis."

Steven smiles at me again, but it's a sad smile this time. A pitying smile.

It makes me mad.

So I keep talking. "All this Valentine's Day stuff comes from big business capitalizing on the delusion of love. All the candy, the candlelit dinners, the flowers . . ." I meet Steven's gaze and hold it for a second and then look away. "It generates more than a billion dollars in revenue every year. Because people want to believe in love. But it's not real."

Mrs. Blackburn shakes her head, frowning. "But have you considered the notion that what we believe in—what we choose to believe in—*is* real? It becomes real, for us."

I push my glasses up on my nose and stare at her blankly.

"Perhaps you're right," she adds, "and what we feel as love is nothing more than a combination of certain chemicals in our bodies. But if we believe that love is this powerful force that binds us together, and if this belief brings us happiness and stability in this tumultuous world, then what's the harm?"

My chin lifts, like I have something to prove here. Maybe I do have something to prove. "In my experience, love doesn't bring happiness and stability. But believing in love can cause a substantial amount of harm."

Like with my parents.

Like with my brother.

Mrs. Blackburn straightens her wedding ring on her finger for a minute before speaking again. "I find that love is a concept much like bravery, Miss Riggs. I, for instance, have been married to the same man for thirty-two years. And, in all that time, I haven't felt 'in love' with him every day, not in the way love is described in romantic comedies and romance novels, but I have loved him. Love is a choice I've made. A verb. And that, because I believe in it, because I act on it, is real. Love is a very real thing to me."

The class goes silent. The discussion has veered off into weird too-personal territory. We don't want to think about the romantic lives of our teachers.

I stare at my hands for a minute. I know I shouldn't argue with her. I don't even know why I want to argue with her—because I don't want to let Steven get away with the rose?—but I can't seem to help myself.

"There was this study," I say finally, "where a scientist made people 'fall in love' with a simple series of actions: he had them talk about certain personal topics and look into each other's eyes for a determined period of time and have this specific physical contact, and if you put those factors all together then, bam—anyone can fall in love with anyone. Some of the people in that study got married later, and they had a lower divorce rate than the national average. It's that simple. You do these certain things, you fall in love. It's biology. Period. That people believe in it as anything else is just proof of how deeply ingrained the delusion is in our society."

Mrs. Blackburn gazes at me all red-faced like she'd like nothing better than to send me to the principal's office, but she can't think of a good enough reason—being the official rain cloud over the V-Day love parade is not going to cut it.

The back of my throat feels tight. I swallow against it.

The round clock over the doorway ticks off its seconds. Then Jill, always the one to come to the rescue in moments of social awkwardness, says, "Hey, I have a word. *Moist*. I hate the word *moist*—it just sounds yuck. Who would come up with a word like *moist*?" She refers to her notebook. "It turns out that it comes from something called 'Vulgar Latin'—whatever that means—*muscidus*,

which means 'slimy, musty, moldy.' Yuck, right? And then somewhere in the thirteenth century it morphed into the Old French
word *moiste*, which means 'damp.'"

Mrs. Blackburn blinks, like she'd forgotten what she was going
to say, then gives a short laugh.

Thank you, Beaker.

"I've never liked that word, either," Mrs. Blackburn says as she
glides smoothly back to the front of the class. "Something about the
way it sounds is unpleasant, I agree." She laughs again. "The study
of words always brings out an examination of our feelings, which
I think has become evident today, hasn't it? That's what words do.
At the basic level they are simply a collection of symbols grouped
together in order to represent an object. *C-H-A-I-R* represents
this"—she puts her hand on the back of her empty seat—"chair.
But each word represents something different for each of us."

The bell rings.

"For Monday," she says, raising her voice above the shuffle of
papers and feet, "write a thousand words about the meaning of one
word, and how the word makes you feel, and why."

Oh, brother. The class gives a group sigh.

"Class dismissed," she says. "Enjoy the rest of your day of Saint
Valentine's."

"Hey, Lex, wait up."

Beaker's running to catch me as I flee the classroom. I stop in
the hall and wait. She pulls up in front of me, her bright, curly hair

falling wildly around her shoulders and getting stuck in her hoodie as she puts it on. She tugs at it and smiles breathlessly.

"El and I, we're going to have an anti–Valentine's Day party at El's house tonight. It's not a party, really; it's an un-party, just pizza and a couple of slasher movies and maybe a game or two of Settlers of Catan." She bites her lip and stares up at me hopefully. "Will you come?"

I love Settlers of Catan.

I love pizza.

I even love slasher films.

For all of two seconds I let myself imagine it: me and Beaker and El in our pj's in El's basement, the way things used to be. And maybe I'd tell them. We'd curl up on El's old ratty couch with mugs of hot chocolate, and I'd spill out everything that's been going on: Mom and her theory that Ty's still in our house and how I'm not so sure now that she's wrong, the letter to Ashley so I could ask them what they think I should do with it, and maybe I'd even talk about what happened that night Ty checked out. With Steven. With the text.

But the instant I really let myself picture it, I feel the hole coming on. If just thinking about this stuff makes me feel like I'm going to die, what would saying it out loud do? And then I consider how Beaker tends to laugh when she's nervous. I imagine El's face, that look she gets when someone has said something too ridiculous to be believed. And I think, No. No. I can't tell them. I can't.

"Lex?" Beaker prompts gently.

I shake my head. "I should be home with my mom tonight, you know?"

And that would be true, if my mom wasn't working tonight. So it's not technically a lie.

Beaker's mouth goes into a frustrated line. I can see her considering her options and then deciding there are none. Nothing trumps sad, lonely mother.

"Anyway, why aren't you going out with Antonio?" I ask.

She tucks a curl behind her ear. "Oh. We're not together anymore. He's a skeez."

"I'm . . . sorry," I say lamely. I never liked Antonio. He was the kind of guy that always wanted to make out with Beaker, but never seemed to want to talk to her.

He was unworthy.

Beaker waves her hand like she's dismissing the thought of him, makes a *pfft* sound. "Well, love isn't real, like you said, right? And Antonio's hormones decided to react chemically with someone else."

"That sucks."

"Yeah, it kind of does," she says with a bitter laugh. "Are you sure you won't hang out with us? I miss you. We all . . . miss you, Lex. That was boss the way you kind of took down Mrs. Blackburn."

We all, she said.

"Is Steven going to be there?" I ask.

"He doesn't have to be," she answers, which means yes, he's supposed to be, of course he is, he's their friend still even though he's no longer my boyfriend, but she'll uninvite him if it would make me feel more comfortable.

I can't face Steven. But I can't kick him out of the party, either.

"Like I said, I have to keep my mom company tonight," I say. "Sorry. It sounds fun."

"Okay, well." She puts her hand on my shoulder. "Hey, if there's anything I can do . . . If you ever want to talk . . ."

"Right. I have to go," I say. "I have class."

She knows that. She has class, too, the same class—AP History—and then third-period calculus, fourth-period physics, fifth-period computer programming, sixth-period calc lab, and then lunch, all of which she and I have together until seventh period, when she takes French and I take German, and then eighth period, when I am a teacher's aide in Mrs. Seidel's chemistry class, and Beaker has a drama class that serves as the first hour of the afternoon rehearsal for the school play.

But she lets go of me, and I back away, and then I walk off before I have to look too long at the disappointment on her face.

8.

FOR DINNER I MICROWAVE a frozen chicken pot pie and sit watching the news on our tiny kitchen television while I pick at it, until the coverage of all-things-love-related for Valentine's Day becomes too nauseating. I turn off the TV. Outside, snow is falling, the passing of yet another winter storm.

I should shovel the driveway, I think. That would make a nice surprise for Mom when she gets home.

But that would mean going into the garage.

I don't go into the garage.

The phone rings. I pick it up, but there's nobody there—just silence for a moment while I say hello a few times, and then I hang up. It's the old phone in the kitchen, so I can't see the number.

I wonder if it's Steven, checking up on me.

I wish he would have said something, if it was him.

Not that there's anything left for him to say. Not that I'd know how to respond if he did say anything.

I finish my pot pie. It's not a candlelit Valentine's Day dinner while I'm being serenaded by a string quartet, but as freezer meals go, it's not too bad.

There's a noise in the hallway, the sound of something heavy hitting the floor.

I go to investigate.

A picture has fallen off the wall. I pick it up, turn it over in my hands. The photograph is missing. I search the floor, but it's not there. The back of the frame is fastened, so someone must have removed the photo and then hung the empty frame up again.

That's weird.

I know the missing picture. It's a photo of Dad and Ty, four years ago, pre-Megan, as they were about to head off on Ty's first deer hunting expedition. They were wearing neck-to-toe camo and neon orange caps. They were both smiling, holding up their rifles, but Ty's smile was strained.

He didn't want to go. He'd been dreading it for weeks.

But he went because he thought it would make Dad happy.

I remember the day they came home from that trip. They had a deer, a small scraggly little guy with a tiny rack.

"Uh-oh," I said when I went out to watch them hang it from the rafters in the garage. "Bad day for Bambi."

Ty smiled at my joke, but he was quiet. Dad was proud, talking about the difficulty of the shot that Ty had made, what a clean shot it was, so the animal didn't suffer, but Ty didn't say anything. He didn't have much of an appetite at dinner. He went to bed early that night. When Mom framed this photo and put it up, he never stopped to look at it as he passed in the hall.

I feel the beginning of the ache in my chest. The hole.

Then all of a sudden I'm flooded with the sense that I'm not alone. If I turn and look, I'll see a shadowy figure at the end of the hall. I'll see him.

Ty.

The hairs on the back of my neck stand up at the thought. I never knew they would actually do that, before—stand on end like that—but they do. I have goose bumps up and down my arms. My shoulders are so tight it hurts. My mouth is dry. I suck in my bottom lip to wet it.

I won't run this time, I think. I'll face it.

Slowly, I turn.

There's no one there. The hallway is empty.

I let out the breath I was holding, then try to laugh at myself. Delusion, I think. A belief that, though false, has been surrendered to and accepted by the whole mind as a truth. Not a ghost, not a hallucination. A delusion.

I hang the empty frame back in its place on the wall.

14 February

Sometimes I miss being kissed.

It seems like such a small thing, a trivial thing, my lips meeting his, but sometimes, like tonight, I lie in bed unsleeping and stare up at the ceiling and remember what that felt like, not just the kissing part but that moment right before, when our faces were so close together, when I could feel his breath and see his eyes up close, the curve of each dark eyelash, the tiny crease where his neck met his jaw. The seconds before he kissed me. The anticipation. The rush of his lips on mine.

The average person, or so the internet tells me, spends 20,160 minutes of life kissing.

I wonder what our total was.

God. V-Day has infiltrated my brain.

The first person I ever kissed on the lips was a boy by the name of Nathan Thaddeus Dillinger II. I was 14, and Nate was the kind of guy whose parents bought him a sports car for his 16th birthday, which he would total (but survive to tell the tale) before he got halfway to 17. He was tall, dark, and handsome, wore designer jeans, and had one of those high-wattage smiles that made the female teachers go easy on him.

Yes, he was hot. Yay for me.

But for all his many qualities, Nate Dillinger was not the sharpest knife in the drawer.

He was failing algebra.

You see where this is going.

The first kiss happened in a study room of the Williams Branch public library. I was teaching Nate about the systems of equations. We were doing a story problem:

John buys 3 goldfish and 4 betas for $33.00. Marco buys 5 goldfish and 2 betas for $45.00. How much would Celia spend if she bought 6 goldfish and 4 betas?

Our heads were close together, bent over my notebook, where I had just finished writing out the equations

$3g + 4b = 33$

$5g + 2b = 45$

when suddenly, without any kind of warning, Nate Dillinger kissed me.

Hmm, I remember thinking as his lips moved over mine. This is not entirely unpleasant.

Then he tried to stick his tongue in my mouth, and I thought something like, Ew, no, gross, and pulled away.

"Sorry," Nate said, smiling in a very non-sorry way.

"That's okay," I said, stunned. I mean, he had just stolen my first kiss. I was never going to get it back. That was it.

He took my "that's okay" for permission to do it again, and leaned in. I leaned away.

"Wait, do you even like me?" I asked.

He frowned, confused. "What do you mean?"

"Do you find me, well, I don't know, attractive?"

He shrugged. "You're all right."

Be still my heart.

"Just all right?" I snorted. "Then why did you kiss me?"

Another shrug. "I was bored."

He was bored. He stole my first kiss because he was bored.

Oh, the horror.

I sighed and resisted the urge to say something hurtful. He was a boy, thus biologically engineered for stupidity of this type. We could get past it, I thought. I could still get through this tutoring session and receive the $50 I'd been promised. "Let's get back to John and Marco, okay?" I suggested. "Now, the first thing we want to do is multiply the second equation by -2, so then we have a +4b and a -4b, which will cancel each other out, and then we'll add—"

That's when he tried to kiss me again.

And that's how:

Nate Dillinger + bloody nose = me - $50

Yeah, so my first kiss was no big deal.

My second kiss, the one that matters, didn't happen until last summer.

That day I was supposed to meet the gang at the SouthPointe Pavilions Barnes & Noble to chill for a bit, then go see a movie at the theater next door. As usual, Steven arrived early; he was already there when I showed up. But El had texted that she had one of her headaches (read:

Downton Abbey marathon) and Beaker had called to report that she and Antonio were "having car trouble" (as in they were busy in the backseat of her car) and she didn't think they'd make it out before the film started.

"It looks like it's just going to be you and me today," I told Steven when I found him flipping through a *Scientific American* in the magazine section. "The others are flakes."

"Good," I remember he said, with a quiet, knowing kind of smile he gets sometimes. "It's been too long since I had you all to myself."

I laughed, but I was suddenly, inexplicably, nervous at the idea of having Steven "all to myself." Maybe I could sense that something was going to happen. A change in the equation.

I told myself I was being silly. Steven and I were friends. We'd known each other since we were 12, when we decided that the smart-kid types in our middle school were better off sticking together. Safety in numbers, you know. I thought Steven was cute even back then. But his attractiveness wasn't really about how he looked, because there were periods when he had bad acne and braces and he was skinny as a beanpole. There was just something about him. The way he got excited about stuff like Tolkien and quantum physics and Doctor Who. He still had a sense of wonder that gets shamed out of the majority of the teen-age population by the time we turn 18. He still loved things about the world. I found that inherently sexy.

That and I could always tell he liked me. There'd been the paper flower on Valentine's Day, and sometimes I caught him looking at me in a way that went beyond friendly. Interested.

But Steven was too reasonable for romance, I thought. Like me.

We wandered over to the science fiction and fantasy section and bonded over our adoration of <u>Ender's Game</u> and discussed how Hollywood hadn't screwed up the film too badly but it would never come close to the experience one gets reading the book, and I relaxed. Everything felt the same between us as it had always been.

Then Steven pulled out <u>Contact</u>.

"You should read this," he said.

"Carl Sagan, as in the astrophysicist?" I squinted at the cover, which had a picture of Jodie Foster on it for some mysterious reason. "He wrote fiction?"

"It's an amazing book," Steven said. "It shows how the belief in religion and the belief in science are fundamentally alike. We believe, even when we can't prove it, even when we can't see."

"But in science, there's evidence," I argued. "There's proof."

"Read it. You'll see what I mean. You'll like it."

I put my hand on my hip and smirked up at him. "How do you know what I'd like?"

Looking back, I can see that this could have been construed as a lame attempt at flirting on my part.

And it worked.

"Oh, I think I know you, Lex," Steven said, the sound of his voice changing from what it had been a minute ago. "I know what you'd like."

"Okay," I murmured, and reached for the book, but he didn't release it.

"While we're on the subject, you know what else you'd like?" He cleared his throat and glanced around. We were alone, at least in that

particular section of the bookstore. "You'd like to go out with me. On a non-friend type of outing. A date, I mean."

Boom. A date.

I sucked in a breath. "Is that a question?" *I asked stupidly.*

"Yes. I mean, would you consider . . . would you go out with me?"

I stared at him. A dozen reasons why this definitely would not be a good idea marched through my brain: This kind of thing would only complicate matters, make a mess. I hated messes. My life was enough of a mess as it was. I was just starting to feel like I had the ground under me again after my parents' divorce. I needed to focus on school, keep up my perfect grades, get into college, figure out my life's trajectory. I liked Steven—I liked him so much; that was easy to admit; he was one of my favorite people—but if we were together like that, it would make the other members of our group feel awkward. It would ruin our friendship.

We'd end up hurting each other.

"Steven—" *I started to brace myself to say all of the hard things.*

"Wait," *he said.* "Hear me out." *He extracted the book gently out of my hand and returned it to its place on the shelf, then took my other hand in his.* "I know a romantic relationship could be considered risky at this stage. We have a year left of high school before we go our presumably separate ways. I know the purpose of romantic engagement, on a biological level, is for procreation, and neither one of us wants that, of course. But . . ." *He glanced down at our joined hands.* "That's not all there is to it. There's the social aspect, of learning to interact with someone, as a partner, which could be useful for our future experience. And* *it's been proven that romantic companionship is good for your health: it promotes the release of endorphins, relaxation, a sense of greater security, and . . ."*

We were both blushing by this point. *We're so similar,* I thought. *When we get nervous, we both start talking like idiot savants.*

"You're babbling," I observed.

"I know." He sighed and then kept talking. "I think we could be good together, Lex. I promise I wouldn't pressure you, about . . . anything, and I won't have any kind of expectations about what's going to happen a year from now. I just want to find out what we could be like. An experiment, of sorts."

I bit my lip. He was making it sound reasonable. Logical. Tempting. That and he was gazing at me with those unbelievably warm brown eyes of his, and his expression said:

PLEASE SAY YES.

"So the experiment would be whether or not there's chemistry between us," I said.

He let go of one of my hands to push his glasses back up on his nose, and smiled. "Exactly. A simple experiment in chemistry."

Which made sense. There was nothing Steven loved more in the world than chemistry.

"So this would entail you and me going on dates," he continued, moving onto the logistics of how it would happen. "Maybe once or twice a week, or more than that, if you want. Whatever you prefer, really . . . We could—"

"Yes." The word was out of my mouth before I could talk myself out of it. "I'll go out with you. Yes."

"Excellent," he said, looking so thrilled I thought he might start dancing right there in the bookstore. "You won't regret it."

And that's how it started.

He held my hand during the movie. I sat in the flickering dark stunned by the idea that it had happened so easily, after all this time knowing each other. He asked me to think of him romantically, and I said I would. Just like that.

"This isn't too weird for you, is it?" he whispered after a while.

"No." I squeezed his hand. "This is good."

And it was.

After the movie he drove me across Lincoln to the Oven, an Indian restaurant downtown. He opened the door for me, pulled my chair out as we were being seated, and insisted on paying for dinner.

That was a little weird.

Then he drove me home and walked me to the front door. And at the porch, he stopped.

"Can I kiss you?" he asked hoarsely. There was so much in his expression, and I could read it all. He liked me. He really liked me. He didn't want to mess this up. He thought it might be too soon, but he wanted to kiss me. He wanted to know that I felt what he felt. It was a real part of the experiment, this kiss. It was:

Does me + Steven + dating = chemistry?

That's what kissing is supposedly for, on a biological level. It's a taste test, to see if you'd be a good match.

"Yes," I said, and stepped closer to him. "You can kiss me."

Slowly he lowered his head until his lips almost touched mine. He smiled, and I felt light-headed with how much I found I wanted this.

I dragged my bottom lip between my teeth to wet it and smiled too. Breathless. Waiting.

"Okay," he whispered, his breath hot against my cheek. "Here we go."

His mouth came down on mine gently, without pressure, and I don't have words to describe what it was like outside of warm and wonderful and alive, and none of those words even come close. After a minute our mouths opened and my tongue touched his, and the furthest thing from my mind would have been the words ew or no or gross. He tasted like red curry and sweet tea. Electricity zinged down my body and pooled low in my belly and I thought, Wow. So this is how it feels. All this time, I'd wondered. I was almost 18 years old and I'd never felt so connected with another person.

I curled my hand around the solidness of his shoulder and pulled him closer. He made a small rough noise deep in his chest and changed the angle, and our glasses banged against each other. We broke away from each other, laughing.

"That was . . . ," he started.

"Spectacular," I breathed.

"Spectacular," he repeated, his brown eyes sparkling. Because the results of our experiment were conclusive:

Me + Steven + dating = spontaneous combustion

He tucked a strand of my hair behind my ear, his thumb lingering on my cheek. I shivered. I wanted to kiss him again.

"Good night, Lex," he said, and then he turned abruptly and jogged back to his car. He sat there for a few minutes without driving off, and I wondered what he was doing until my phone buzzed with a series of rapid-fire texts. Which read:

There are some things I didn't get to say before.

You are an amazing girl, Lex. You're smart and funny and kind and beautiful. You're the whole package.

Thanks for saying yes.

I'll see you tomorrow?

I texted back that yes, I would love to see him tomorrow. We grinned at each other through the glass of his car window, and he drove away, and I went inside.

It was June 20.

I'd get six months with Steven, six months to the day, 183 days of kisses, before the equation would change again.

9.

TY AND I ARE WALKING IN THE WOODS. There aren't a lot of woods to choose from in Nebraska—we're more of a plains-type state—but when we were kids Mom and Dad took us to this one part of the Nebraska National Forest where there were tall trees and a lake and a campground. We camped in tents, Ty and me in one and our parents in another. I can't remember how old we were, but little, I think. Little enough that our very own tent with just the two of us seemed like the greatest adventure. We stayed up half the night whispering, making shadow puppets with our flashlights, gazing up through the see-through mesh at the top of our tent at the dark shapes of the tree branches swaying over us, imagining the stars. The next morning, we got up early to fish on the lake. Ty caught five fish to my four, but he threw his back into the water. He was tenderhearted, even then, too sweet to murder an innocent fish. But Dad bashed mine in the head with a special hammer and fried them up over the campfire for lunch. And then he said to Ty, "This is reality. Eat up."

Dad's not so much with the sentimentality. My apple didn't fall far from his tree, I guess.

Anyway. It's those woods, I think. Where Ty and I are walking now.

He's wearing a white tee and dark jeans.

The sun is going down somewhere behind us. I don't know where we're walking. I'm wearing my backpack, and it's heavy. I want to stop, just so I can get a good look, in the fading light, at Ty's face. I'm starting to forget it. The shape of his nose. His ears. His lips, which were perpetually chapped. I used to say to him, "Dude, invest in some ChapStick already." Now I just want to memorize him, every detail I can get, chapped lips and all, to push the image of him yellow and stiff and covered in a layer of funeral-home makeup out of my brain.

"Hey," I say to him. "Can we rest for a minute?"

He turns to me. "You're tired already? We only just started." But he sits down on a large rock. "Give me some of your water."

I find I'm carrying a large water bottle. I hold on to it. "What's the magic word?" I tease.

"Puh-leeze," he says, reaching, smiling, and I shake my head. "Nope."

"Moist," he says. "The magic word is *moist*."

"Ew. No."

"It's not *delusion*, I'll tell you that much."

"Shut up. I was improvising."

"What word are you going to write your essay about?"

"I'm not planning to do that assignment," I inform him.

"You. Aren't going to do your homework. You."

"How do you even know about that?"

He shrugs. "What word?" he persists. "What word would you write about?"

"Doofus," I retort.

"Brilliant. It fits you," he says with a roll of his eyes. "Now give me the water, Lex. I'm dying here."

I arch an eyebrow at him.

He smirks. "Figuratively speaking."

I hand him the water. He gulps down like half of it, wipes his mouth with the back of his hand in a gesture so familiar it makes my chest ache, and hands the bottle back.

I miss you, I want to say. It's on the tip of my tongue, but I think, If I call attention to the fact that this is a dream, then I'll wake up.

I don't want to wake up.

Something snaps in the woods. A flock of birds startles from a tree and takes flight, their wings crackling in the air. The light is fading by the minute. I look at Ty. He's staring off into the darkest part of the woods.

"We should go," he says as he gets to his feet.

"Okay."

We start walking again. I still don't know where we're going. There doesn't seem to be a path, but Ty acts like he knows the way. He keeps looking over his shoulder, behind us, like he's afraid, and this makes me afraid. It's suddenly so dark. The shadows are coming at us from every direction.

We walk faster. I'm out of breath. I stumble on a tree root or something.

I fall.

Ty grabs my hand and helps me to my feet. In the woods behind us there are more snapping branches and crunching leaves, the sounds of something moving toward us. Something stalking us. Something big.

I've hurt my ankle. Bad.

"It's a bear," Ty says, when I open my mouth to tell him that I'm not going to be able to run. "A grizzly."

"There aren't grizzlies in Nebraska."

"We should climb that tree." Ty picks a huge, spreading oak, which also shouldn't be in these woods. "Can you climb it?"

I don't have any experience climbing trees, but I try. I scramble up the trunk, ignoring the pain in my ankle, reaching at branches. Ty follows behind me, helping me balance, pushing me up, coaching me. But I'm slow. I don't climb high enough or fast enough. I'm clumsy.

"Hurry!" Ty cries. "It's here." It's so dark I can hardly see, but I can make out the huge silver-tipped shoulders of the bear below us, impossibly big. It makes a kind of chuffing noise, like a bark. It stretches up toward us. Then it has Ty's foot in its mouth. It starts to pull him out of the tree.

I grab his arms. I hold on.

Ty looks into my eyes. He smiles, and it's a sad smile, because he knows how this is going to end. We both do.

He says, "Don't watch. Stay up here, where it's safe. It will be over soon."

"Ty, no." I clutch his arms tighter. "Don't."

The bear is too strong. I can't hold him. He's yanked away. He falls. In the blackness of the forest, I hear him scream.

This is a dream, I tell myself. This is only a dream. He can't die again.

But he does. I hear the bear kill him. There are roars, Ty's yells of pain and terror, the ripping of fabric and the cracking of bones. I press my face into the rough bark of the oak tree, and I squeeze my eyes closed, and I listen to him die. Even then, in my dreams, I can't cry for him. I can't stop it. I can't help.

I am completely useless, I think. I can't save him.

Then, when it's over, when the woods fall silent again, I wake up. In my own room. In the dark. Alone again.

I've been having these dreams for weeks now. They're always the same, me and Ty, doing something we used to do, talking the way we used to talk, and then, after a while, something goes wrong and Ty dies. So far he's died in a plane crash and gotten shot by a gang member and been struck by lightning during a thunderstorm. In one he fell down a set of stairs and broke his neck. In another he got hit by a car while we were riding our bikes to school. It's like my own personal version of Kenny from *South Park*, except that Ty never dies the way he actually died. And every time he dies, every time I watch him, it feels real.

My stomach churns like I might vomit. I take a few deep, steadying breaths, like when Dad was in his Pilates phase and made us all learn to breathe from our core, and I sit up. I push my tangled hair out of my face. And then my heart lodges itself in my throat like a chunk of ice.

In the dim light from my bedroom window, I see a figure standing there. A silhouette. A person.

"Ty?" I croak.

The figure shifts slightly, as if he's been looking out at the street but now he's turning around. He doesn't speak. I fumble for my glasses on the nightstand. I'm bat blind without my glasses. When I was a kid I used to freak myself out in the middle of the night, thinking that if a monster came out of my closet to get me, I wouldn't see it until it was too late.

My fingers close around the frames. I unfold them carefully, bring them to my face, and look again at the window.

He's not there. There's just the shadow from the weeping willow tree outside.

I fall back on my pillow.

A shadow. A stupid shadow. From the stupid tree.

Ty's not ever going to be here when I open my eyes, I tell myself sternly. Not for real. No matter what I dream about.

I turn onto my side, my face to the wall. I will myself to go back to sleep. I go with the tried and true method: numbers. 0, 1, 1, 2, 3, 5, 8, 13, 21, each number the sum of the two numbers before it. The Fibonacci sequence, it's called, after an Italian mathematician who wrote about it in 1202. Fibonacci numbers are everywhere, in nature, even, in the pattern of leaves on a stem or the way the circles present themselves on the skin of a pineapple or the arrangement of seeds in a pinecone. Math. Safe, reliable math.

There is nothing more real than numbers.

My heartbeat starts to slow. My shoulders relax. I let myself breathe.

34. 55. 89. 144.

I remember that I'm wearing my glasses, and I take them off, fold them, and reach behind me to set them on the nightstand. The room goes dark and blurry, like an impressionist painting, colors but no distinct lines. Like a Van Gogh painting, I used to tell myself. *Starry Freaking Night.* I pull the covers up to my chin.

233. 377. 610. 987. 1,597. 2,584.

And it's right then, as my eyelids begin to get heavy, as I start to drift off to the gray space where Ty isn't dead, that I smell it.

A mix of sandalwood and basil and a hint of lemon.

Brut.

I smell my brother's cologne.

10.

SOMEONE'S KNOCKING ON THE FRONT DOOR.

I ignore it. I've got my hands full, literally. My sleeves are rolled up, and I'm wearing the rubber gloves and apron and everything, up to my elbows in hot, soapy water, in the middle of the mountain of dishes that's been piling up on our kitchen counter all week, since neither Mom nor I have the energy for dishes.

I haven't been sleeping well.

Now, I've decided, is not a good time for a visit from the sympathy parade.

Whoever-it-is pounds on the door again.

I'm annoyed. Mom's still asleep. Yes, it's after three o'clock in the afternoon on a Sunday, but she's been out cold all day. She didn't even get up for church, which is a bad sign. Until now she's always managed to get up for God.

The knock comes again.

Hey, that's okay, I think, still ignoring it, putting a dish in the dishwasher. Mom doesn't have to go to church. We're allowed to be antisocial. We're permitted to sleep as much as we want to. We get a pass. It's the only real perk that comes with the whole lose-your-brother gig: an indeterminate amount of time to make excuses. I don't have to open the door.

But this knock. It's loud. Persistent. A knock that isn't going away anytime soon.

Then it occurs to me that whoever-it-is could be bringing us dinner. That's how American culture teaches people to deal with a death: They bring a casserole. A pie. A fruit salad. This ritual provides the person giving it the feeling that they've done something useful for us. They've fed us. That's how they show us they care.

The first week people cared a lot. We had so much food that most of it went bad before we could eat it. Mom and I weren't even remotely hungry at that point; we just kind of sat in various positions on various pieces of furniture, and people would orbit around us, bringing us tissues, water, every few hours asking us if we thought we might eat something. I always waved the food away, but Mom tried. She wanted to be polite. I'd watch her sit at the table, forcing herself to go through the motions of eating, chewing each bite carefully, swallowing, trying to smile and reaffirm how good she thought it was, how very thoughtful.

The second week the people were mostly gone, and we picked at the best stuff they'd left us: the chocolate cream pies, the roast chickens, the sweet rolls. I tossed the rest. By the third or fourth week I started to get a bit of my appetite back, but right about then was when the food stopped coming.

People move on with their lives.

Even if we can't.

Which is too bad, since I can't cook to save my life, and Mom's becoming less and less reliable in that department.

I'm suddenly hopeful as I go to answer the door. A casserole sounds amazing. I'm starved.

I open the door, and there's Sadie McIntyre, our neighbor from three doors down. Voilà. But something's off. She doesn't follow the regular visitor protocol when she sees me, doesn't smile, doesn't ask how I am. She's not holding a plate of cookies or a pan of enchiladas or any kind of offering whatsoever. She's just standing there, one leg crossed over the other, staring at me with bright blue eyes, her expression neutral.

"Hi?" I say, a question.

"I'm going to Jamba Juice," she says in her cigarette-husky voice. "Do you want to go?"

This request makes no sense for a number of reasons:

1. It's February. In Nebraska. Today's a particularly chilly one; my cracked phone reports that it's hovering at around four degrees right now. Fahrenheit. When Sadie asks me, the question comes in a puff of steam.

Do you want to go to Jamba Juice?

Presumably to get a frozen drink.

2. Sadie and I haven't spent any real time together since elementary school.

When we were kids, when we were really little, I mean, we

101

practically lived at each other's houses. I had my own secret path from my back door, across Mr. Croft's porch, along the big stone wall that stretches across Mrs. Widdison's backyard, through a gap in the lilac bushes that edges the McIntyres' property, and across their lawn to Sadie's bedroom window. I could have walked that route in my sleep.

Sadie was my first friend. I can't even remember a time before I knew her, although our parents liked to tell a story about how Sadie ran away from home when she was two and ended up in our backyard sandbox, which is how we met. *A firecracker* was what my parents called Sadie. She was my best friend for years. If the other kids called me Four Eyes or Coke Bottles or Squinty (the glasses were a big liability back then), I could always rely on Sadie to come to my defense. She had four older brothers, and if anybody picked on either one of us, Sadie would set her brothers on the bully the way you sic a pack of dogs. I survived elementary school, in large part, on account of Sadie and the McIntyre boys.

I can still picture Sadie from those days: scrawny and tan, her curly, float-away hair bleached almost white by the summer sun, wearing a clean but faded T-shirt handed down by one of her brothers, which was always so long on her it would flap at her knees as she ran. Sadie loved to run. She never walked anywhere if she could get away with running there. And because I liked her so much, and because she was my friend, I always ran after her.

Until one day, when Sadie stopped running. She got a bike, and picked up a paper route from her older brother, so she could buy her own clothes when she started sixth grade. She started wearing makeup, and smiling in a different way. She made herself over into a whole new Sadie.

To be fair, I changed too, that year. I started hanging out with Jill and Eleanor and Steven. Sadie and I grew apart. It happens. As a sophomore Sadie had an unfortunate incident with shoplifting, which the entire neighborhood knows about but doesn't speak of. She hangs out with the stoner crowd. I'm in the geek brigade. We're still friendly, but our social circles don't often overlap.

Now she's standing on my doorstep in a worn red plaid jacket and jeans with deliberate holes in the legs, her blond curls tucked under a black knit hat. She's wearing gloves and too much eyeliner. I wonder why the stoners always feel the need to wear eyeliner.

"Lex?" she prompts, because I still haven't answered her question.

Oh, right. Jamba Juice.

I can't fathom what she wants from me, what she could be up to, but I also can't think of a good excuse, and honestly, the idea of getting out of the house for a while appeals to me. So I nod and remove the rubber gloves.

"Sure," I say. "Just let me get my coat."

Jamba Juice is deserted when we arrive. Big surprise. The guy behind the counter acts startled to see us, like we must have wandered in by mistake.

"Whew," Sadie breathes with a playful smile as she saunters up to the counter. "It's a scorcher out there. I am parched."

She's joking, but it doesn't compute with Counter Guy, who puts down his phone mid-text and stares at us like this has to be some kind of punking situation, like any second now he's going to spot a camera crew filming this.

"I'll have the Matcha Green Tea Blast," Sadie says without even consulting the menu, like she's here every day. "With the antioxidant boost." She turns to me. "You get one, too, Lex. My treat. Got to combat those free renegades."

Free radicals, I think, but I don't correct her. I order the same.

"Can we sit anywhere?" Sadie asks Counter Guy after she pays. "Or do we need to wait for a table to become available?"

He waves a hand across the empty shop and goes back to his phone, annoyed like we're interrupting his free time. Sadie picks a table in the far corner, slings her sizable leather purse over the back of her chair, plops herself down, and goes right to her drink, which is, I should mention, about the same color and texture as fresh guacamole.

This should be interesting.

"Some people," she says, "have no sense of humor."

I take a tenuous sip of the smoothie. It's surprisingly good.

"So," Sadie says after our smoothies are about a quarter of the way depleted. "I want to talk to you about something."

Here it comes. The "I'm so sorry" speech. The sympathetic squeeze of the hand. The "how can I help?" offer that I will actually feel guilty about when I refuse. The part where I will become Sadie's new pet project.

"I saw you the other night," she says. "Running."

Oh. That. I blink up at her. I try to imagine what I must have looked like, out there without my coat on, tearing through our neighborhood like I was being chased by wild dogs.

An insane person, that's what I looked like. A stark raving lunatic.

"Are you taking up running?" Sadie asks.

The idea is so preposterous that I almost laugh out loud. Even in those days when I used to run around after Sadie, I always hated it. I despised every aspect of running: the sweating, the huffing and puffing, the weird taste I'd get in my mouth, the way my shins ached afterward. I make it a rule to avoid physical exertion if at all possible.

But what can I tell her, I was running away from the ghost of my dead brother?

"Something like that," I mumble.

Sadie nods like she's confirming a rumor she's heard about me. "That's great," she says. "I've been thinking about running again myself. I got this app on my phone that's supposed to take you from the couch to running five K in like a month. You start out alternating running and walking and then end up running the whole time, by the end. It burns like five hundred calories per hour."

"That's what I've heard," I say.

"So maybe we could run together," she suggests casually, and fixes me with this strange stare, like she's throwing out some kind of challenge.

Uh-oh. Danger, Will Robinson. Red alert.

"Uh, sure," I manage to get out. "We should totally do that. I mean, I'm kind of busy right now, but maybe in a few weeks. And I don't know if it's a great idea to run in the cold, bad for your lungs or something. Maybe in the spring. But then I have Physics Bowl, and I have to take a bunch of AP tests, and my schedule gets pretty hairy. Maybe in the summer . . ."

Sadie's eyes narrow.

"Oh, Lex," she says then. "Whatever."

When we were in fifth grade, we went through a phase where we played this game called Whatever, which is where you're basically trying to get rid of all your cards by lying about what you have, but if someone says *whatever* and catches you in the lie, you have to take the whole pile. Sadie was a master of that game, I remember. She could always pick out my fibs.

She's calling me a liar.

"Sadie . . . ," I begin.

"Something's going on with you," she says, folding her arms across her chest. "You were scared, that night on the road. I want to know what you were running from."

I stare at her helplessly. "I wasn't running from anything—"

"Whatever, Lex," she says. "What-ever. You're in some kind of trouble. I can feel it."

Silence builds between us. I think, Of course I'm in trouble. Haven't you been paying attention for the past two months? And: What do you care if I'm in trouble? We haven't been close for years. It's none of your business. But then the urge to tell somebody—the urge to get the past week off my chest—crashes over me like a tidal wave. Sadie's still my friend. And she's not like my other friends;

she's not super rational and scientific, and maybe she won't jump to conclusions about my dubious mental health. She could be open-minded.

She could listen.

I do a quick survey of the shop. Counter Guy is nowhere to be seen, probably in a back room somewhere. The Jamba Juice is empty.

"I was running, because . . ." I take a deep breath. "Because I thought I saw Ty. And so I had to get out of my house, for a while."

Sadie leans forward. Her eyes are absolutely serious.

"Okay," she says after what I swear are the longest sixty seconds of my life. "Tell me everything."

An hour later we're holed up in my bedroom watching *Long Island Medium*. After I finished giving Sadie the basic details of the Ty-could-be-a-ghost story, she insisted that I bring her home and take her down into the basement to show her the mark on the wall from where I threw the phone at Ty, like she wanted to see the evidence herself, even though there's no real evidence. She peppered me with a barrage of questions: At what time of day, precisely, did I see my brother? Did I feel hot or cold in his presence? Was he wearing white or black? Did he look normal or was he altered in any way?

I tried to answer the best that I could.

Then she stood in the middle of his bedroom gazing into the mirror like she expected him to appear at any moment. I didn't know whether to be relieved or disappointed when he didn't show.

"Is this the note?" she asked, her eyes lingering on the Post-it in the center of the glass.

Sorry Mom but I was below empty.

I nodded.

She stared at it for a few more seconds, and her voice was low when she asked, "Did he talk to you?"

"No," I answered, and I thought, This is crazy. How is it possible that we're having a conversation about this like it really happened? "He was only there for one or two seconds, both times. It was like a flash."

"Well," she said gravely, "he'll definitely try to find some way to express what he wants. He's here for a reason, and you have to figure out what that reason is."

Right.

"How do you know so much about ghosts, anyway?" I asked.

And that's how we ended up watching *Long Island Medium* on my laptop upstairs. I've never seen the show before, but apparently Sadie's caught almost every episode.

"Theresa's hilarious," she says now, stretched across the foot of my bed on her stomach with her feet dangling in the air. "It's almost like she can't help herself. She has to talk to the spirits wherever she finds them."

This is true. So far in this episode Theresa—the medium, who has a thick Long Island accent and huge bleached platinum hair—has felt compelled to deliver a message from beyond to the guy at the Chinese takeout place and a girl she meets at a cooking class.

"She always bites her lip when she hears the spirits," Sadie adds. "I love how she tells people, too. She just comes out and says, 'I'm a medium. I talk to dead people.'"

I'm not sold. Not that the show isn't entertaining, because, if I'm being honest, it is. But it seems to me that the medium is simply telling people what of course they want to hear: that the person who died is safe and happy and at peace, and they shouldn't feel guilty about whatever they feel guilty about, and everything's okay.

In my experience, everything is not okay.

"So," Sadie says after the show wraps up. "What do you think Ty's trying to tell you? Why is he here?"

I hesitate. Then I retrieve my backpack from where I left it in the corner and dump the contents out on my desk.

"Whoa, is that rose made of paper?" Sadie asks, swinging herself around to sit up. "That's amazing. Where'd you get it?"

"Nowhere." I stab a pin through the wire stem and tack the rose up next to last year's daisy before Sadie has a chance to inspect it. I really, really don't want to get into my love life right now. Instead, I pull Ty's letter out from between the pages of my notebook. I hold it for a minute, feeling its weight in my hand, unwilling to relinquish it, and then I hand it to Sadie.

"I found it in his desk," I explain, a detail I'd kind of skimmed over before. "After I saw him—later, I mean, I found it."

"Who's Ashley?" she asks immediately.

I sigh. "The girl he took to homecoming. Outside of that, I have no idea."

I show her my typed list of prospective Ashleys.

"Damn," she says, scanning down the page with her finger. "That's a lot of Ashleys."

"You're telling me."

"And you don't have any other clues?"

I swallow. "She's blond. I only saw her once, from the back."

"That's not a lot to go on." She looks at my face and scoffs. "Ah, don't feel guilty. I never know who my brothers are dating. It's like an episode of *The Bachelor* in my family these days. I have to find out what their relationship status is on the internet."

This makes me feel about 5 percent better.

And then the answer hits me.

I gasp and grab my laptop. "Of course. I'm so stupid sometimes."

"What?" Sadie peers over my shoulder.

"The internet. Ty could have posted about homecoming."

I don't spend any real time on social media, but I do have an account for most things. I log in to one of them. I go to Ty's page. It's flooded with posts from other people, messages like *We miss you, Ty* and *Why'd you have to leave us so soon?* and *We won't forget you.*

We really should close this down, I think. I can't put my finger on why it bothers me, the idea of Ty's internet presence still being active when Ty himself is not. But it bothers me.

"When was homecoming, again?" Sadie asks. "September? I never go to the stupid dances."

"October." I scroll down to the bottom, press OLDER POSTS, then scroll to the bottom again, back and back through his timeline until I get to October.

And suddenly, just like that, there it is. A picture of Ty and his date at homecoming. He's standing behind her in front of a blue satin backdrop, his hands on the waist of her gossamer pink gown, smiling wide. She's turning her head, looking up at him, her mouth slightly open like the camera has caught her in a laugh.

I wonder if she noticed the makeup.

Her hair is long and blond, like I remember, and I can't tell the color of her eyes from this angle. But I recognize her instantly.

She must have cut her hair. She must have dyed it.

Because I know the girl in the picture. I drag the mouse over her face, and her name pops up. He tagged her.

Ashley Davenport.

The letter belongs to the cheerleader after all.

16 February

The first time Ty ever liked a girl, at least that I was aware of, he was 8 years old. He came home from school one day and announced that he was going to marry Melissa Meyers, a girl in his second-grade class. Because she was pretty, he said. And because she was "the nicest." Apparently, he'd proposed at recess, and she'd accepted. So it was a done deal.

My parents, ever the sensitive types, burst out laughing when he told them.

"Did you kiss her yet?" Dad inquired between chuckles.

"Ew, no, gross," Ty replied. "Girls have germs."

This answer only made Mom and Dad laugh harder, and Ty caught on that he was the butt of some kind of joke. He reddened and scowled, then skulked off to his room to contemplate his undying love for Melissa in private.

That was the first time that Ty ever volunteered information about his love life to the family. It was also the last.

I remember the incident well, because at the time my 10-year-old self had a crush on one of the McIntyre boys: Seth, who was 2 years older than me and kind of a tough kid, always getting in fights at school, but to me was, as Ty phrased it, "the nicest." I saw what happened to my brother and took a mental note never to tell my parents about my romantic experiences, either.

Not that there would have been a lot for me to report. I didn't exactly brag about my little encounter with Nate Dillinger.

I used to tease Ty about girls, not excessively, but enough. It was my sisterly duty, I thought. "Nice cologne," I might have said occasionally. "Trying to impress a girl?" "Who are you texting?" I'd ask if I caught him checking his phone. "A girl?" "Was that your girlfriend?" I'd prod if he smiled at a girl as we were walking into school together. "What's her name?"

He typically had a two-part response:

1. No.
2. Shut up.

But I only teased him because I knew there was nothing serious to tease him about, and he knew that. When he said his "No, shut up" line, he always wore a wry smile, because he knew it was a game we were playing, the big-sister-harasses-little-brother game.

It was different with Ashley. That night before homecoming, when he admitted that he liked this girl, he really liked her, I didn't joke, because I sensed that it was serious. I didn't push to find out the details: Did she go to our school? Was she a sophomore too? Did they have *classes together? What kind of person was she? What was it that he liked about her? Had he kissed her yet?*

He would have hated it if I'd asked whether or not he'd kissed her.

He'd tell me about her when he was ready to tell me about her, I thought. In his own time.

I didn't pressure him, didn't tease, but I watched him. I noticed things. Like how all through October and November he was on his cell a lot, and his voice when he spoke into the phone was softer and sweeter than I'd ever heard him talk. He started wearing his cologne every day, and shaved even though he didn't really need to, and spent more time in the mornings styling his hair. He walked with his chest out. He whistled as he came up the driveway. He even seemed more relaxed during our dinners with Dad.

I was glad for him. It was nice to see him smile when he saw her name come up on his phone.

I didn't think about the fact that he was 16 and so the happy part wouldn't last.

I didn't think about the fallout.

I don't know what day it ended exactly. I became aware of it the first week of December, when Ty got into a fight at school with one of his jock friends. He didn't give us the specifics, but the way the principal described it to my mom, Ty threw the first punch. He was only suspended for a day, on account of the fact that it was his first offense, but I noticed a subtle shift in the way people were acting around him at school after that. Like he was on suspension from the cool club, too, maybe not permanently, but for now. And Ty was trying his best to act like he couldn't care less.

He stopped talking except in the barest possible terms: please pass the salt, I'm going out, etc. . . . He stayed in his room, mostly, and played his music too loud, the bass throbbing up through my bedroom floor.

Happy was over.

This kind of behavior went on until December 10th, when a huge snowstorm passed through town. It dumped three feet of snow in a matter of hours, and the district called off school. Ty and I spent an afternoon watching TV in the den. He was sullen. He'd hardly strung 3 words together at breakfast, he'd rolled his eyes when Mom suggested that it was his turn to do the dishes, and, by the smell of it, he hadn't showered in a couple of days.

Something needed to be done.

I decided to see if I could make it better.

"So," I said as he flipped through channels. "What happened with that Ashley girl?"

I never was much for subtlety.

He made his face into a mask of careful indifference, but there were a few seconds there, before he composed himself, when pure pain flashed in his eyes.

"Nothing happened," he said.

"Weren't you going out or something?"

He looked at the television, considering what to tell me. "We went out for a while. But not anymore. It's fine."

It was not fine. Clearly.

"Uh-oh, am I going to have to beat her up?" I asked. "Because I will, you know."

He smiled faintly. "No."

"Who is this chick, anyway? Ashley who? What's her last name? Because I am totally going to kick her butt," I said, and the word butt came out so sharp and unnatural that Ty gave this tiny laugh, but he kept saying no, he wasn't going to tell me her last name, it wasn't necessary for me to beat her up, he could handle himself, thanks.

I had no real intention of confronting Ashley. I was just trying to cheer Ty up with the ridiculous notion that I, with my glasses and my twig-skinny arms, was capable of beating anyone up. So I kept going on about it, kept asking, and he kept telling me everything was fine. Then I dragged him out into the backyard to build a snowman effigy of Ashley and pelt it with snowballs, which he did reluctantly but then shifted to chucking snowballs at me, which evolved into an outright war. Then, when we were both snow-plastered and worn out, I suggested that we go in and do the girly thing and eat a whole lot of chocolate.

Operation Cheer Up Ty worked. Ty smiled. For the rest of the day he seemed lighter. He even cracked a joke at dinner.

He was going to snap out of it, I thought. He was going to get over this Ashley girl. He was going to be okay.

11.

THERE'S SOMETHING ABOUT THE HIGH SCHOOL gymnasium—maybe the odors of adolescent sweat and disinfectant and rubber, the way the grunts and the shouts bounce off the walls, every noise amplified, sneakers squeaking on the floor, the perpetual chilliness of the air—that sets me instantly on edge. I associate this place with physical punishment, PE and running the mile and the amount of pull-ups I've inevitably failed to do to meet high school fitness standards. I hunch uncomfortably on a metal bench in the back corner of the empty bleachers and gaze down at the shiny-floored basketball court. I don't belong here. My world has always been the classroom, with its smell of chalk or whiteboard, or the library, the safety of books and facts and soft lighting, not the bright fluorescent wash of the gym.

And yet, here I am. It's eighth period. I'm skipping my last class of the day so that I can sit in the cold gym and watch the cheerleaders practice.

I take out my five-subject notebook.

New subject: Ashley Davenport.

She's easy to spot in the group of girls in maroon uniforms on the far side of the gym. Her red hair against all the blonds. She's tall, too. Not towering, but taller than most of the other girls. Slender. Her voice, when she's shouting out the cheers, is clear and bright.

> *Let's G! Let's G!*
> *Let's O! Let's O!*
> *Let's go, mighty Gators!*
> *Let's go!*

I watch her for a while, take some notes, and in the next forty-five minutes of observing her, here's what I learn:

Ashley Davenport can kick really high.

She can also do the splits. And three back handsprings in a row.

She's strong. She makes it look effortless when she stands with another girl balancing on her shoulders.

That's about all I've got.

I shouldn't have sluffed eighth period.

I try to remember Ashley from other times I must have seen her at my brother's basketball games. But back then she was just another cheerleader, another set of waving pom-poms in a pack of too-short polyester skirts. I didn't have any reason to pick her out from the rest.

There's a sudden click, the noise of a camera going off, and I suddenly understand the phrase *jumping out of your skin* with much more clarity. I turn, ready to see the principal or campus security here to bust me for truancy.

I have a good excuse. Just as soon as I come up with one. Also: Can it be truancy if I didn't leave school property?

But it's Damian. He's sitting on a bleacher two rows above mine, wearing his usual gray hoodie and baggy jeans, holding a camera with a big lens and focusing on the cheerleaders.

"Oh, hi, Damian," I say reflexively. I'm not even that surprised to see him, once my heart rate goes back to normal. "What are you doing?"

"I take pictures for the yearbook," he explains as the camera clicks again. He lowers it and turns to look at me. "What are *you* doing, Lex?"

"Just hanging out," I say. As if the gym is so relaxing.

He nods like this makes perfect sense.

"I didn't know you were a photographer," I say.

He sweeps his shaggy hair out of his eyes with the back of his hand. "I've been dabbling in it. Seeing if I can get the camera to speak through me or whatever. I'm invisible to people, you know, which makes it easy to get interesting candids."

That sounds mildly creepy. "You're not invisible," I say. "I see you."

He smiles the timid smile again. "I know. But with some people—most people, really—I just fade into the background. If I disappeared one day, really disappeared and never came back, they wouldn't even notice."

I'm just the opposite, I think. I feel like I've disappeared already, the Lex that I was before, and some people have definitely noticed I'm gone. But them noticing I'm missing doesn't mean I get to come back.

I must look tragic and contemplative, because Damian tries to lighten the mood. "That's high school for you, though," he says. "Everybody's caught up in their own thing. We're all the stars of our own movies. Anyway, that's my big superpower. Mister Invisibility."

Right. I rub my shoe against the metal ridges on the back of the bleachers. Damian takes another picture of the cheerleaders as they line up for another cheer.

We've got pride! (clap clap clap)
On our side! (clap clap clap)
You know it! We show it!
We've got pride!

"Who comes up with these things?" I say. "Seriously."

He nods. "Hey, they are excellent rhymers. Pride and side. Know and show. Like, whoa."

We both laugh. Nothing gives nerds more innate satisfaction than poking fun at cheerleaders.

"Did you ever cover the basketball games?" I ask. "For the yearbook, I mean?"

He nods again. "Sure. A few."

"Did you see Ty play?" My voice catches on my brother's name, because I don't say it that much anymore, not out loud, in public, and saying it makes me feel vulnerable or slightly selfish, like I'm asking for sympathy or attention. I didn't mean to bring Ty up, but I can't seem to help myself. Because Damian knew Ty, he really knew him, probably better than any of Ty's jock friends ever did.

"He never missed a shot," Damian murmurs. Then his eyes widen over how that sounds, in my own personal context. "He was good. They haven't won a single game since he . . ."

And there's the pause.

This time I don't fill it in. I let the silence drag.

"I might have a few pictures of him from this year, if you want them," Damian says after a minute.

"Yeah. I want them," I answer.

He coughs into his sleeve. "I would have given them to you earlier, but I didn't know if you'd . . ."

"I want them," I say again. "Please."

"Okay."

He's uncomfortable now. I've made him uncomfortable. I shouldn't have brought up Ty. I check my watch. "Anyway," I say. "The bell's about to ring. I should . . . We should . . ." I stuff my notebook in my backpack and start to climb down out of the bleachers. Damian follows me. He helps me get over the metal bar at the bottom of the seating area.

"Thanks, Damian," I say.

"See you later, Lex," he says, and then he slouches off.

The bell rings.

I take one more look at the cheerleaders as they head for the locker room. Ashley Davenport lags behind. She stops and kneels to tie her shoe. The others drift away.

Who is this girl, I wonder? What happened between my brother and her? What happened?

She finishes tying her shoe and stands up, but she doesn't follow the others. She looks across the basketball court, past the bleachers.

At me.

I'm torn between the urge to duck and the urge to wave, but I don't do either. I simply stand there, staring at her, as she stares back at me. For a minute we're suspended in time.

I have the letter with me. I always have it with me. I could give it to her. I could go right now, down the bleachers, and I could put it in her hand.

"Hey, Ash," some girl calls, peeking out of the locker room. "Are you coming? We're going over to Starbucks, remember?"

She lowers her head quickly. "Yeah. I'm coming."

She doesn't look at me again as she walks to the locker room door.

12.

ON THE BUS RIDE HOME, Sadie slides into the seat next to me. I don't think I've ever seen her ride the bus before, but here she is, in ratty black jeans and green Converse sneakers, her shoulder brushing mine as the bus bumps along the street.

"Do you want to have dinner at my house?" she asks.

My mouth waters just thinking about dinner at the McIntyre house. Sadie's mom is a culinary genius—pot roasts and lasagnas and fried chicken with mashed potatoes, all the various meals I've eaten at the McIntyre home cycle through my mind, bite after wonderful bite.

I get out my phone to text my mom and tell her that I'm going to be home late. *Out with a friend,* I type. She should be happy with that.

See Lexie socialize.

But when we get to Sadie's place, the house is strangely quiet.

I remember it always being a bustle of activity and noise before—Sadie's brothers talking and joking and jostling, music blaring, her mom screaming for them to keep it down—but now there's nobody home, by the sound of it. Sadie leads me down the stairs to the family room in the basement. It looks the same as I remember, same couch, same paint colors, except the TV is bigger now. It still smells faintly of popcorn, from when Sadie's parents bought an old popcorn maker from a theater in Lincoln when it went out of business, but the machine is gone, a patch of slightly lighter carpet outlining where it stood along the wall. We used to love to watch it heat and pop, the burst kernels spilling out like a delicious volcano of buttery goodness. We spent hours down here, hours upon hours. A decent percentage of my life.

"Have a seat," Sadie says, and plops herself down on the couch.

"Where is everyone?" I ask.

She frowns like she doesn't understand the question.

"Your brothers?"

"Oh. They all have their own places now, except Seth. Josh is married. Austin's in law school. Matt's studying child psychology at UNL, though he changes majors every few months. They're around, though. They come for Sunday dinners and show up if they need to do laundry." She puts her feet on the trunk that serves as a coffee table and sighs contentedly. "It's nice having the TV to myself."

Everything changes, I think. That's the only constant. We all grow up.

Almost all of us.

"I remember watching *Jaws* here," I say, sliding down on the cushions next to her. "What were we, eight? My mom would have killed me if she'd known."

Sadie shudders. "It took me years to get over that movie. I couldn't even swim at the lake without imagining a shark in the water under me, waiting to rise up and bite me in half."

She turns the TV on and brings up the DVR, where I see, predictably, a bunch of episodes of *Long Island Medium*. But there's also *Ghost Hunters* and *Paranormal State* and *My Haunting* and pretty much every other ghost-related show on television. Which for some reason I didn't expect. I wouldn't have pegged Sadie as someone who would obsess over the occult.

"Do you have a preference?" she asks. "We don't have to watch ghost stuff. We can watch anything. We can just veg, if you want."

"Why do you like those shows?" I ask, because I don't get it. I don't understand how any rational person who isn't wrestling with the idea of her dead brother possibly being a ghost watches those shows.

Sadie shrugs. "I'm morbid, I guess. I like the idea that we don't stop, after we die."

"You believe in heaven and all that?"

Her eyes meet mine, startled. "Well, yeah. I do."

"But if heaven exists, what's this ghost thing about?" I gesture at the TV. "So everyone Theresa hears on her show is a person who didn't go to heaven, who's just sticking around earth hoping to chat with whatever medium comes along?"

"No," Sadie informs me matter-of-factly, like this is scientifically proven. "Theresa deals with spirits, not ghosts."

"There's a difference?"

"Spirits are people who've passed on to the other side. It's like another dimension, and they can visit us and watch over us and pass along messages, but they're at peace. Ghosts, on the other hand—" It occurs to her then that I might not want to hear this, and she falters.

"What about ghosts?" I ask, sitting up. "Tell me."

"Ghosts haven't crossed over. They have unfinished business in this world, so they linger."

I want to laugh it off and say it's all a bunch of crap, but I can't. Not after everything. "So you think what I've been . . . experiencing . . . is a ghost," I surmise. "Not a spirit."

"Well, you saw his figure, but he didn't speak," Sadie explains, "which is more consistent with ghosts. Spirits are talkative. And he's a suicide."

"But why does that matter?" I find myself asking, my voice sharper than I mean it to be. "I mean, with suicide, they want to leave this earth. They want to cross over, right?"

She bites her lip, and I wonder if she's not telling me that she believes suicides go to hell or being a ghost is a kind of purgatory. A punishment. I wonder if she's judging him like everyone else.

"I think with suicides a lot of times they're hanging on to something," she answers finally. "Some anger or some pain or something they've got to work out."

"So you think my brother is trapped in my house because he has something he has to work out," I say. "Unfinished business."

It's a ridiculous notion. Stupid. Crazy. Dumb.

Sadie doesn't answer.

I take the letter out of my backpack and sit for a minute holding it.

Ty's unfinished business.

"I don't know that he meant to give this to her," I say flatly. "What unfinished business could he possibly have with Ashley? I mean, they broke up. He's dead. That's finished business, I'd say."

"You haven't read it, have you?" Sadie asks in her raspy voice.

I've wanted to. I have so wanted to. "It's sealed. He wouldn't have sealed it if he wanted anybody else to read it."

She stares at the envelope thoughtfully. "Well, you have more self-control than I do. I don't know if I could not read it, if I had a letter like that."

"It's sealed," I say again, as if that settles it.

"You should read it. Then you'll know what Ty wants you to do with it."

"Sadie," I say, shaking my head. "It's not real. Ty's not a ghost. He doesn't want anything. He's dead."

Her eyes flash up to my face. "You don't think he's real? But what about—"

"I saw him for maybe a total of five seconds. I don't even know what I actually saw. The first time, I might have fallen asleep watching television and dreamed it, and the second time . . ." I think about the way Ty's face loomed up at me in his bedroom mirror. "I don't know. I don't know what I saw. Maybe it's me that's the problem. Maybe I'm . . ."

She folds her arms across her chest. "Crazy? You think you're crazy?"

I smooth down a corner of the letter. My nails are short, jagged, bitten. I don't even remember biting them; it's a bad habit I've never had before. That all by itself is like proof that there's something wrong with me.

Sadie shakes her head. "You're not crazy."

I glance up. "How do you know?"

"Because crazy people never wonder if they're crazy. Come on, Lex. If you're insane, then the rest of us are in big trouble, is all I'm saying."

I don't find this very reassuring.

"Even if you are crazy, which you're not, and even if the ghost isn't real," she points out, "the letter's still real, and it's definitely intended for Ashley. So you should give it to her."

I should give it to her, she says. This girl who broke my brother's heart. This cheerleader.

I shake my head. "No," I murmur.

"Don't you think you should respect his wishes?" Sadie asks.

My shoulders are instantly tight. My lungs start to close up. It feels like it's all coming down on me at once—bad dreams, bad memories, bad choices. It's too much. "What wishes did Ty respect?" I throw back at Sadie. "Why doesn't anyone ever ask that, I wonder. Where's the respect there?"

"Lex, hey, it's okay . . . ," Sadie begins. "I know—"

"You *don't* know." I cut her off. "I didn't ask for this. I'm not Ty's messenger boy. If he wanted this girl to have the letter, he could have mailed it. He could have left it where someone else would find it. Not me. Why does it have to be me?"

"Maybe he wanted you to r—"

"No. I don't believe in this stuff. I won't. I don't want—"

I can't finish the sentence. The hole ratchets itself wide open in my chest. I'm out of air.

"You don't want him to be in your house," Sadie murmurs.

It's the most horrible irony, Ty hating his life so much that he chose to end it, only to wind up right back in our house, back in his room, stuck, as helpless to change his situation as ever.

It's the worst thing I can think of.

I won't believe it.

I sit for a minute not-breathing. Sadie lays her hand on my shoulder and squeezes. She doesn't say anything but pulls me into a hug, and I let her. When we were younger she smelled like cheap laundry detergent and Ivory soap and kid sweat, from all her running. Now the aroma coming off her is a fruity perfume, some kind of melon, mixed with a whiff of cigarettes.

After I regain the ability to take air into my lungs, Sadie pulls back. "Do you need to punch something?" she asks. "I find that punching something is therapeutic."

I shake my head, embarrassed, wheezing. Nobody has had such a front row seat for the hole in my chest before. "I'm sorry. I've been kind of a spaz lately."

She flaps a hand at me, like whatever. "Don't be sorry. It is what it is. When my dad died I thought I was going mental for a long time. I had all this pain and I didn't know what to do with it, so I just puked it out on people. My mom and Seth got the worst of it."

I stare at her.

Her dad died. I knew that, somewhere in the back recesses of my brain. It happened three years ago, the summer we were fifteen. Her dad had been playing catch with her brothers in the backyard, and then he just sat down on the grass and said he was out of breath. And then he died.

I was at math camp in Vermont that summer. My mom called to tell me. I didn't go to the funeral. Sadie and I, we'd grown apart by then.

God, I think. What kind of selfish, horrible friend am I?

I forgot her dad died.

That's why her mom's not home. Her mom had to get a job. That's why the house is so empty.

"It's okay," Sadie murmurs.

It is not okay. It is *not* okay.

I don't know what to say. I suck.

Right then, the door behind us opens, and Seth wanders out. He's wearing camo pajama bottoms and nothing else, his short blond hair tousled. He rubs his face and gives us a sleepy grin.

"Hey. What's going on?" His gaze moves over to me. "Hey, Lexie."

"Hey, Seth."

He's different than I remember, too. He's taller, obviously. Filled out from the lanky teen he used to be, with muscles and tattoos splashed across both biceps, a black dragon stretching down his ribs. He raises a pierced eyebrow at me.

"Long time no see," he says.

I nod. "Are you just getting up?"

Sadie snorts. "He sleeps all day. Slacker."

"I am not a slacker," Seth argues, unfolding his half-naked frame unceremoniously on the couch next to me. Where Sadie has just a hint of nicotine on her, Seth has a cloud of stale cigarette smell floating over him. "I work nights."

"He's a desk clerk at the Residence Inn off the Cornhusker Highway," Sadie informs me, like this is the most slacker job ever. "He basically sits on a stool all night and brings people extra towels."

The side of Seth's mouth quirks up. He turns his attention to the television. "Don't tell me you're watching the ghost stuff again. That stuff's bullshit, you know. Do they ever get a real ghost on tape? No. They get strange orbs, weird floating lights, mysterious creepy sounds. No real evidence of a ghost. It's a fucking scam."

I'm inclined to agree. Plus I'm jealous at the way the swear words can simply flow off his tongue, like it's no effort to produce them.

"Hey, Lex, I think I've found something for you to punch," Sadie replies fondly.

"I could tell you a ghost story better than anything you'd see on TV," Seth boasts.

Sadie scoffs. "Okay, smart guy. Go ahead. Tell us a ghost story."

"Are you sure you want to hear it?"

"Oh, we're sure."

He looks at me. I nod. "Okay." He leans forward, elbows on his knees, and puts on a serious expression. "A few years ago I worked at Circuit City on O Street."

I almost laugh. Somehow when I heard the words *ghost story* my mind didn't jump straight to Circuit City on O Street.

"It's closed down now, but I worked there for like a year. It was a pretty normal job. A slacker job." He smirks at Sadie. "Mostly I hung out in the DVD section and tried to keep the punks from shoplifting movies. They always stole weird stuff, too, like *The Notebook* and *Mary Poppins* and shit."

"Ooh, terrifying," Sadie mocks.

He ignores her. "So one night after we'd closed up, I went into the back office to get some receipt paper to restock my register, and I got this weird feeling."

"A weird feeling?" Sadie's skeptical. "Like maybe the feeling that you should get a real job?"

He looks at me again. His eyes are the same cool blue I remember. "A feeling like there was someone watching me. At first I thought maybe someone was in the room with me, like a customer or a burglar or somebody. I said, 'Who's there?' and I picked up the baseball bat that my boss kept in the corner of the office. I went into the back room, and I turned on the lights and checked all the corners and stuff, but there was nobody. Still, I couldn't shake the feeling."

I wait for Sadie to make another snarky comment, but she doesn't. She's leaning forward, waiting to hear the end of the story. So am I.

"So I put the bat away and turned to go back out on the floor, and that's when I noticed it." He leans back, clearly enjoying the fact that we're so interested. "The shadow."

I can't help it; a chill goes down my spine. I shiver.

"Shadow?" Sadie repeats hoarsely.

"On the wall, there was a shadow of a man. And then I like whipped around to see what was casting the shadow, and I saw this dude standing there, just looking at me. He was an Indian. He was wearing the buckskins and moccasins and the feather in his hair and the whole Native American ensemble, which was weird enough, but what was weirder was that I could sort of see through him, to that sign on the wall that counted how many days since the last accident."

It's quiet for several seconds. Sadie and I are holding our breaths.

"So, go on," Sadie prompts. "What did you do?"

"I took a couple quick steps back," Seth says.

"And what did he do?" I want to know.

"He nodded, all solemn, and then he lifted his hand up like this." Seth raises his palm. "And then he said, 'How.'"

"'How'?" I repeat. "'How' what?"

"Like, 'How, white man. I come in peace.' And after that we were totally friends, me and Tonto, and every night after work we'd knock back a beer."

He starts laughing.

Sadie smacks him on the shoulder. "You doofus!" she cries. "God, can't you be serious for two seconds?"

He keeps laughing. I sink back into the cushions, part relieved, part disappointed, while Sadie chews him out.

Doofus, she called him. I swallow.

"But seriously, though," he says, catching Sadie's wrists when she tries to pummel him. "That Circuit City was built on an old Indian burial ground. Look it up on the internet if you don't believe me. And sometimes, for real, we'd hear footsteps or things would be moved in different places when we left the room. Seriously."

"Come on, Lex," Sadie says, disgusted, jumping up. "Let's get away from this loser."

"Love you too, baby sis," he calls after us, grinning wickedly. "You should have seen your faces. Priceless."

She takes my hand and tows me toward the stairs. When we get to the kitchen she gets out two paper plates, unwraps two frozen burritos out of the freezer, microwaves them for two minutes, and then scoops one up with a spatula and sets it in front of me.

Plop.

"Ladies and gentlemen," she says. "Dinner is served."

Mom's still up when I come in a few hours later.

"How's Jill?" She's sitting at the kitchen counter flipping through a *Better Homes and Gardens* magazine and sipping a glass of white wine. "Did you have a nice time?" she asks.

"Actually, I was hanging out with Sadie McIntyre," I confess.

A mix of surprise and disapproval crosses her face—Sadie's not what she would think of as a "good influence"—but she covers it up quickly. "What brought that about?" she asks, keeping her voice light. "I didn't think you and Sadie had much in common anymore."

"We have more in common lately."

Comprehension dawns in her eyes. My mom has no trouble remembering that Sadie's dad died. Mom's a decent human being.

"Well, I think that's nice, you and Sadie," she says after a moment. "You two used to be like peas in a pod."

I nod, remembering Sadie's face when she talked about her dad, the tension in her mouth like she was trying to keep her lip from quivering, even after all this time. She believes that her father is in a better place now, but that doesn't stop her from obsessing about ghosts and spirits and what happens after we die.

I think about what she said about the letter for Ashley, that it doesn't matter if the ghost is real or not, that Ty intended for Ashley to have it. That I should respect his wishes.

"You look lost in thought," Mom says, startling me. "Long day?"

"The longest," I say. Which is what every day feels like.

"Do you want to talk about it?" she asks.

That's nice. I wish I could tell Mom about the letter situation. I can imagine telling her, the way I used to occasionally ask for her advice, and then she'd help me work out the insignificant problems I had in my life before. But my mother isn't that Mom anymore, and I'm not that Lex. The woman in front of me now, pouring herself a second (or however many) glass of wine, is almost a stranger to me, but I do know one thing about her: she's fragile. She's barely hanging on. If I told her now about me seeing Ty, she'd lose her grip. She'd fall.

"Rain check, okay?" I tell her, giving her a brief hug. "I'm wiped."

In the hallway I notice that the empty frame, the one with the missing picture of Dad and Ty, is on the floor again. I pick it up. The glass in one corner is cracked. I turn it over and inspect it, but there doesn't seem to be anything wrong with the loop on the back or the hook on the wall. It just happens to be on the floor. Again.

I sigh. Just once I'd like to get through a day with nothing weird happening

I go back to the kitchen.

"Hey, Mom," I ask. "Did you do something with this picture?"

She frowns. "What picture?"

I hand her the frame. "It's the one with Ty and Dad going hunting. Did you take it out?"

She shakes her head, staring at the empty space in the frame. "I remember that day," she murmurs. "Your father was so proud. And Tyler . . ."

She doesn't finish her sentence, but she doesn't have to. I know.

Ty never wanted to kill anything. Not a fish or a deer or a spider, even. That's just how he was.

How is it, then, that he managed to do such damage to himself?

Mom wipes at her eyes. "No. I didn't take it."

And now I've started my mother crying again. Perfect.

"There's another picture missing, though," she adds. "From the stairwell."

"What?"

"Your father's graduation picture. I noticed it the other day when I . . ."

When she went down to sleep in Ty's bed.

I go straight to the stairs. There are dozens of pictures on the wall here as you descend into the basement: all the awkwardly posed family photos and pictures of both sides of relatives. A picture of Dad and his two older sisters standing in front of their house with seventies hair when Dad was just a toddler. A portrait of Gram and Pop, Mom's parents, at their wedding on the steps of a stone church. Dad with a dorky little beard, holding a wet and naked baby (okay, that's me) in a fluffy orange towel. Grandpa at his sixtieth birthday party. Christmas card photos of my cousins. Terrible class photos. And Mom's right; there is a picture missing, on the bottom right side of the wall. The frame's still there but the photo is gone. It was a black-and-white professional photo of Dad wearing a suit and tie, smiling serenely like there was nothing in the world he'd wanted so much as to graduate with a BS in accounting from the University of Nebraska–Lincoln.

Sigh. Just one freaking day.

When I was a kid I had a thing for Sherlock Holmes, the way he was able to ascertain so much by using deductive reasoning and simple observation. I went through a phase where I told people that I was going to be a detective when I grew up. But now I've got this seemingly simple mystery in front of me and I have no idea how to go about solving it.

I head back up the stairs. Mom's still sitting at the kitchen counter. Still drinking. Still crying.

She glances up, sniffles. "Yes," I affirm. "The photo's missing."

"I thought your dad might have stopped by and taken it," she says. "He still has a key to the house. Maybe he took the one in the hallway, too."

That explanation makes sense, I guess. Both missing photos are of Dad. But (a) I hope Dad doesn't feel like he can sneak into the house whenever he likes and take stuff. He could ask me, if he wanted something. I wouldn't give him any grief about it. And (b) why would he take the photos but not the frames? Why would he take the time, mid-sneak, to carefully unfasten the frames, slip the photos out, and then return the frames to their proper places? And, finally, and maybe most importantly, (c) why would he take the photo of himself at graduation and the hunting photo and not take, say, the picture of his sisters or of Grandpa or the one where he's holding me?

"We should change the locks," I say to Mom.

She sets her glass down on the counter. "Because we have a photo thief on our hands?"

"Because Dad shouldn't have the key to the house anymore. Or I can ask him to give it back, I guess. Whichever you prefer."

She folds her hands in her lap and looks down at them, her decision-making pose. "I don't know, Lex. That seems excessive."

It's not excessive. It's been three years since he moved out. They're divorced.

Dad's never coming back, I want to say to her, but I don't. I don't want to push her. But I wish that Mom was stronger. That she didn't cry. That she hadn't been so devastated when Dad left. That she'd done that woman-scorned thing and piled up his stuff in the yard and burned it all. Maybe, I think, if she hadn't been so weak, then Ty could have let go of the rage he felt whenever he saw her hurting like that. He could have moved on. And then maybe he would never have made that first attempt with the Advil. And maybe it would have occurred to him to fight back when life got tough.

Maybe he'd still be alive.

So in that moment, even though she's kind of the only thing I have left in this world, I blame her.

But there's nothing to do with that emotion but swallow it down.

"I'll ask him," I say to her, although I don't clarify whether I'm referring to the photo or the house key. I turn away. "I'm going to bed." I tilt my head toward the hall and my waiting bedroom. "I'm thrashed."

"Night," she says. "Sleep well, sweetie."

Yeah, right.

17 February

The last basketball game I saw of Ty's was in the first week of December. December 3rd, if I remember correctly. A Tuesday night. On Thursday morning Mom would get called into the principal's office because Ty had punched one of his jock friends. Broke his nose, so the story went. By Friday people at school were giving Ty that we're-so-over-you look. So Tuesday night might have been when he and Ashley broke up.

That was the week Ty made shooting guard on the junior varsity team. It was a big deal. He was proud of it, I could tell by the half jog he did as he came out onto the court that night, wearing the black jersey with the number 02 on his back. He tried to look confident through his nervousness: nonchalant, unruffled, oh-so-cool. Then he gazed up into the stands the way he always did, scanning the crowd. He never said so, but I knew he was searching for Dad's face.

Dad was the reason Ty started basketball.

Basketball had been one of Dad's obsessions back when Ty was around 12. *Dad was like that, before, always looking for a new week-end hobby, finding something that interested him and then getting consumed by it, spending all his time and extra cash on procuring the best equipment and how-to manuals and clothes. I used to chalk it up to Dad having the most boring job in the world, so he was looking to get some excitement in his life. Every few months it was a different thing. Tennis is the first one I remember, a string of early Saturday and Sunday mornings where Dad went off wearing white shorts and carrying a racket. Then sailing—Dad bought a sailboat (yes, a sailboat in Nebraska: landlocked state) and a different set of white shorts, and spent 2 entire summers gliding back and forth across Branched Oak Lake before he lost interest in that. Then came inline skating, which was mercifully short, only a few weeks that he dragged us out to the empty church parking lot laden with pads and helmets to practice pivoting and stopping. Then mountain biking, which ended in Dad breaking his leg. Then chess, while the broken leg healed. And then, if I remember correctly, it was basketball.*

We woke up on a Saturday morning to the sound of a ball hitting the concrete in our driveway, Dad wearing some kind of jumpsuit, throwing and missing and cursing as the ball bounced off the hoop he'd just installed over the garage door.

"Hey, kiddos," he said when we went out on the porch to watch him. "Want to shoot some hoops?"

I declined. I'd borrowed a book about Einstein from the library, and I wanted to spend the day curled up in my room trying to get my 14-year-old brain around the theory of general relativity. But my brother's eyes lit up.

Finally, something he could do. Something he and Dad could do together.

After that, Ty was always out there practicing. Dad moved on to hunting and guns and target practice that year, but Ty stayed with basketball.

The team was up against Omaha North that night, in the last game I saw Ty play. Math Club was running concessions, per usual, but they let me sit out in the stands for most of the game and then rush back at halftime to help fill sodas and pour nasty molten nacho cheese over stale chips and run the register. So I saw him play. I caught the look he sent into the crowd, the search for Dad, and when he glanced in my direction I held up my hand and smiled. He nodded, glad to see me and disappointed that I was alone, and turned away. He didn't look up into the bleachers again.

Dad came to a few games in the beginning, but that petered out fast. I guess he couldn't bear to be away from Megan for that long. It's a shame, though, that Dad didn't get to see Ty play. It was a thing of beauty to watch him. And it would have made Ty so happy—even though he never would have admitted it—if Dad could have seen just how stellar he'd become on the court.

He was the best shot on the team. No question. Sometimes I wonder if that's how the math gene presented itself in Ty—his ability to calculate angle and force with the muscles of his arm, so he could hurl a ball from half a court away and then stand back to watch it swish effortlessly through the net. He wasn't the fastest player, or the tallest, and he wasn't great at blocking or guarding or slam dunks. But my brother could shoot.

I want to remember that game. I've tried so many times in the past week, since I figured out that the letter belongs to Ashley Davenport. I try to bring up even one shot he made that night. He must have made several—we won the game 97 to 33. I remember the freaking score, the red digital numbers lit up on the board, I remember what happened right before, as he came out with the team, and what happened after, but no matter how many times I go back through it, I don't remember any specific moment with Ty during the actual game.

When I try to think about it, instead I remember 17 days later.

Sorry Mom but I was below empty.

And then everything goes mercifully numb. Or I get the hole in my chest. One or the other.

Here's what I do remember about December 3:

Steven came down from the concessions stand about 10 minutes in, said El and Beaker had it covered. He took my hand, and he held it for a while, and then he turned it over and ran his index finger up and down the length of my palm. All my nerves started firing. I shivered and laughed and told him to quit, but I liked it. He laced his fingers with mine, and we watched the game, but I was really watching Steven, the jerk of his Adam's apple when he swallowed, the small freckle he had next to his right ear, the way he pushed his glasses up on his nose a bit awkwardly with his left hand, because his right hand was holding mine, the way his eyelashes were long enough to brush the lens if he pushed the glasses too close to his face.

I remember that at the beginning of halftime Beaker did an imitation of Principal Boone that was so funny that El snorted soda up her nose, and we were trying not to die laughing almost the entire 15 minutes of the break, as we counted out the people's change and served their food, and they were looking at us strangely, because what could possibly be so hilarious, which made us laugh even harder.

I remember Mom showed up 20 minutes before the game was over. She looked tired but happy that she'd made it. She smelled like the hospital when she sat down next to me, like Clorox and burned plastic and antiseptic. She said hello to Steven, and he produced a Hershey bar with almonds (Mom's favorite) from his jacket pocket and said he'd snagged one from the booth just for her. Oh, the smile she gave him, the approving-mother smile, like a ray of sunshine in that cold gym.

Steven knew how to bask in it.

"You're a total kiss-up," I told him, bumping my shoulder into his. "Where's _my_ candy bar?"

He shrugged, but his eyes said that there were things in this world better than candy.

Yes, there were.

I remember we stayed parked outside the house for longer than usual when he brought me home, until Mom flipped the porch light on and off, which was her way of saying, Enough necking. Time to come in. Good night, Steven.

"Mom. Please. You don't have to do that," I told her when I slipped inside the house. "I'm perfectly capable of deciding when I should call it a night." My lips were swollen and my hair a total mess and my face felt flushed, probably red because I was embarrassed that I looked like I'd been making out. Which I had been. Excessively. And my mother was standing just inside the door like the chastity police.

"Are we going to have to revisit 'the talk'?" she asked.

"God, no. Once was enough for this lifetime, thanks."

"Okay. Do you want me to take you in and get a prescription for birth control pills?"

My mouth opened and then closed. I frowned. "No. Well, maybe. I don't know."

"Condoms break," she informed me.

Now I knew for a fact that my face was fire-engine red. "I am aware of that. Good grief, Mom. Where's Ty?" I asked, sure he was going to jump out from the hallway with a giant smirk. I did not want to be having this conversation in front of him.

"Ty's not home yet," Mom said.

"Ah. Maybe he needs 'the talk.'" I started past her toward the safety of the hall and my bedroom, a full-scale retreat, and for once I was glad that Dad didn't still live with us. One parent in this situation was bad enough. I didn't need Dad and his shotgun.

"I just want you to be safe," Mom called after me.

"I'm safe," I answered, and then I went in my room and closed the door and took a deep breath. Because I was safe. Steven and I hadn't been past, er (what were the bases, again?)—second base yet. But we were definitely on second, taking a few steps in the direction of third.

Maybe it was time for us to discuss it, I thought. Maybe it was time.

I wanted it to be Steven, the first time. I knew that much. I didn't know when or how or where something like that could happen, but I did know who.

And sitting there in my bedroom, thinking about it, I blushed and I smiled.

December 3. I remember all that. In detail.

Steven. El and Beaker. Mom. Steven.

But I don't remember Ty playing. I don't remember him interacting with any of the cheerleaders.

I wasn't paying attention. I was too busy being the star of my own movie, while my brother might have been out there that night, in the dark somewhere, getting his heart broken. And 17 days later, he was dead.

13.

"SO, HOW'S THE WRITING COMING?" Dave asks from his comfortable chair.

"Swell," I reply.

He waits for me to give him a straight answer.

I shrug. "I don't think it's doing me much good."

I glance at the clock. God. Forty-two minutes to go.

"Why do you say that?" he asks.

"There's no real point to it. No purpose."

"We discussed this. The purpose is to release some of the pain, express it onto the paper so you don't have to carry it around with you in your day-to-day life. It's cathartic."

"Yeah, that's not happening," I report.

I'm still carrying around plenty.

His eyebrows bunch together. Dave has very expressive eyebrows. "Are you writing about Tyler?"

"Look, I did what you asked. I wrote about the firsts and the lasts." I sigh. "I think it's time to try something else. Let's just call it done with the writing part of the healing process, okay?"

He rubs his hand over his mouth, then says, "But how does it feel, when you're writing?"

"Honestly? It sucks to try to remember. It hurts. I don't want to do it anymore."

"Ah. It hurts. Good," he says.

Wait, I think, good that it hurts? But then it hits me: Dave knows about the numbness. Somehow, he knows. And this writing thing isn't his attempt to get me to express my feelings so much as it's trying to get me to actually have feelings.

Dave's sneaky that way.

"Maybe I want to forget," I say, just to be contrary. "Maybe it'd be easier to forget, and get on with my life. Isn't that healthier? Moving on?"

"Is that what you really want?" Dave asks.

"Would you please stop answering my question with a question?"

"What would you like me to say? Aren't there some vital questions that you must answer for yourself?"

Dave doesn't play fair.

I sit back and consult the clock again. Ugh. Thirty-eight minutes.

"I think you should continue with the journal. Humor me for a while longer," he says. "What I think you might need, to make the writing seem more relevant, is a recipient."

"A recipient?" That doesn't sound good.

"Someone you are writing to."

Oh, this just keeps getting better and better.

He sees the look on my face. "Alexis. I'm not suggesting that you give the journal to anyone. It's for your eyes only, I understand. But perhaps if you use the journal to express something to someone specific, you'll be able to get some of the weightier issues off your chest."

I arch an eyebrow at him. "You're saying I need an imaginary audience, so to speak. Do you have someone specific in mind?"

"Well, let's see," Dave says, as if he hasn't already given this a lot of thought. "Maybe you could write to a future version of yourself. Many people write their journals to future selves, I think. It demonstrates a kind of hopefulness."

"So my audience would be some wise Alexis who's made it through all this crap and occasionally cracks open this journal to see how far she's come and says to herself, Whew, I'm glad that's not my life anymore."

"Exactly."

I wish I could be her, I think. Fast-forward through this part of my life.

I shake my head. "But maybe she's just as messed up as I am. Maybe all of this has twisted me irrevocably, and I will forever be incapable of a healthy, normal future. Maybe it would only torture Future Me, having this record of where it all went south."

"Is that what you think?" Dave asks. "That you're twisted?"

He takes a few seconds to write something in the yellow legal pad he keeps his notes on. This makes me nervous.

Time for a change of subject. "Or I could write to aliens or robots or whoever's left in ten thousand years. An extraterrestrial will lift this book in its gray fingers and think, Hmm, so this was the life of a female Homo sapiens. How interesting."

"Yes," Dave says, like he is taking me completely seriously. "You could write to aliens."

Who am I kidding? Nobody's going to care. Not future me. And certainly not an alien species.

This is pointless.

"You could write to God. That has been known to be therapeutic to many people," he suggests.

"No. I don't have anything to say to him. I mean, I don't believe in God."

Dave writes more in his notebook.

"You could try writing to someone else," he says then. "Someone you want to talk to. You could speak to him or her by writing. Even if that person never reads it. Even if that person can't hear."

That's when I understand where he's been leading me all this time. That person. "You mean Ty."

"If you'd like."

"I don't want to write to Ty," I say without hesitation. I had my chance to talk to him, when it counted, when it would have meant something, and I missed it. "He's gone."

"The people we love are never truly gone."

"Yeah, you know what, you should design bumper stickers or something. That's profound. That's catchy."

He sits back. "You seem tense today, Alexis. Has something happened?"

My heart rate picks up. A part of me still wants to tell him everything, ask him what I should do about the letter and talk about the times I've seen and smelled Ty, the dreams I'm having about him, just get it all out there in the open, see what he'll have to say, but my desire to confess is still considerably less than my fear that he will think I'm crazy, and if a mental-health professional thinks I'm crazy, I probably am.

"Lex?" Dave prompts. "What are you thinking about?"

"Nothing," I say automatically. "Nothing's happened."

Thirty-one minutes.

He sighs and writes something else in his notebook. "Well, I think your assignment this week should be to figure out some kind of audience for your writing."

"A recipient," I say.

"Yes."

"Great," I answer. It's fruitless to argue with Dave; he's so freaking calm. "I'll get right on that."

I can't wait.

14.

THIS TIME TY AND I ARE SWIMMING in Branched Oak Lake, the water cool and green and deep under us. At first it feels just like the old days. He says he'll race me to the shore, and we start out swimming steadily side by side. Then I become aware that I am swimming alone.

I've lost sight of Ty.

I tread water and look for him. He's gone. Nothing but dark water all around me. I call his name. I turn in the water, searching, and then suddenly he comes up right beside me, spraying me, laughing.

"Gotcha," he says. "Look at your face. What, did you think I drowned?"

"Jerk," I say as my heart rate begins to slow. There was another dream I had, a couple of nights ago, in which he drowned in a swimming pool, a lifeless shape at the hazy blue bottom that I was trying to fish out using the pool net.

"You know you love me," he says now.

I do.

"Hey, what's that?" He looks off over my shoulder at something in the water.

I think he's still joking around with me, but I turn. There's a fin cutting its way toward us, maybe twenty feet away. Then ten. Then five. Then it glides under us, out of sight.

"Uh-oh," Ty says gravely. "I knew we shouldn't have come out here. It's not safe."

"Don't worry," I say, with that weird logic that exists inside dreams. "This is fresh water." As if my stating this fact will negate the existence of this inevitable shark.

He pivots in the water. "There," he says, pointing down. "Do you see it?"

I see it. A huge dark form taking shape below us, closing in.

It's on us before I can catch my breath.

Ty screams. He thrashes and goes under. There's billowing blood in the water. Ty pops up again, sputtering, caught in the middle by a massive great white. I try to grab him as the shark shakes him the way our dog used to shake her toys.

"Ty!" I cry. "Tyler! Ty!"

I can't get a grip on him. He's too slippery.

Then, as suddenly as it came, the shark is gone. Ty comes to the surface, gasping. His face is white as milk, his lips tinged with red.

"Lex," he chokes.

I turn him over onto his back, grab him by the shoulders, and start to tow him toward shore. Blood trails behind us as I swim, so much blood, too much, but I don't stop to think about that.

"Lexie," Ty says again, this time like a warning. "I . . ."

"No." I kick hard, swim with as much power as I can, but the shore doesn't seem to be getting any closer.

"I have to . . . go," he says.

I stop. "No. Stay with me, Ty."

"It hurts," he whispers.

"Stay with me," I plead. "Stay."

His eyes close. His breath rattles in his chest. And then stops.

"Ty!" I scream, and then I sit up with a jolt, tangled in sheets. Another dream.

My hands are shaking. My breath jerks in and out of my lungs. I can still feel the cold of the water. I can still smell the blood.

A bad one this time.

Really bad.

There's a soft tap on my door, so soft I wonder if I really heard it. I try to make my breathing quiet so I can listen. Which is hard.

Another tap. Louder. Real.

"Honey?" It's my mother's voice behind the door. "Are you all right?"

I fumble for my glasses, pausing before I put them on to wipe my wet face. Was I crying? I couldn't have been crying. I don't remember.

I straighten out the blankets before I answer. "I'm fine, Mom."

The door opens. She pokes her head in. "I heard a noise. It sounded like you were upset."

I wonder if she heard me yell Ty's name.

"I had a nightmare, is all," I say. "I'm okay."

She comes in and sits at the edge of my mattress. When I was little and had nightmares, sometimes she would crawl into bed with me and stay there for the rest of the night, her body so warm and soft and safe that the nightmares never came back. And then, after Dad left, for the rest of that lousy summer, I slept with her because she couldn't bear to sleep in their big bed all alone without him.

She snored. Loudly. Like a wounded pig. But then again, the times she stayed with me when I was little, in the twin bed so small she had to sleep sideways to fit, I used to wet the bed.

The things you do for the people you love.

She tucks a strand of my hair behind my ear. "Sometimes I dream about your brother, too."

She meets my eyes. There's a painful knowledge there. She heard me call his name.

"Yeah," I whisper.

I can't explain it to her, how they make me feel, these dreams where Ty dies. They're bad, and it feels like they're getting worse, more graphic in nature, but I don't want to stop having them. In some morbid way, I like having them. Because at least then I get to see Ty. I get to talk to him, sometimes. At least, when I'm there, when Ty is dying in whatever way he's dying, I'm with him. I'm hanging on to him. I'm asking him not to go.

In those moments I can do something for him that I didn't do in real life. I can answer the text. I can be there.

"Valium helps. Do you want a Valium?" Mom asks. "I don't

dream when I take them."

What is it with people trying to force-feed me drugs? I shake my head. "It wasn't that bad."

She hesitates.

"I'm fine, really," I insist.

"All right, honey." She leans to kiss me on the temple. "I love you."

It wasn't fair for me to be blaming her, before. Not for Ty. All she's ever been guilty of is loving too much.

"I love you, too," I say.

She gets up and goes out, closing the door quietly behind her, as if there is someone else in this house she doesn't want to wake up. I lie back.

0. 1. 1. 2. 3. 5. 8. 13. 21. 34. 55. 89. 144.

But sleep doesn't come for a long time, and when it does, the dreams are all still waiting.

21 February

~~The last time I saw Ty~~

22 February

~~Dear Dave,~~

~~This writing thing is killing me. Can I please stop now? I've been~~ ~~hanging out with a new friend, by the way. Well, an old friend, tech-~~ ~~nically. But a new friend. Healthy, right? Cathartic, right? I'm the~~ ~~picture of sound mental health, I swear~~

Dear alien race in the future:

Please don't read this journal as a representative of the typical life of a human adolescent. It will screw up your research for years to come. In fact, it's probably best if you simply disregard what's written here entirely.

Also, if you haven't already, please don't annihilate the human race. We can be charming.

Yours truly,

Alexis P. Riggs

15.

MY CAR WON'T START. I'm in the parking lot at Dave's office, after yet another scintillating hour of non-productive conversation, and now, to top it off, the Lemon is screwing with me. It does that sometimes—some kind of electrical short that would cost me more than the car is worth to have fixed. I put the key in the ignition and turn it, and nothing happens. I do all the stuff that normally works in this situation. I open and close the door, bang on the dash a few times, turn the heater to the off setting, jiggle the key, and try again. Nothing happens.

I wait five minutes and try again.

Nothing.

This is a problem.

I'm all the way across Lincoln, at least twenty miles from home. It's getting dark.

I take out my phone and stare at my contacts list. I can't call

Beaker—she's at play practice for *Brigadoon*. Eleanor doesn't have a car—her mom drops her off everywhere. My own mom is working until ten.

Crap.

I could call Dad. We were supposed to have dinner tonight, Tuesday, as usual, but he left me a message earlier that he wanted to reschedule for Saturday morning.

I check my watch—5:17. He might be home by now. Megan's house is only a few miles from here. I know he'd be happy to come pick me up.

I sigh and try the key one more time.

Nothing.

I've never called Dad, is the thing.

Not since he left.

He calls me, if there are plans that need to be made. We meet at a rotating set of restaurants every week, and these meetings last about an hour at most. We talk about work. We talk about school. Sometimes he gives me money, an offering that communicates that he is sorry he messed up my life, words I know I will never hear him say out loud. I take his money. The bad-father tax, I like to call it. Which I don't feel bad about, since most of the savings my parents had put away for my college education was eaten up by the divorce.

We have our rituals. Our unspoken rules.

We don't talk about Megan.

We don't talk about Ty.

I don't go to Megan's house.

I don't call Dad at home.

If I did that, it'd be like me saying it's okay, what he did. Like I'm accepting his new life, the one he built without us.

I won't do it.

I dial Sadie's cell, but she doesn't pick up. I dial her house. The phone rings and rings, and I'm about to hang up when I hear a disembodied voice.

"Yeah," it says. "I'm here, yo."

"Seth?" I ask, but who else could it be?

"In the flesh," he says with a sleepy laugh. "What can I do you for?"

I try to ignore his atrocious grammar. "Hi, it's Lex. Is Sadie home?"

"Sadie? Nope. Did you try her cell?"

"Yes, Seth. I tried her cell."

"Well, I don't know what to tell you, then. Do you want to leave a message?"

"No." I try the key one more time. Nothing. I beat my fist against the steering wheel. Stupid, stupid Lemon. "I was just hoping she could give me a ride home. My car's . . . stupid. Never mind."

"I could give you a ride," Seth says. "Where are you?"

"A ride? On your bike, you mean?" I've seen Seth tearing around the neighborhood on that thing. It makes so much noise you can hardly miss it.

He snorts. "On my Kawasaki Ninja 300. Her name is Georgia. Because she's a peach."

Right. I try to picture it, me balancing precariously behind Seth on his motorcycle, clutching him around the middle as we careen twenty miles over the icy roads across town.

"No thanks, Seth," I decline as politely as I can. "I can get someone else to pick me up. I only called because I thought Sadie might want to hang out."

"Oh, so me and Georgia aren't good enough for you?" he says, his voice teasing. "Come on, Lex. Where you at?"

"It's okay," I say quickly. "You probably have to be at work soon, and I'm all the way downtown, and I don't want to inconvenience you."

"Lex."

"There's someone else who can come get me," I say again. "It's no problem. Thanks for the offer, though. Some other time I'd love to ride . . . Georgia, okay?"

"You sure?"

"Positive. Thanks."

I hang up. I try to start the engine again.

Nothing.

I hate the Lemon.

"Crap," I say to nobody. "Crap!"

I get a flash of Ty's face, a memory of his brow furrowed in frustration, when I taught him to drive.

"Crap," he said. He tugged on the shift, making the Lemon groan in protest. "I'll never get this."

"You will," I told him. "But hopefully you'll get it before you ruin my transmission."

The car died.

"Crap!" Ty roared. He'd been so moody lately, every ten minutes switching to a different wild emotion. I chalked it up to shifting hormones. It's a terrible thing to be a teenage boy.

I put my hand over his on the shift, and for a minute I was mad too, that it was me teaching him and not Dad. It should have been Dad.

"Hey," I said to Ty. "It's okay. Take a breath."

He leaned back in the driver's seat, exhaled forcefully through his nose, and rubbed at his bloodshot eyes. He'd started wearing contact lenses a few weeks earlier. I was still trying to get used to seeing him without his glasses.

"I suck," he said. "I should just take the bus."

"You do suck," I agreed. "But, you know, pretty much everybody sucks at first, and everybody learns to drive, sooner or later, the same way everybody learns how to walk. Step by step. Put your foot on the clutch." I reached over and turned the key in the ignition, and that time, which happened more than a year ago, the Lemon started right up.

"You can do this," I told him. "No big deal."

He nodded. Smiled faintly. "Thanks."

And then he drove. Not well, not that time, but he got us from point A to point B.

I blink against the memory.

I turn the key, but the engine doesn't make a sound. Maybe the battery's dead this time. Maybe my crap car has finally gone belly-up.

I'm hosed.

Of course, there is someone else I could call. I wasn't lying when I said that to Seth.

Someone who would definitely come and get me.

Someone not Dad.

I stare at my phone.

It would be awkward. Embarrassing. Pathetic, even. But what other choice do I have?

I swallow, hard.

"I can do this," I whisper, and then I press send. "No big deal."

Twenty minutes later, Steven's little car—a blue Toyota Corolla that he shares with his older sister Sarah—pulls up next to the Lemon. His brakes squeak as he comes to a stop. He rolls down the window.

"Do you want me to try to jump you?" he asks.

"Don't bother." I want him to expend as little effort here as possible. "I just need to get home."

He leans to unlock the passenger door and clears a bunch of books and papers off the seat so I can sit down. He waits while I put my seat belt on, then clears his throat and backs us out of the parking lot.

We head north on O Street. It's fully dark now, and a light snow is falling, catching the street lights. We make small talk for a while: the weather (cold, as always), Ms. Mahoney (awesome, as always), and college plans (still waiting to get our acceptance letters). Then we hit Wyuka Cemetery, its heavy black iron fence stretching along the edge of the road, the graves, old trees, and mausoleums looming beyond it.

Steven and I stop talking as we pass. He clears his throat again, his expression suddenly clouded.

"Lex . . . ," he starts.

I say, "I know I shouldn't have called you, but there was nobody else. I'm sorry. Won't happen again."

"Of course you should have called me," he says sharply. "We're still friends, aren't we? I thought we were still friends."

"I don't know," I admit. If the definition of the word *friend* is someone you're comfortable with, someone it feels good to be around, then Steven and I are definitely not friends.

"I'd like us to be friends, Lex," he says.

But even coming from him it sounds like a lie.

"Do you want to get something to eat?" he asks as we turn onto 27th. "There's the Imperial Palace coming up."

My favorite Chinese place.

That's where we went out to dinner that night. Does Steven remember?

"No," I say quickly, before he can turn into the parking lot. "I have dinner waiting for me at home." An obvious lie. "Plus I have a ton of homework I need to get to," I throw in for good measure.

He doesn't call me out on it. We drive for a while, past the restaurant, past a video arcade we always used to go to, past the flower shop where he bought my corsage for the homecoming dance and where we got Ty's funeral flowers. It's so quiet I feel like my head is going to implode.

Steven reaches for the radio dial but pauses before he turns it on. "Music?"

Oh God, yes. Music.

"Yes, please."

We're flooded with Yo-Yo Ma's cello playing Bach's Suite No. 1 in G Major. I close my eyes and let the notes wash over me. This was a bad idea, I think for the thousandth time. But at least we're more than halfway home.

"So," Steven says, just when it feels like I might survive this little joyride. "You still won't call your dad, huh?"

My eyes open. He's looking at the road, the light from the oncoming headlights moving in lines across his face, but it feels like he's looking at me.

"No, I don't call him. Nothing has changed on that front."

"That's too bad. I thought maybe, with Ty, it might bring you two together," he says.

"I don't want to be together with my dad," I snap.

We stop at a red. Steven looks at me. The Bach is suddenly not enough to drown the silence.

"Why not?" he asks.

"If my dad hadn't left us, Ty would still be alive." It surprises me when I say it. I didn't know I actually believed it—not in such simple terms, anyway—until the words left my mouth. But I do believe it.

"You don't know that," Steven says.

"I don't need you to be my therapist, Steven," I say, my sudden anger welcome against whatever else it is that I'm feeling. "I have a therapist."

"Then what do you need me to be?" he asks, and pins me with those well-meaning brown eyes. "Tell me what you need, Lex, and I'll do that. I'll be that."

I look away. "It's green."

"What?"

"The light's green."

"Oh." He steps on the gas. Then he reaches up and turns off the music. Sighs.

"I wish you'd talk to me," he says. "Tell me what's going on with you. I know we're not together anymore, and I respect your wishes about that, but that doesn't mean I've stopped caring about you. I—"

"I'll tell you what I don't need," I interrupt. "I don't need sneaky love poems. I don't need you calling my house to check up on me. I don't need to feel like you're always there breathing down my neck. That's what I don't need."

He looks confused. "What?"

"I don't want to talk about it," I say. "I need a ride home. Okay?"

His jaw tightens. "Okay."

We go the rest of the way—ten long minutes—without saying another word.

I jump out before we've even fully stopped in my driveway. "Thanks for the ride."

I'm gone before he can form a response. I duck through the first door that's available: the side door to the garage. But I don't close the door behind me all the way. I leave it open a crack and watch Steven as he sits for a while, his eyes closed, his hands gripping the wheel.

I'm hurting him. Still.

I was right to hesitate, when Steven asked me to go out with him. Of course I was right. We were destined to break up, the way all early romances are doomed. And now things are awkward with our friends. And we are hurting each other.

I was right.

He opens his eyes and backs the car out, then drives off fast, spraying snow and gravel.

I close the door.

That's when I realize that I'm in the garage.

I gaze at the spot.

Where my brother died.

They cleaned it up after, some company that does that. There's no blood here now, no dark stain to mark the place, but there is a chip in the cement. I can't remember if it was there before, or if it was created by the bullet after it passed through. Which makes me immediately start considering angles and trajectory and velocity, and I don't want to think about that.

I look around at the last things Ty would have seen: the rusty rakes and shovels lining the wall, the grass-encrusted lawn mower, our broken snowblower, the old wheelbarrow with a flat tire, the barrel of dog food that's still here even though our dog died a year ago. It smells like dust and motor oil and plants decaying.

It's a depressing place to die. Dark and cold and dingy.

I imagine the shot, how it must have filled this space with its noise, how it must have deafened him in those few seconds he could hear. I imagine the gunpowder, curling in the air. The smell of blood. The chill of the cement against his cheek as his vision faded.

He would have felt so alone here.

I go inside to the kitchen. I stand for a few minutes staring into the refrigerator, which is like a barren wasteland, it's so empty, but that's fine because I'm not hungry anymore. I take out a bottle of Mom's mandatory Diet Coke—which I've been trying to get her to quit on account of the nasty chemicals—and I chug it. The bubbles burn my nose.

I'm almost finished with it when I think I see, out of the corner of my eye, a figure in the reflection of the kitchen window. A flash. Ty.

But when I lower the bottle, when I turn, he's gone.

Of course.

I toss the bottle in the recycling bin and put my back to the window. From here I have a view of the top of the stairwell. The empty frame of Dad's graduation photo gleams at me, like it's trying to get my attention.

Oh, that's right, I think. The mystery.

How would Sherlock Holmes go about solving this case?

Well, I reason, first it might be a good idea to check to see if there are any other photos missing from where they ought to be. Or if the hunting picture and Dad's graduation picture are the only two. That'd be a start.

I do a quick mental rundown of where there are pictures. Then I check the mantel over the fireplace in the living room, but nothing's out of order there. I try Dad's office, where there's still a silver framed photo of him and Mom on their fifteenth wedding anniversary. Dad didn't take it when he left. Mom's never taken it down. It's still there, a dusty example of the kind of parental units I used to have. I try the guest bathroom, where years ago Mom framed several photos of Ty and me taking baths together as toddlers, all the private places covered with bubbles but humiliating nonetheless. All those pictures are still in place. Outside of the mother lode in the stairwell, I can't think of anywhere there are framed photos.

Nothing else is missing. Back to square one.

Clearly I'm no Sherlock Holmes.

But who says they have to be framed photos? it occurs to me suddenly. That sends me to a particular shelf on the bookcase in the basement den, where there's a row of photo albums. Mom and Dad's wedding. Their honeymoon. Family vacations. And then our baby books, mine and Ty's both.

Mine is full and well maintained. Mom carefully filled out the family tree and all the details about my birth, like that I was born at 9:46 at night after eleven hours of labor, and I had excellent Apgar scores, and the first three months of my life I spent approximately three and a half hours a day crying for no good reason at all, which is just under the clinical definition of colic. She has the dates and times of all my first accomplishments: my first bath, my first smile, my first steps and words (*Da-da*, then *dog-gy*, then *Ma-ma*, which totally offended my mother), my first teeth, my first haircut, my first friend, where it says *Sadie McIntyre* in Mom's perfect cursive. As if I really want to know that stuff.

Ty's baby book is slimmer. By the time Ty came along, Mom

had her hands full with me and no time to spend lovingly documenting every moment of his life. The second kid always gets shafted in the picture department. He's lucky, I suppose, that he has any photos in his book at all.

It's hard to thumb through it, but I do.

Ty as a fat and purple sleeping lump.

Ty as an adorable chubby toddler.

Ty on a camping trip, wearing Dad's Jeep baseball hat, drinking a can of grape Fanta with a straw.

Ty petting Sunny.

Ty in bed, on Elmo sheets, with his dimpled hands clasped and his eyes closed, saying his prayers.

Now I lay me down to sleep.

I skip over the pictures of Ty and me, because something in my chest twists when I look at them, all this carefully archived evidence of what we've lost.

His first word was *Ma-ma*, incidentally. Kiss-up.

It doesn't take long for me to realize that there are photos missing in this book, too, not just places Mom was too busy to fill in, but empty spaces with the residue of double-sided tape still marking the page. But unlike the framed photos that are MIA, his baby book photos aren't something I have memorized. I don't know what's gone. All I can do at this point is make an educated guess here and there and count the spots where I conclude that a photo has been removed.

Eight photos, in all. Which brings us to a grand total of ten missing photos.

I'm still no closer to understanding what's going on here. Or why.

I hear footsteps on the floor above me. Part of me freezes for about three seconds, until I recognize the sound of Mom's jingling keys. She has a rhythm when she gets home: open the coat closet by the door, hang up her coat. Walk to the kitchen and set down the mail in the tray on the kitchen counter. Open one of the cabinets and stick in her purse and her keys. Make herself a cup of instant coffee—or, more recently, a wine cooler or glass of wine.

I'm starting to fear for her liver.

I glance at the clock on the cable box near the basement TV. 6:07.

Mom shouldn't be home yet.

I take the stairs two at a time. Mom yelps when I pop up at the top.

"Hey," I say. "Get off early?"

"How was your day?" she asks me, sliding by my question.

Oh, you know, Mom, I think. Fan-freaking-tastic.

"The Lemon died," I report. "I don't know if she's coming back this time. She's still in the parking lot at Dave's."

"Oh no," Mom exclaims. "How did you get home?"

"I had to get a ride with Steven."

"Oh." This has got to be the most loaded "oh" a person has ever uttered.

"Yeah," I affirm. Awkward city.

Her expression softens. Mom understands breakups. She gives

a stilted laugh. "That car of yours definitely has the right name, doesn't it?"

I nod.

"If only we had some—" she starts to say, and then stops herself.

If only we had some money. To buy a new car.

I try not to scrutinize our family's financial situation, because if I do, it becomes abundantly clear how my parents' divorce was the key contributor to all our current cash-flow troubles, and there's nothing I can do with that information but be mad about it. But I pay attention to numbers. I know that Ty's death cost $10,995: the casket alone was $2,300, plus all the funeral home fees (embalming, body storage, a cost to rent the mortuary space for the wake, etc., which added up to around $3,895), plus what they charged for the body retrieval and cleanup ($400), plus the flowers ($200), plus the grave space at Wyuka ($1,300) and the cost to dig the grave ($1,000), and finally the headstone, which was an even $2,000.

Mom is a registered nurse, but she's been on the job for less than a year, so she makes $20.25 an hour. She had a life insurance policy on both Ty and me, but because Ty's death was a suicide, the insurance company declared that his policy was void. Dad pitched in for half the cost, of course, but he's not rolling in cash, either. See divorce lawyers and court fees and the money he had to fork over for Mom's nursing school after he left.

In other words, we're broke.

See Lexie drive a clunker.

"I don't really need a car," I tell Mom now. "When I'm at MIT next year I'll take the subway. Cambridge has excellent public transportation, which is safer, statistically speaking, than driving a car."

She smiles sadly and pats my hair. I don't know if she believes that I'll get into MIT, but she'll act like she does. She'll indulge me. "Good. Then it will be one less thing to worry about," she says. "Now let's go figure out what we're going to do with the Lemon. Then we can get dinner."

Ironically, the Lemon starts right up for me when we go back for it. Without a hitch or a sputter or anything. She just purrs to life.

"Wouldn't start, huh?" Mom says from her vantage point in the next parking space over. "Are you sure that's what happened?" She gives me a look like maybe this whole charade with Steven giving me a ride home may have been a ruse on my part. To spend time with Steven. Because of course I still must like Steven. Because he's such an upstanding young man.

Maybe Mom doesn't understand breakups.

"I swear. The car likes to mess with me," I say. "She's temperamental."

Mom nods knowingly and then moves on to the dinner plan.

"How about the Imperial Palace?" she suggests. "You love that place."

"Meh." I shrug. "It's only marginally good."

She accepts what I say at face value. "All right. We can do better than marginally good, I think."

"How about the Spaghetti Works? We haven't been there in

forever." Because it's too expensive. Not ridiculously expensive, but too expensive for us. "I heard they have a six-dollar spaghetti special. All you can eat."

"Spaghetti sounds wonderful," she says. "I could use a glass of red wine about now."

16.

TIME PASSES. THAT'S THE RULE. No matter what happens, no matter how much it might feel like everything in your life has frozen around one particular moment, time marches on. After my brother died, time passed slowly, with me trudging through all the obligatory activities that I was still expected to do: class, eating, sleeping, brushing my teeth, drying my hair, pretending like I gave a crap. Either that or time disappeared: I found myself on the other side of Christmas without remembering more than an ambiguous pine-scented blur. A calculus final, gone. Whole conversations that I don't have any memory of.

Now, suddenly, I find that it's March 3. A big day. A day I was waiting for: the first possible day that I could have expected to hear anything from MIT. After school I go to the mailbox, and there, tucked in the shadows, big and beautiful, is a fat envelope.

I've been trying not to think about MIT too much, to refrain from obsessing like some people do or get my hopes unrealistically high—there are other schools, after all, other perfectly decent institutions of higher learning. But MIT is *the* institution. And somewhere deep inside me, I expected this. I hoped for it, anyway. I dreamed.

I don't bother going inside. I tear the letter open and read it standing next to the mailbox.

Dear Alexis,

On behalf of the Admissions Committee, it is my pleasure to offer you admission to MIT. You stood out as one of the most talented and promising students in the most competitive applicant pool in the history of the Institute. Your commitment to personal excellence and principled goals has convinced us that you will both contribute to our community and thrive within our academic environment. We think that you and MIT are a great match.

I swallow down the hard lump in my throat and scan past the details: I have until May 2 to let them know whether I accept their offer, they invite me to attend something called Campus Preview Weekend in April to get a sense of what life on campus would be like, an MIT student will be calling me in the coming weeks, and they urge me to look over the details of my financial aid package. I flip forward and my breath catches—more than forty-three thousand dollars in scholarships.

I read on:

*And now for the requisite fine print—I must remind you
that this offer of admission is contingent upon your completing
the school year with flying colors. Have fun for the rest of your
senior year, but please keep your grades up!*

*I hope you'll agree with us that MIT is the perfect place
to prepare for your future. As a member of our community,
you'll join builders, scholars, entrepreneurs, and humanitar-
ians. Together, you will all make a difference in a world that
desperately needs you.*

*Many congratulations, and once again, welcome to MIT!
Now stop reading this and go celebrate.*

This is happening.

This is what I've wanted from the time I knew what college was
about: to get out of Nebraska, to study math with the country's best
instructors, to bounce my ideas off the sharpest minds. To become
someone of consequence. I don't want to be rich or famous, but I want
to contribute something significant to the history of human thought.

The Riggs theorem.

That's my immortality, my idea of heaven. Something people
will remember me for after I die.

As I walk back to the house I'm surprised by how, with this letter finally in my hands, I'm not that excited. Not the kind of excited
I thought I'd be.

I'm going to MIT. Okay. Yes. This is what I wanted. Yes. This
is, without a doubt, the most awesome thing ever to happen to me.
Yes. Yes.

But that will mean leaving Mom all alone in this house.

I sit down on the living room couch and read the letter again. I force myself to imagine it: me standing at a blackboard at MIT, going all Will Hunting on some problem, me curled up on a twin bed in a tiny-but-mine dorm room, reading about quantum mechanics, me strolling along some tree-lined sidewalk, chatting with the other students, a stack of heavy books under my arm.

It's nice, thinking about the future as something that won't entirely suck.

But things are different now than they were when I filled out my college applications.

March 5. I haven't told my parents. Not Dave, when we had our session yesterday. Not my friends. I don't know how to slip it into the conversation at school. I guess it should be as simple as *Guess what? I got into MIT. Hooray-hooray!* But whenever that pause happens, when I could make the announcement, I choke.

If I tell people, they're all going to watch me for my super-elated reaction. And I'm not Beaker; I'm no great actress. I'm happy I got into MIT, I am. But I don't know if I can do happy at this stage in my life. Not in public. Not at the level they're all going to expect.

Still, I bring the acceptance letter with me, tucked in with the Ashley letter in the front pocket of my five-subject notebook, and every now and then I open the notebook and stare at the envelope and think of all the promises collected in this one place, all the hope.

Maybe that's it, what's holding me back from telling people—
the hope.

I'm not used to hope anymore.

It's hardest to hold the MIT news inside me during calculus.
We're learning how to find volumes of rotations using integrations,
and Steven is up at the board writing out these gorgeous equations,
his handwriting so much neater than mine and so much more careful,
which is why Miss Mahoney called him up there, so he could show us
the answer the way a painter might create a still-life that looks like:

$$V_{C\,one} = \pi \int_0^2 (f(y))^2 \, dy$$

$$V_{C\,one} = \pi \int_0^2 \left(\tfrac{3}{2}y\right)^2 dy = \pi \int_0^2 \left(\tfrac{9}{4}y^2\right) dy$$

$$\pi \int_0^2 \left(\tfrac{9}{4}y^2\right) dy = \pi \left(\left(\tfrac{3}{4}\right)y^3 \,\Big|_0^2\right) = 6\pi$$

"So," Miss Mahoney says when he's nearly finished. "Let's say
Steven is a glassblower, crafting a vase. He could use this method
to understand the different shapes he's making and the amount of
water the vase would hold."

"Yeah, Steven," El snickers. "You're a glassblower."

He grins and shrugs one shoulder. "It's a job."

"What kind of vase are we talking about, here?" pipes up Beaker. "What color of glass? I've always been fond of blue glass. Can
you do a blue glass vase for us, Steven?"

"All righty," he says, and turns back to the board. "Blue glass
coming up."

The class laughs, and we understand it's a tad lame, but I've always appreciated the way Miss Mahoney tries to give us real-world applications for the things we learn, so it's not just math in a box. She wants us to see the beauty in the equations, how absolutely cool it all is, but she also wants it to be real for us. It never fails to amaze me, in these moments, that the numbers explain something tangible and true about life. The numbers make sense of things. They make order of a disordered world.

I want to say thank you to Miss Mahoney. For giving me that. For trying to make it fun and not just "neat," unnecessary knowledge.

I want to say, *Hey, Miss Mahoney, I got into MIT.*

Then I want to tell Beaker. And El. After all the daydreaming we did. MIT is a real place, and I am going there. I'm going there.

I want to tell Steven.

But I can't find the words.

Words were never really my forte.

17.

WHEN I GET HOME I FIND MOM'S CAR in the driveway.
That's twice now that she's been home when she's supposed to be
working. I go inside and call for her, but she doesn't answer. Some
part of me goes into panic mode, and I run to her bedroom, holding my breath until I can confirm that she's not sprawled across the
bed with her arm trailing off the mattress, a spilled bottle of pills
scattered on the carpet.

Where did I get that image, I wonder, the go-to scene of fatal
overdose that you always see in movies? Why did my mind go
straight to the worst possibility?

Because it happened, I answer myself. The worst possibility
already happened once. It could happen again.

"Mom?" I yell.

There's no answer. I check Mom's bathroom, Dad's office, and
the kitchen without success, which gets the adrenaline flowing again.

She could be out with a friend, I reason. Then I come across her purse on the kitchen counter, her phone inside it. Her coat is slung across a kitchen stool. Everything here but nothing in its proper place.

"Mom!" I scream. "Mom!"

I stand still for a minute, holding my breath, listening. Then I hear it.

Music. Very faint music.

Coming from downstairs.

I find Mom in Ty's room. Led Zeppelin is pouring out of Ty's clock radio: "Stairway to Heaven," a song that he and Patrick and Damian used to play on a constant loop back in middle school, again and again and again until Mom and I could have sung the lyrics in our sleep. Mom is standing with her back to me, hands pressed to a Kevin-Durant-making-a-slam-dunk poster on the far wall.

My heart sinks. She's taking down his room.

It was going to happen at some point, I suppose.

"Hi," I rasp. "I was looking everywhere for you. Did you hear me calling?"

She shakes her head. Her small shoulders are trembling. She's crying again.

"Are you okay?" I ask.

"I've been better." She takes a deep breath and then smooths the poster down, pinning a corner with a gold thumbtack.

She's putting it back up, I realize. Not taking it down.

I scan the room and spot a large cardboard box near the bed that contains more of Ty's stuff: his basketball jersey, a mason jar of

184

fifty-cent pieces he collected from the tooth fairy, a tie he wore to church sometimes, a belt, his baseball cards.

"There's a lady who's sure all that glitters is gold, and she's buying a stairway to heaven," intones Robert Plant.

The smell of Ty's cologne is so heavy it makes me want to cough.

"Mom, what's going on?" I ask.

She wipes at her face. Then she reaches and turns down the music.

"I called in sick." She goes to the box and removes another poster—*The Hangover Part II*—and goes about realigning it in its former place on the wall. "Could you help me?"

I unfreeze my feet and hold the paper up for her as she carefully guides the tacks back into their original holes.

"Redecorating?" I venture.

"Gayle was here. She brought that." Mom indicates the box. "She thought . . . it was time . . . for me to pack up . . ." She bends her head, gasps for air as the tears drop into the carpet. "Tyler's things. She said it would help me . . . move on."

I bite my lip to keep from bursting out with furious words for Gayle. How dare she, I think. How dare she come here and decide what's best for everyone?

"Gayle wants me to sell the house," Mom continues. "She wants me to move to Lincoln, closer to the hospital so it's not so much trouble to drive in to work. She says I should get a smaller place, since Tyler's gone and you're going off to school and it will only be me. She also wants me to take a new job that's come up in the neonatal intensive-care unit—work with the babies instead of having to deal with all the people who keep dying on me in the surgical wing."

"Sounds like Gayle has it all figured out." I sit on the edge of Ty's bed.

Mom reaches into her pocket for a crumpled-up tissue. She blows her nose and goes back to the box, where she takes out an old catcher's mitt, from when Ty was in Little League.

"Where did this go?" she whispers. Her eyes dart around the room. "I can't remember."

"Top right corner of the bookshelf," I answer automatically.

She nods. "That's right. Of course. You always had such a perfect memory. A photographic memory."

She makes no move to return the glove to its place. She stands there holding it, rubbing her fingers along its smooth leather surface.

"I volunteered to coach T-ball that one year, do you remember?"

I remember.

"I got this book called *Coaching Tee Ball: The Baffled Parent's Guide*. I didn't know anything about baseball."

"You learned."

"Tyler was mortified to see me standing up there in front of everybody with that book."

"He got over it."

She stares at the mitt. "I tried," she says after a minute.

"I know."

"No, I mean, I tried to do what Gayle said. I tried to take it all down, put it away. I even thought about calling his friends and asking them if they would want some of it. But . . ." She takes a shuddering breath. "I can't. I can't let go."

She starts crying for real now, in big, gasping sobs. I jump up to hold her.

"I can't," she cries against my shoulder. "I can't."

The hole opens up in my chest and I cling to her, and it's as if the pain passes back and forth between us, until she goes limp in my arms.

I guide her to sit down on the bed.

"I have big news," I say softly. "Good news." Because we could both use some good news right now.

She looks up at me, bewildered, tear-streaked. "What?"

"I got into MIT."

Her face opens up like a flower in the sun. She pulls away and stares at me for several moments, not talking, just looking at me with an expression that says maybe there is a God after all. Who has answered her prayers.

"I'm glad," she whispers when she regains her powers of speech. "I'm so glad, Lexie."

I try to smile. "Me too."

"Now you can go," she says fiercely.

"I can go?" I don't understand.

She takes me by the shoulders and gives me a gentle shake. "You can build a new life for yourself. That's what I want, for you to get away from this place. I want you to go to Massachusetts and never look back."

She says it like we're the last people in line for a lifeboat on a sinking ship, telling me to leave her. Telling me to let her drown.

"It doesn't have to be like that," I croak. "You can build a new life for yourself, too."

She lets go of me and turns away. "No. My life is over."

I'm shocked to hear her say it that way. She was always an optimist, before. Even when Dad left, after she got over the initial shock, she kept saying, "He'll come to his senses. He'll come back. We'll go along the best we can until then. This isn't the end of the world." Even though it clearly was. The end of our world, anyway.

And now she's saying her life is over.

"Mom . . ." I don't even know where to start.

She's not looking at me anymore; she's staring at the mirror with the Post-it and the words *below empty*.

"You're not dead," I say, my voice sharper than I mean it to be. "You're alive. It's hard now but . . . you'll heal. You can still be happy, someday."

She goes to the bookshelf and returns the catcher's mitt to its proper place. "No, sweetie," she says in her official parenting voice, like I'm ten all over again and she's telling me the facts of life. "I'll never be happy. How could I, when he's not here? When I have failed him this way? No. No. I will not heal from this. My life is over," she says. "If you weren't here I'd . . ." She trails off.

"If I wasn't here, you'd what?"

She shakes her head. "Nothing." She tries to give me a reassuring smile. "Don't worry about me, Lexie. I'll be fine. I won't be happy—I can't be—but I'll be fine."

I watch in silence as she continues unpacking the box, helping her find where an item belongs if she doesn't remember. Then there's only one thing left to deal with: the collage frame that Ty filled up in the days before he died, the one with the pictures of his friends and family.

That doesn't have a place where it belongs. After the funeral somebody stuck it behind his bedroom door, and it's been there ever since.

Mom lays it on the bed and looks at it.

"I don't know what to do with this. I could take the photos out and send them to the people in them, but I can't remember their names. Isn't that silly? I honestly don't know who most of these people are." She points to a picture on one edge. "I remember Damian and Patrick. The three amigos, I used to call them. And I remember the boys he played with when he was in elementary school. But his friends now . . . I was in nursing school by then. I didn't pay as close attention as I should have. I don't know them. What kind of mother am I, that I didn't know his friends?"

"It's okay, Mom."

She shakes her head. We stand for a few minutes looking at the pictures. One depicts Mom giving Ty a bath when he was just a baby, which seems odd, that he would want people to see that picture, but Mom is so beautiful in it. She's wearing curlers and a plaid shirt with the sleeves rolled up, one hand cupping Ty's round baby head, the other dragging a washcloth over him. She's looking up into the camera with half a smile, chagrined to be caught so undone, and she looks incredibly young and vibrant and, at the same time, maternal and sweet. She looks like a different person from the woman standing beside me now.

In another corner I spot the picture Mom took of Ty and me the night of homecoming, me in my green dress, Ty in his tux and his flawlessly makeup-covered forehead. He wanted people to see that, too. Us together. His arm around me. That's something. It's not an explanation or a goodbye, but it's something.

And suddenly it hits me: the missing photographs. This is where Ty must have put the missing photographs.

I scan the collage again, but there's no picture of Ty and Dad hunting. No picture of Dad at graduation. No picture of Dad here at all.

Like she can read my mind, Mom points to an empty slot in the collage, the only empty slot, which makes it seem deliberately empty. I noticed it at the funeral, but didn't give it too much thought. Now, though, Mom is looking at it with a sorrowful expression.

"Your dad should have gone here," she murmurs. "That was cruel of Tyler, leaving him out."

Cruel is not a word that I would ever use to describe Ty.

"Dad probably didn't even notice," I say.

"He noticed." Mom touches her finger to the glass. "I watched him that day, keeping in the back of the church, out of our way, because he wanted to stay by . . ." Her lips tighten. "But near the end, when the crowd was thinning, he came up and looked at this. He went from picture to picture, looking. And he never found himself there."

"Maybe Dad doesn't deserve to be there," I argue.

She sighs. "Maybe not. But you should have seen his face when he realized he wasn't included. He looked about as hurt as I've ever seen him. Then he just put his hands in his pockets and walked away. It was cruel. I didn't think Tyler had that kind of vindictiveness in him."

"Ty was angry," I say. "He had every right to—"

Mom lifts her hand to stop me. "I know. I just wish he hadn't ended things that way."

I chew on my bottom lip, thinking. I look at the collage again, and then I suddenly notice that right in the middle, in a place of prominence, even, there's a picture of Ashley Davenport. Not the homecoming picture of Ty and Ashley, but a black-and-white candid shot, taken by someone who was obviously trying to be artsy with the camera. It shows Ashley and two other cheerleaders in what must have been the seconds right after the basketball team made a basket, wearing their uniforms, smiling and jumping for the crowd in the background, their eyes bright, so full of action even in the picture that I can almost hear their shouts.

Mom sees what I'm looking at. "They're so pretty, aren't they?" she says. "Teenage girls are at the height of pretty, like flowers just as they bloom."

I cock my head at her. "Me too? Am I a flower?"

She gives me an attempt at a smile. "You're a flower."

"Did you know this girl?" I ask, tapping the glass over the cheerleader photo.

"She was Tyler's girlfriend," Mom says. "Ashley. He brought her over to the house for dinner once."

My mouth falls open. "He did? Where was I?"

"A Math Club competition, if memory serves." She sighs, remembering. "We had pot roast I made in the slow cooker. She actually brought an apple pie that she baked herself. She was lovely, inside and out, that girl. You could see it in her. A good girl. Sweet. Just the right kind of girl for Tyler to be with."

She looks away.

"Do you know why they broke up?" I ask softly.

She shakes her head. "He didn't tell me."

"I thought she dumped him, but . . ." My gaze returns to the picture. "I guess he wasn't too mad at her if he'd put her picture up here."

"I don't know if you could really be mad at a girl like that," Mom says wistfully.

Wow, I think. She was imagining grandbabies and everything, it seems.

Mom's mouth pinches up, like all this talk about Ty's lost romantic prospects is painful to her. She picks up the collage and moves it behind the door, then takes one last long look at Ty's room. She sighs, pulls a tissue out of her pocket, and blows her nose.

"Come on," she says. "We're done in here."

She turns out the light.

I don't know why, maybe because I love torturing myself, but I keep going back to the first day Steven and I were officially together. Not to the bookstore, or the date, or the kiss after, although I think about those things often enough, my own personal memory playlist that's on a continuous loop, but to a conversation I had later about Steven. With Ty.

After Steven dropped me off, I floated inside on cloud 9, bursting with all that had happened in the past few hours. Mom was working, so I couldn't girl-talk with her about it. I found my brother in the basement, bowling on the Wii.

"Where have you been all day?" he asked when he saw me coming down the stairs, his arm swinging back as he delivered the virtual ball to the gutter. He groaned.

"Around. I saw a movie at SouthPointe." I replied. "Wow, you're not even good at virtual bowling."

"Shut up," Ty said good-naturedly, and reset the Wii so that we

could both play. "Loser buys the winner McDonald's."

Then he proceeded to kick my bowling butt.

"How was the movie?" he said after a while.

"Okay. Heavy on visuals, light on plot," I replied. I was going to leave it at that, but I wanted to tell him. I wanted to share part of this monumental day in my life. So I said, "I went with Steven."

Ty's eyes didn't leave the TV screen. "The guy from your math club or whatever?"

"Steven Blake. Yes."

"What did you used to call him? Like his geek nickname?"

"Oh," I said, laughing that he remembered. In middle school we all used to have nicknames: Mine was Luthor, after Superman's Lex Luthor—the world's greatest criminal mastermind. Eleanor's was Roosevelt, which she loathed and rallied to change to Rigby, after the Beatles song, but never pulled off. Beaker's was the only one that actually stuck past 8th grade. And Steven's was—

"Hawking," I told Ty.

"After the star guy."

"After the world-famous astrophysicist and cosmologist, which means he studies the origins and structure of the universe." Sheesh. Star guy.

"Yes!" Ty rolled a perfect strike. I was beginning to suspect that he was hustling me for McDonald's. "So you went on a date. How was that?"

"It wasn't supposed to be a date, but it ended up that way. It was good. Really good, actually." I picked up my controller and immediately bowled a gutter ball. "Crap."

"I approve of this Hawking dude," Ty said as I lamely managed to knock down a few pins on my next roll. "Of course, if he breaks your heart, I'm going to have to beat him up. Brotherly duty, you know."

"Thanks." I smiled and nodded and didn't say anything else Steven-related that night. We bowled, and I lost. We must have gone to McDonald's, but I guess I blocked that part out.

That was the last time I agreed to play Wii with my brother.

It was also the last time we had anything resembling a "real" conversation about our personal lives. When he said he approved of Steven.

I wish I'd told him more. I could have talked about Steven—although not about the kissing, because no brother wants to hear about his sister making out. I could have told him about how brave Steven had been, to just ask me point-blank like that, how gentlemanly he'd been for the rest of the time, and how, in spite of my modern-feminist misgivings, I'd kind of liked that. I could have told him about the paper daisy, or the things I liked about Steven: the way he made me laugh, how he infected me with his enthusiasm, his wonder, and made me feel like I was pretty when nobody else had ever really made me feel that way, which shouldn't have been so important but was.

I could have shared that with Ty. If I had, maybe he would have felt comfortable doing the same. Maybe he would have let me in, that snow day when we talked about Ashley and the breakup, instead of insisting that it was nothing, that nothing had happened, that everything was fine. Maybe he would have given me the details I need to understand what went down between them, the facts I'd use to *figure out what to do with this letter.*

Because he didn't hate Ashley. She might have broken his heart, but he still put her picture up in his collage.

Which meant that he still considered her a friend.

18.

ON THURSDAY I CAUSE some general confusion among our respective friends by asking Sadie to eat lunch with me. I pick a table for us in the cafeteria where I can keep an eye on Ashley Davenport. The letter is stuck under the edge of my tray, where my food sits untouched. I'm too busy to eat. I'm watching this girl who was so important to my brother that he wrote her a letter before he died. I'm planning to make my move.

I'm thankful that seniors and sophomores, by sheer coincidence, have the same lunch period. So far I've learned way more about Ashley in the cafeteria than I did in the gym. Like: she waves at nearly everyone who passes as they make their way down the lunch line (she's friendly), and they wave back (she's popular). She picks all the tiny chopped carrots out of her salad (she's trying to lose weight?), which she nibbles with her fingers (she has bad table manners?), and she laughs a lot (she has good teeth).

She seems like a nice girl. A lovely girl, like my mom said. Inside and out.

Over at my regular table, Table Dweeb, as we like to call it, Beaker catches my eye. She keeps looking worriedly from me to Sadie and back again, like she can't believe this turn of events: me and the shoplifter. What the heck is going on? She may be forced to stage some kind of intervention. Next to her, El glances over and gives me a smile, which I don't know how to interpret. I don't know what to make of her smiling at me. Maybe now it's easier for her to like me at a distance?

And then, of course, there's Steven. He's reading, his tall frame curled awkwardly in the metal cafeteria chair, his head bent over his book. He pushes his glasses up on his nose and drags his lower lip between his teeth, something he does when he's thinking all the deep thoughts. He rests his forehead against his fist, then jots something down in the margins.

I love that he writes in books.

"Hey," Sadie whispers to me urgently. "Here's your chance."

I look up at Sadie. "What?"

She jerks her head in Ashley's direction.

I turn back. Sure enough, Ashley's friends are getting up. They give their faint "see you at practice"s and "love you"s and then they're gone. Ashley sits picking at her carrot slivers alone.

It's like the universe is giving me this opportunity. If I believed in that sort of thing.

Ashley reaches into the backpack at her feet and pulls out a book: *Persuasion*, by Jane Austen.

Yes. She even freaking reads classic literature. This girl is too good to be true.

It's time. I slide out the letter and stand up. All of a sudden my heart starts beating like a brass band. *Whomp whomp whomp.*

"You can do it," Sadie whispers.

I can do it. I can take twenty steps across the cafeteria and hand a letter to a girl.

I can say: *Hi, Ty left this for you. So . . . here.*

And then I can give it to her and I can turn around and walk away.

So I won't see her face when she reads it.

Or maybe she won't read it here, with all these people around. Maybe she'll go to the library and find that empty corner behind the stacks. That's what I would do. Or maybe she'll wait until she gets home.

And maybe I should be more discreet. We're in the middle of a crowded cafeteria. People will notice. People will be listening.

I could say, *Hi, can I talk to you?* and lead her to that empty corner of the library, and give it to her there.

If she'd come with me.

But people would notice that too, and then they might ask her about it.

I could mail it to her.

But then maybe her mom would find the letter first, and read it, and maybe there's sensitive information in there. Ty could have mailed it to her if he'd wanted that. Maybe her dad would read it and maybe she and Ty had sex and he wrote about that and it would ruin her relationship with her father forever.

All of this goes through my mind and more, more questions, more junk, more variables.

I'm ten steps in the right direction now. Ten to go.

Someone says Ashley's name. She looks up from her book and lays it on the table and smiles blindingly, a happy, excited smile. She jumps up and throws herself into a guy's arms.

Not just any guy, either. Grayson.

One of my brother's friends.

"I was just thinking about you," Ashley says.

They kiss. Not a long kiss, nothing passionate or showy or French, but a quick peck that says, *We're together. We kiss all the time, and it's no big deal.*

I've stopped walking. I'm standing there five steps away, watching them kiss. They pull back from each other and Grayson says something I don't understand in his deep, rumbly-jock voice, and then he glances over Ashley's shoulder right at me.

It's clear that he recognizes me. His expression tightens into one part pity, one part I don't know what, like the sight of me brings an unpleasant taste to his mouth. The same look on his face as when he and Fauxhawk brought that box to our house three days after my brother died, when the school gathered up all remaining evidence of Tyler James Riggs and delivered it to our front door.

They took Ty's name off the roster. They even expunged his school records for the year, as if they could erase his existence altogether.

I'd bet good money they didn't do that kind of thing with

Hailey McKennett, who lost her battle with cystic fibrosis two years ago, or Sammie Sullivan, who died of complications from pneumonia, or Jacob Wright, who was killed in a car crash driving home drunk from a party at Branched Oak Lake last summer. Jacob got a tree planted for him at the front of the school, a plaque under it that I pass every day walking in that reads WE'LL MISS YOU, J. Sammie got a moment of silence during first period that year and an entire page of the yearbook devoted to her memory. They read Hailey's name at graduation.

But Ty got his locker packed up and delivered promptly back to my mother, before we'd even had a chance to bury him.

Because it was suicide.

Because they don't want to seem like they're condoning it.

Ashley sees Grayson's expression and turns to see what he's looking at. She sees me standing there frozen. All at once a myriad of emotions pass over her face: confusion, pity, embarrassment over kissing Grayson, and, oh yes, there it is, an emotion I'm most familiar with these days, rising in her deep blue eyes.

Guilt.

I know guilt when I see it.

I do a quick 180. I leave my tray on the table and walk stiffly past Sadie and her questioning expression, past my other friends, who are looking at me too, out of the cafeteria. I go to my locker, set the letter in its place in the five-subject notebook on the top shelf, and slam the door.

I'm angry, it turns out.

The image of my mother's face swims up in my mind, when

she took the box from Grayson after he rang our doorbell, the way she tried to smile at him, to thank him, before she brought it back to the kitchen table and opened it and started crying all over again, lifting out Ty's gym shoes and his extra deodorant and the tiny magnetic mirror that he used to smile into every day.

A-holes. All of them. A-holes.

And Ashley was kissing Grayson. My brother's a-hole friend. The guy, if the slightly crooked nose is any indication, who Ty punched that day when he got suspended from school.

Over Ashley. Ty punched him over Ashley.

I have to consider the possibility that Ashley Davenport, that lovely girl, inside and out, the right kind of girl, the nicest, might be the biggest a-hole of them all.

"Is there still a shredder in Dad's office?" I ask Mom when I get home.

She frowns. "Yes. Why?"

"I got a credit card application in the mail," I explain smoothly. "I would have just thrown it out, but then I remembered that you and Dad always shred that kind of thing."

It's getting marginally easier to lie to my mother.

"Oh," Mom says. "Yes, that sounds like a good idea."

Still in the cold anger I haven't been able to shake from school, I head down the hall to Dad's old office. The door to this room is usually shut, as if Mom can't stand the sight of his absence. When he lived with us he kept the door open, so he could catch us as we walked by. "Hey there, Peanut," he'd always say when he spotted me. And I would stand in the doorway for a few minutes "shooting the breeze with the old man," as he called it, telling him about my day at school or whatever book I was reading or the square root of some number I'd memorized.

I don't stop to look around as I enter the office. I go straight to the shredder. I turn it on.

I take the letter out of my bag.

I want to destroy it. I want this whole mess to be over with, Ty's unfinished business, his presence, real or not, lingering in this house, his problem, his, not mine. I want to go to college and leave this part of my life behind. Start over. Be someone else besides the-girl-whose-brother-died. I've earned that, I think.

I don't want to think about Ty anymore.

I finger an edge of the envelope that's curling up, the glue there coming unstuck. I've been handling it too much and the paper is showing some wear.

It would be so easy to open it and find out everything.

I want to get his explanation. In his own words, I want him to tell me why.

I catch a whiff of my brother's cologne.

"What? You want me to give it to her?" I say.

There's no answer.

Then I ask him the question that's been on my mind all this time. Even though he's probably not even here.

"Why her? Why Ashley? Why would you write her a letter, and not write one to me? Didn't you have anything worthwhile to say to me?"

No answer. But the silence feels like an answer.

I swallow.

I think about the text.

"I refuse to feel guilty about something you did," I mumble, but I don't mean it.

I do feel guilty.

Every single day.

I turn the shredder off. "I got into MIT," I whisper to the empty room.

He would have been proud of me, if he were alive. He would have known how much it meant.

19.

FRIDAY. I'M ALREADY ON EDGE when I get to school. I haven't burned the letter or shredded it or thrown it away yet, all things I've been tempted to do so I don't have to get involved in this Ashley/Ty/Grayson affair. I have it with me, still stuck in the pages of my notebook. I can't leave it home on the off chance that someone else—insert: Mom—will find it. I can't let anybody else find it. In that way, it belongs to me.

I'm hungry. I walk to the vending machine in the corner and fish out a crinkled dollar. I missed breakfast (i.e., Mom didn't get up to make it, and I didn't have the energy to pour myself a bowl of cereal). I put the dollar in. The machine spits it out. I put it in. It spits it out.

It's worse than the Lemon. "Come on," I plead. "I require sustenance."

Not that there's anything good in the machine to eat. Dried

fruit. Granola bars. Whole-grain pretzels. Organic gluten-free seaweed chips. This is Nebraska, for crying out loud, land of meat, potatoes, corn, corn, and corn as the five basic food groups.

I'm suddenly struck by a memory of Ty standing in this exact spot, banging on this exact machine until a bag of dried apricots dropped into the slot. He picked it up. Scowled.

"I don't care what the First Lady says," he complained, loudly enough that the people around us started nodding in agreement. "This is not a Pop-Tart. I need my junk food, man. How's a growing boy to survive on all this healthy stuff? Am I right?"

He's right.

My throat closes. I miss him I miss him I miss him. The hole in my chest explodes. I can't breathe I can't breathe. There are people waiting for the machine behind me, so I don't have time to let the hole pass on its own. I stumble to the side and force my legs to move away, down the hall to the restroom, where I almost run to the last stall and sit down on the lid of the toilet and bend my head over my knees and gasp and gasp and think maybe this drug thing Dave suggested isn't a bad idea after all.

I'm not doing well, here. Clearly.

When the hole fills in again, my body feels achy, like I'm coming down with something. I flush the toilet as if I was in there for a good reason. I go out, take my glasses off, and splash some water on my face. The girls on either side of me don't say anything; they just return to meticulously washing their hands.

I lean forward to take a long look at myself in the mirror. There are dark circles under my eyes, and my lips are chapped and colorless. I swipe at a wet tendril of hair that's clinging to my fore-head, but then it just sticks to a different spot. The whites of my eyes look like road maps, veiny and red-rimmed and swollen, like I've been crying, even though I haven't been crying.

I look wrecked.

This whole thing has warped me, I think. I'm a board left out in the rain, and it's impossible to go back to being straight and undamaged ever again. This is who I am now.

The girl whose brother died.

Plus there's the fun fact that I am losing my mind. I'm here at school freaking out about a stupid letter that my dead brother wrote for his ex—why exactly?

Because some part of me thinks that Ty's still around. Because I think maybe that drawer being open that night and that letter being in that drawer means that he wants me to deliver it. Because, no matter how much I try to be rational, some part of me wants to believe that I am seeing his freaking ghost.

This, for some reason, makes me laugh. The sound is sharp and bounces off the tight white-tiled walls of the bathroom.

Hilarious.

One of the girls next to me gets the heck out of there—she just bolts for the door. But the other girl waits for me to pull myself together. She hands me a paper towel to dry my face. And when I put my glasses back on, I realize it's Ashley Davenport.

Awesome.

"Hi," she says. "I saw you come in here, and I wanted to talk to you, so . . ."

So she witnessed my little breakdown. Even more awesome.

She's wearing a bright pink cardigan over a white sequined tank top, silvery lip gloss gleaming off her Cupid's-bow lips, and a gold heart-shaped necklace that's resting in the hollow of her throat. She's beautiful. What sticks out to me most about her is that she looks . . . *healthy* is the word that comes to mind. Not just in her athletic legs and shiny red hair and bright eyes and dewy porcelain skin. It's more than that. She has all the signs of a person who life has left almost completely undamaged. I bet her parents are still together and still hold hands and still kiss. I bet she volunteers for some kind of charity. I bet the most tears she's ever shed in her whole life were over her childhood dog when it died of old age.

She's not an a-hole, I think. She's a nice girl.

But that doesn't change how I feel.

"There's nothing I want to talk about," I say. "Not with you."

She puts her hand on my arm. Gently, but insistently. "Wait. I know you saw me and Grayson in the cafeteria yesterday. You looked upset, so I thought, you might have thought . . ."

"I might have thought what?" I challenge. "That you cheated on my brother?"

Her eyes widen. "But I didn't cheat on Ty. I would never. He broke up with me, not the other way around. I would never have cheated on Ty. I—"

"But what about the fight? When Ty punched Grayson? Why would he do that?"

She bows her head. "I was . . . sad after Ty broke it off. He didn't even tell me why. He just came up to me that morning and said things weren't working out between us. He said he was sorry, and then he walked off. I was shocked. I thought we were—I cried. I was upset. People thought he was being a jerk. And the next day Grayson said something rude to Ty about it, and . . ."

"Ty hit him," I fill in.

She squeezes my arm. "I wasn't into Grayson back then. We just started dating like a week ago. I swear."

I don't know what to say.

Her lip starts trembling. A tear shines on the edge of her eye.

I wish I could cry so easily.

"Your brother was an amazing guy," she continues. "Everybody liked him. They were only mad at him because of me, but they would have gotten over it. . . . I don't know why he would . . ." She pauses, of course she does, but then she looks at me like I'm going to tell her now, why Ty did it, why someone like my brother, who everybody liked, who was cute and funny and popular, thought his existence was so terrible that he chose to end it.

Because I'm his sister. I should know the reasons why.

"I should have realized that he was . . . I didn't know . . ." She lets go of my arm and presses her lips together, like she's about to start really crying. "I'm sorry. I'm really sorry, Lex."

"I have to go." I back away from Ashley, then push out of the bathroom and into the noisy, crowded hall. I walk on autopilot back to my locker. I lean against it, watching everybody pass by, ready to head toward class, ready to start their days.

I lean my head back until it touches the cool metal of the locker, and close my eyes.

She didn't dump him. She didn't cheat on him.

It's not her fault.

She doesn't even know why he broke up with her. Which makes Ty the a-hole in this scenario.

My eyes snap open. I unzip my backpack, pull out my five-subject notebook, and retrieve the letter. I don't give myself any time to think about what I'm doing. I don't make a plan.

I just head down to room 121B.

I wait outside the door for the students to trickle in.

"Hey, Lex," Damian says, slinking up to me. He gives his head a little shake to get his hair out of his eyes. Smiles. Fidgets. "Fancy meeting you here."

"Yeah."

"Did you finish *Heart of Darkness*?"

I nod distractedly. "Oh, the horror."

He laughs. "The horror. So what are you doing here? Not that I'm complaining. But aren't you a little old for this class?"

"An errand," I say. "I'm running an errand. Hey, uh, it's good to see you, Damian, but you should probably . . ." I gesture toward the classroom. "I don't want to be responsible for you getting marked tardy."

"It's good to see you, too," he says, smiling his painful-looking smile again, and then he goes to take his seat.

Ashley shows up just as the bell rings. This time she doesn't bowl me over when she appears from around the corner. She slows down when she sees me, suddenly unsure of herself. Then she stops.

"Hi," she says.

"Hi," I say back. "Sorry about before. Sometimes I get overwhelmed by . . . everything."

She bites her lip. For some reason she looks frightened. Maybe she can sense what's coming.

"I was wrong, earlier," I say quickly, and before I can lose my nerve, I pull the letter from the inside pocket of my coat and hold it out. It trembles between us. "This is for you. From Ty."

If it's possible for her face to get any whiter, it does. Even her lips drain of color. She doesn't reach for the letter.

"Take it," I say, thrusting it at her. "He wants—he wanted you to have it."

She takes it.

I feel lighter the second the envelope leaves my hand.

Ashley stares down at it, her eyes tracing Ty's sloppy letters spelling her name.

"I didn't read it," I feel compelled to tell her. "I don't know what it says, but it's for you." I can't think of what else to say, and we're both late to class, so I whisper, "I'm sorry," although I don't know what I'm apologizing for, for Ty or for me, and then I walk away.

I hope it's the right thing. It feels like the right thing. Probably. Maybe.

But at least it's all over with now. It's done.

9 March

My parents used to tell this story, over and over, year after year, about the first time I ever saw Ty.

According to family legend, I was playing at the park by my house when it happened. I was on the swings being pushed by my grandmother, who'd been looking after me while my mother was at the hospital. When my parents came into view, walking slowly across the grass toward us, Grandma lifted me out of the bucket swing, set me on the ground, gave me a little push, and said, "Go. Meet your brother."

I ran to my parents.

They'd prepped me about this, of course, with months of talking about a new baby brother and what a good big sister I'd be, feeling Mom's distended belly, singing to it, reading books about how we have to be quiet when the baby's sleeping and we have to sit down to hold the baby and never poke the baby in the eye. They'd shown me the new baby's freshly painted room and moved me into a "big girl bed" so he *could have my crib. They'd even bought me a T-shirt that had the words* BIG SISTER *in silvery sparkly letters across the chest. I was wearing it, that day. Or so they tell me.*

It was a lot of hype. Too much hype, probably.

When I reached them, my dad knelt and showed me the blue-wrapped bundle in his arms: a tiny disgruntled person with a round, purplish face, eyelids that were so swollen it was hard to tell what color the eyes were, and a head that bore only a small thin tuft of brown hair.

He wasn't the best-looking baby, my brother.

I looked at him.

He looked at me.

Then he went cross-eyed.

"He's not cute" is what I famously said, clearly disappointed. "I thought he was going to be cute."

Apparently I've always had a problem with calling it like I see it.

But then I laid my hand on the top of the baby's nearly hairless head. "Hello, brother," I said, by way of introduction.

"Tyler," Mom provided. "His name is Tyler."

"Ty," I confirmed. "Can I hold him?"

I sat down cross-legged right there in the grass, and Dad laid Ty carefully in my lap. I looked up at Mom and smiled. "He's mine," I announced. "My baby. Mine."

Yep, that's how the story goes. 2 minutes into meeting my baby brother, I claimed him as my own personal property. He may not have been cute, but he was my brother. Mine.

I realize that almost everybody has a story like this. It's not unique. I read somewhere that approximately 80% of Americans have at least one brother or sister. There's a predictable formula to these stories: Older sibling meets younger. Older sibling says something cute (or rude, or funny, but always cute) and everyone laughs, and the older sibling eventually gets used to the idea that he/she isn't the center of the world anymore. There's a reason we tell these stories again and again— because they define us.

The first time I was a sister.

The first time we were all together as a family.

Now I try to remember that day as more than a story I've heard. I try to call up the wind on my face as I ran across the field. My heart thumping. My dad smiling as he crouched down. The smooth heat of Ty's head under my fingers. The smell of baby powder and garden roses. The grass prickly against my knees.

But I don't know if any of that is real, or just a bunch of happy details I imagine to fill in the blanks of my parents' fairy tale, which they've told so many times it's started to feel like memory. I was 2 years old when Ty was born.

But I do remember this:

He cried. I think he cried every night, really, but I remember this one particular night. I woke to the sound of him crying, a thin wail that filled the house. I got out of bed and padded in stocking feet into his room, then boosted myself over the railings of the crib and lay down beside him.

He stopped crying to look at me.

I pulled his blanket back over him. He'd kicked it off. He was cold.

"Don't worry," I said. "I'll take care of you."

We stayed that way for I don't know how long, looking at each other.

Then Dad was there, smiling down at both of us, his hand cupping the back of my head, and he said, "Well, look at you two, all quiet and cozy. You calmed him right down. Well done, Peanut. Well done."

And I remember being proud. I had made things right when they were wrong.

20.

ON MONDAY, SADIE SHOWS UP at my back door before school. Just like when we were eight years old, when she'd stand on the steps and tap on the glass sliding door, like *Can Lexie come out to play?* until Mom heard her and let her in.

"Lex!" Mom calls down the hall. "You have a visitor."

I come running.

"Think fast." Sadie throws me a Pop-Tart, cherry, my favorite—she still remembers my favorite. "Breakfast is served," she says.

I glance over at Mom to see if she's offended by the notion that Sadie apparently believes she has to feed me, but Mom is leaning against the kitchen doorway smiling the nostalgia smile.

"I thought we'd wait for the bus together," Sadie says cheerfully, even though I know she doesn't typically ride the bus. "Two freezing ass—backsides are better than one, I always say."

"Indeed," I say.

Mom laughs in that muted way she has now of just breathing out her nose. "It's good to see you again, Sadie. How are you?"

"I'm stellar, thanks," Sadie answers. "What's going on with you?"

It's an awkward question these days, but better than "How are you?," which we can never answer truthfully, and Sadie asks it in a completely casual tone. Mom doesn't lose the smile.

"Lex got into MIT, did she tell you?"

Sadie swings her gaze to me. Blank face.

"Massachusetts Institute of Technology," I explain, my cheeks heating.

Mom puffs. "It's the best mathematics program in the country."

Sadie gives a low whistle. "Congrats, Lex. Wow."

I stare at my sneakers. "Thanks."

"She's going to do amazing things," Mom says.

Sadie nods. "No doubt."

This is getting to be too much. "Come on." I grab my backpack in one hand and readjust my grip on the Pop-Tart with the other and lunge for the door. "We have to go if we don't want to miss the bus."

"You girls have a good day at school," Mom calls as Sadie follows me out.

Like we are eight years old again.

"Your mom hasn't changed much," Sadie comments as we stand waiting.

It's funny, her saying that.

My mom has changed so much since Sadie and I were best friends.

I have changed so much.

But every now and then it's like we're allowed to act like our old selves. It comes back. If only for a moment.

"I gave the letter to Ashley," I confess to Sadie when we're sitting in the front seat of the bus, the heater blowing loud and hot across our knees.

"Whoa," Sadie says. "What made you decide to finally do it? Last time I saw you—"

"I talked to her," I say before she recounts her own rendition of the Ashley-kisses-Grayson debacle. "She told me her side. Ty dumped her, not the other way around. Apparently he didn't even give her a reason. So I thought the letter might provide some explanation."

"You still didn't read it."

I shake my head.

"God," Sadie says. "You and the iron self-control."

We don't talk for a while. Sadie plugs some earbuds into her phone and I do the same with mine. Sadie's music choice: rap, by the sound of it. Mine: Rachmaninoff. We cruise along through the endless white cornfields. Then Sadie pulls one bud out and turns to me.

"So, Massachusetts," she says. "That's a long way."

"Yes. It is."

"It's good news, though, right?"

"Right. But it's going to be hard, leaving my mom."

"She's not going with you?"

I frown at her, boggled by the idea. "You don't usually bring your parents to college with you, Sade. That would be weird."

Sadie gives me a half smile. "I'll look after her, if you want."

"What are you going to do after graduation?"

She shrugs. "Find a job."

"You're not planning on college?"

"School's not really my thing." She grimaces like the idea of college is physically painful.

"You're smart, though, Sadie," I argue.

She looks startled.

"You are," I insist. "You should go to college."

She sits back, surprised and pleased, and stares out the window for a while.

"I'm not smart like you are," she says.

"Well." I hold up my hands. "Nobody's smart like I am. Obviously."

She grins. "Right. You're MIT material."

"I'm MIT material," I agree, and it feels good, that someone else knows.

We go back to listening to our respective music for a while. Sadie's head bobs. I close my eyes and try to get lost in the Piano Concerto no. 2.

Sadie taps on my arm. I pull out my earbud.

"You were brave, giving the letter to Ashley." Her black-ringed blue eyes, so close to mine, are earnest, admiring. "That took guts."

"It took forever before I actually did something about it," I say.

"True, but you did something."

True.

"And now Ty can move on," she says, lowering her voice when she says his name so people don't hear. "He can be at peace now."

I don't know whether or not to believe her. But, for once, I hope she's right.

"Yeah," I say. "Maybe now things will start to get back to normal."

When we get to school, it's immediately apparent that something's wrong. It's too quiet. Students are standing in groups, whispering, the boys with their heads down, the girls looking tearful. Even the teachers are somber as they shuffle toward their classrooms.

Something has happened.

I don't like the way people are looking at me. There's a new awareness in their stares, which burns me before they turn away and go back to their hushed conversations. Something has happened that involves me in some way.

My brain goes straight to the letter for Ashley. It must have had something to do with me, and she must be telling people about it.

I knew I should have read the dumb letter. Why didn't I read the dumb letter?

I spot Damian standing by the door to the counselor's office. He's crying. He sees me, and he starts crying harder.

My heart is ice as I approach him.

"Hey," I rasp nervously. "Are you okay? What's going on?"

"Patrick Murphy is dead," he chokes out. "He was a sopho-more. He was my friend. He was—"

I know who Patrick Murphy is. One of the three amigos.

"How?" I ask, but part of me already knows the answer.

"He killed himself." He wipes a fat tear that rolls down his chin and gives me a look that's pure despair. "At the train yard, about an hour ago."

My vision goes white. I lean against the wall and wait for the color to return. When it does, I'm so angry my hands are shaking. I know it's inappropriate and completely selfish, but at that moment, I'm furious at Patrick. Not for doing something so stupid as dying. Not that. But for the way I know my mother's face is going to look when she hears the news. I'm mad at the way, just five minutes ago, I'd finally felt like I had the ground under my feet for the first time since Ty died.

And now this.

Damian goes back to crying, hard, like he doesn't care who's watching, his thin shoulders racked by sobs.

I think, if I put my hand out and touch him on the shoulder, will it make it better or worse for him?

I think, if I put my hand out and touch his shoulder, will I be able to hold it together myself?

I think, no.

"I'm sorry," I murmur. I don't know if he hears me.

Then I back away.

There are so many people crying. I walk among them like a zombie. I think, I have to keep moving. I have a big German test later. I have to keep my grades up for MIT. I have to pass with flying colors. I have to keep going.

But the ground is flying out from under me.

Something roars in my head. I hate everything, in this moment. I hate the world. I hate life.

Ty.

Now Patrick.

Another boy dead.

21.

SOMEHOW, I'M NOT EVEN SURE EXACTLY HOW, I get through the rest of the day. I ride home. I make my way silently up the driveway and into my house. I take off my shoes and coat and set my backpack by the door. I pad down the hall into Mom's bedroom, through the room, into her bathroom. I open her bathroom cabinet and take down her bottle of prescription Valium.

If this were *Brave New World*, I'd take the stupid soma.

I wonder if Mom knows yet. My heart squeezes at the thought. For a minute I'm struck with a childlike desire to have her hold me and stroke my hair and tell me everything will be all right. I'm upset, and I want my mother to comfort me. That's what mothers do. But with this news about Patrick, I suspect it's going to be the other way around.

She's going to need me.

I need to keep it together.

"We must learn to deal with the facts," I whisper. I look at the single bright pill in my hand for a minute, and then I put it in my mouth and lean over the faucet to swallow it down.

I go to my room and curl up on my bed.

0.

1.

1.

2.

3.

5.

8.

13.

21.

34.

55.

89.

144.

233.

377.

610.

987.

1,597.

2,584.

4,181.

6,765.

10,946.

17,711.

28,657.

46,368.

75,025.

121,393.

196,418.

317,811.

514,229.

832,040.

1,346,269.

2,178,309.

3,524,578.

5,702,887.

9,227,465.

14,930,352.

24,157,817.

39,088,169.

My head goes fuzzy. I imagine the Valium doing its work inside me, binding to the receptors in my brain. I can feel myself sliding, sliding, off to the gray space. To sleep.

I don't dream about anything at all.

11 March

Here's my last real memory of Patrick Murphy: the day I caught Ty and his friends smoking in the playhouse.

They were 12.

Oh, yeah. They were busted big time.

Building stuff was one of Dad's temporary hobbies when I was about 9. It started when he decided to construct a custom doghouse for our dog, Sunny. He spent about two weeks on it in careful construction, nailing and sanding and laying real roof tiles on the top to keep the weather out. He even painted it to match our house: green, with white trim.

Sunny hated it. She much preferred the family-room sofa.

It didn't matter. Dad was so pleased with how the doghouse turned out that he decided to try his hand at something bigger. A playhouse. He went to Toys "R" Us to study the pictures of the thousand-dollar playhouses they sold and came home with a solemn promise to Ty and me

that he would build us the best playhouse this side of the Mississippi—
not some roughshod half-plastic monstrosity that would only look good
for a summer or two, he said. Something solid.

Something that would last.

He enlisted the help of Aunt Jessica, who's an architect in Missouri.
She drew up the blueprints for a 500-square-foot, one-and-a-half-story
playhouse, which was basically a square little room with a ladder and
a loft.

Dad bought the materials. He laid a set of pretreated railroad ties
as the foundation for the structure, in case we ever sold our house and
wanted to move the playhouse, he said. He dug a 30-foot-long trench
between the house and the far corner of the backyard, so he could run
electricity to our playhouse. So we could have lights.

It was a big freaking deal.

Dad built the frame first, then the roof. He put real insulation in the
walls, to keep it warm in the winter and cool in summer. Ty and I wrote
our names on the inside of one wall before Dad sealed it up with dry-
wall and painted. He installed real glass windows that opened and closed,
complete with screens to keep the bugs out, and a real full-sized front door
with a little window in it. Then he set down a layer of cheap black-and-
white-checkered linoleum on the main floor, and green carpet in the loft.
The outside he painted to match our house, too. Green with white trim.
Topped off with a tiny front porch with a porch light and everything.

Mom sewed some curtains for the windows. She bought a large
play kitchen set from a garage sale in Lincoln: a toy refrigerator, stove,
and sink, with storage where I could keep my food play dough molds,
my plastic dishes and cups, and my tea set. She even splurged on a

227

child-sized wooden table and chairs.

Suddenly all the neighborhood kids wanted to come to our house to play.

Sadie and I practically lived in the playhouse from ages 9 to 12, our sleeping bags always ready to roll out in the loft. The green carpet became grass for our My Little Ponies and Barbie's front lawn, and the light blue walls were the sky, and we stuck glow-in-the-dark stars to the sloped ceiling.

It was our own private world.

I feel I must guiltily confess that it wasn't Ty's own private world, not until Sadie and I lost interest, which took a few years. Then, after dollies and Barbies and playing at being grown-ups lost their sparkle, the playhouse passed to Ty.

So. That time with Patrick. Mom sent me out to the playhouse to bring Ty, Damian, and Patrick in for dinner. I knew there was something going down the minute I came through the door and heard all this scrambling up in the loft.

I smelled the cigarettes right away. I mean, they hadn't even opened the windows.

"Hey, you guys," I said cheerfully. "What are you doing?"

I climbed halfway up the ladder and stuck my head into the loft. The boys all looked at me with wide, innocent eyes.

"Nothing," Ty said. He gestured to Dad's old boom box, which was playing "Stairway to Heaven." "We're just chilling."

I looked at Damian and Patrick. Damian looked the same as he does now: thin and birdlike, his clothes hanging off him in various shades of muted colors, gray eyes wary like any second he expected somebody to attack him. Patrick was one of those kids who had orange hair like a sweet potato and white, white skin with freckles all over. His face was bright red.

"Are you okay, Patrick?" I asked.

He started coughing. The minute he opened his mouth a puff of cigarette smoke came out. He coughed and coughed and coughed.

I looked down for a minute. "Hmm," I said. Sigh. "Okay, boys. Hand them over."

Ty's face was a little green. He started to say, "Hand what over?" but I gave him a look that said he didn't want to mess with me. Ty brought his hands out from behind his back and produced their hastily stubbed-out cigarettes. They'd put them out on a piece of my porcelain tea set, the thoughtful little sweethearts.

At least it's not pot, I thought. I stared at the plate, then rolled my eyes. "Where's the rest?"

"The rest?" squeaked Damian.

"The pack. Where is it?"

They exchanged glances and then decided there was no getting past me. Ty opened up the My Little Pony Dream Castle, where he'd stuffed the pack of Virginia Slims.

I choked back a laugh. "Where did you get these?"

Silence.

"Tell me or I tell the grown-ups."

"I swiped them from my mom's purse," Damian confessed.

I rubbed my eyes. Sighed again. "You guys. Wow."

"Please don't tell," pleaded Patrick, almost in tears. "My dad would be so mad."

"You know why he would be mad?" I asked. "Because only morons smoke cigarettes." I looked at Damian. "Sorry, Damian, but your mom's a moron."

He didn't argue.

I held up the Virginia Slims pack. "These kill you. It's slow so you don't really notice, but they will kill you. They also make your breath smell bad and turn your teeth yellow and wreck your voice and stain your fingers and empty your wallet and about a hundred other terrible things."

"We were trying it out once," Ty said. "We weren't going to start smoking or anything."

"The girls at school think it's cool," Patrick said defensively.

"Right. The girls in your middle school. Whose center of the universe right now is the fricking Rainbow Loom. I'll tell you what, I would never, ever kiss a guy who smoked. Uck." Not that I would ever kiss a guy period, I thought wistfully. This was a few months before the infamous Nathan Thaddeus Dillinger II.

Damian and Patrick looked thoughtful.

"So are you going to tell Mom?" Ty asked.

I thought about it for like 2 seconds. "No. But only if you guys promise me you'll never do something this moronic again."

"We promise," they said immediately.

I made them pinky swear. The most solemn oath.

"Lexie?" Mom yelled from the back porch. "Boys?"

I turned to the 3 amigos. "Here's what you're going to do. You're going to go straight into the house and say I told you to wash your disgusting boy hands. Which you will do. Then we have to do something about your breath."

"We could use Dad's mouthwash," Ty suggested.

"Too obvious. I'll bring by a box of Tic Tacs while you're in there. You'll come out and have dinner, yum yum yum, and then Damian, you're going to go home and tell your mom you stole her cigarettes, and give them back."

Damian's face went pale. "What?"

"You're going to tell her you stole her cigarettes because cigarettes kill people, and you don't want her to die. She'll forgive you if you put it like that. Okay? Got it? Do we understand the plan?"

3 nods.

I marched them down the ladder and out of the playhouse.

"You have like the best sister ever," I heard Patrick say to Ty as we crossed the yard.

"She's all right."

And that's the last thing I remember about Patrick. Saying I was the best sister.

Wishing that he had a big sister like me.

22.

MOM IS MAKING A GREEN BEAN CASSEROLE.

Her hands tremble slightly as she trims the beans with a sharp knife, but she doesn't cut herself. She scoops the beans up and delivers them into a pot of rapidly boiling water. She waits until they're tender but still slightly crunchy. She drains them over a sieve in the kitchen sink. The steam fogs her glasses. Then she leaves them hot in the sink to open a can of cream of mushroom soup, which she whips together with a cup of milk, a quarter cup of french fried onions, a dash of salt, an eighth of a teaspoon of pepper, and a tablespoon of melted butter. She pours the frothy mix into a glass baking dish. She adds the green beans, stirs them gently, then covers the dish with foil. She puts the dish in the oven. She sets the timer.

We wait.

Outside, a single chickadee is perched on a branch near the kitchen window, chirping. Clouds are moving across the sky.

Snow is falling in slow motion.

The timer goes off. Mom dons a pair of mitts, reaches into the heat of the oven, and draws out the dish. She sets it on a hot pad on the counter and carefully rearranges another layer of french fried onions around the edges.

I'm reminded of Christmas. Mom used to make green bean casserole at Christmas. She was never a top chef or anything, but it was a good casserole. I would watch her, just this way, as she put it together.

This was the part where my hand would snake out and steal some onions.

This was the part where, if she caught me, Mom would smack me on the wrist with her wooden spoon. Then she'd take a handful of onions for herself, and she'd smile, and I'd smile, and we'd eat them like it was some kind of marvelous secret between us. They were salty and left a layer of grease on my tongue, and I loved them.

There was no green bean casserole this Christmas. For obvious reasons. We ate pity food for Christmas this year.

Mom finishes dispensing the onions and returns the dish to the oven, uncovered this time. She resets the timer.

We wait.

The timer rings again. Mom gets the mitts and takes the casserole out. The onions on top have baked to a lovely golden brown. The air smells savory and rich. She puts the dish on the counter to cool.

At the sink Mom scrubs her hands in a way that reminds me of a surgeon prepping. She dries her hands and removes her apron to reveal her simple black sheath dress. She smooths the fabric down her sides and pads off on bare feet with unpainted toes to retrieve her shoes, a pair of plain black pumps. She gracelessly leans against the table to slip them on one foot at a time. Then she goes to the counter and measures out a new layer of foil for the casserole. She takes a black marker out of a drawer and writes *From Joan and Alexis Riggs* across the top. She folds it over the casserole. She puts the dish into an insulated bag that will keep it warm.

Then she picks up her purse and checks its contents—lipstick, powder, a card for the Murphys, which she had me sign earlier.

It says, *With sorrow for your loss.*

We have become the observers of tragedy.

Mom checks her watch. She palms her car keys. Then she looks at me.

"Are you ready?" she asks.

I nod.

She brushes off the shoulders of my black cable-knit sweater.

"All right," she says, her voice as flat as if we were making a trip to the dentist. "Let's go."

Patrick's funeral is held in the Cathedral of the Risen Christ, a different church than where we held Ty's funeral. Practically the entire school turns up, even the teachers and the principal and the office staff. Mom and I sit in the back of the sanctuary, and try to ignore the way people are looking at us, two ways, actually: (a) They know that this funeral is going to be particularly hard for us, and they feel sorry for that, but they need to focus on the Murphys now, please understand. Which we do. And (b) we shouldn't be here. Our kid infected this kid with the suicide disease. We should feel ashamed of this. Which we also kind of do.

Maybe they're right. Maybe we shouldn't have come, but Mom wants to be here, if only to lend silent support, if only to prove to the Murphys that survival is possible.

So we sit in the back.

There's no viewing this time. Closed casket. Because it was death by train.

Patrick's casket is white and shiny and edged with silver, like the hood of an expensive car. On top is a heap of red roses that I can smell from here. One rose by itself smells nice, but twenty-four of them fill the room with such a cloying sweetness that it overwhelms everything else. It makes my stomach turn.

Still, there are worse things to smell than roses.

At the foot of the casket Patrick's dad stands next to a giant framed photograph of a younger, happier version of Patrick. His dad greets the people who line up to pay their respects, like some kind of twisted wedding reception in reverse. With the men he shakes hands, but it's not so much a shaking motion as them grabbing his hand and holding it for a few seconds, then letting go. The women give him awkward, tearful hugs.

I can't hear what they're saying, but I know that it's variants of "I'm sorry," and "Patrick was a good person/kid/student/human being/member of the swim team," and "Call us if you need anything," and Patrick's father is saying, "Thank you," and "I know," and "I will."

Even though he probably won't.

Patrick's mother died when he was a kid. Car accident. So they've been through this before. He has a younger sister, but she's not standing with her dad. I locate her, already seated in the front pew. Her head is down, and I wonder if she's reading the program or praying or staring at her toes.

I stared at my toes, when it was me sitting at the front of the church.

The organist starts to play. People file into the pews and stand, singing.

Mom hands me the program. On the front is a smaller black-and-white picture of Patrick, smiling his awkward smile, and a Bible verse, Romans 8:38–39: *For I am convinced that neither death nor life, neither angels nor demons, neither the present nor the future, nor any powers, neither height nor depth, nor anything else in all creation, will be able to separate us from the love of God that is in Christ Jesus our Lord.*

Ty had the same scripture. It must be the go-to Bible passage for suicides.

The song fades away. Patrick's dad joins the sister in the front row. The priest in his black robes climbs the steps to the podium.

"Good afternoon," the priest says. "We are gathered here today to celebrate the life and mourn the passing of Patrick Michael Murphy."

I don't remember much of Ty's funeral. What struck me about the funeral was that it ultimately felt like some kind of trial. Ty had committed a crime—premeditated murder, if you want to be technical—and we were all assembled there, his family and friends, his teachers and fellow students, as witnesses to testify to his good character.

Everyone who got up to speak said an approximation of the same thing:

Ty was kind—we never heard him say a cruel word to anyone.

He worked hard in his classes, even if he wasn't the best student.

He had some killer basketball moves, even if he wasn't very tall.

He was a good dancer.

He was sensitive. He felt things deeply. "Maybe too deeply," the pastor said, as if that explained everything.

Ty was good. Implication: He didn't deserve to be punished for his crime. He wasn't in his right mind. He wasn't thinking clearly. He didn't mean it.

Please, God, please, have mercy on his soul.

To which God responded: *Neither death nor life, neither angels nor demons, neither the present nor the future, nor any powers, neither height nor depth, nor anything else in all creation, will be able to separate us from the love of God that is in Christ Jesus our Lord.*

Then everyone was allowed to feel better about it.

When Mom got up to speak, she said she was grateful for the sixteen years she got to spend with Ty, wonderful years, she said. She thanked people: his piano teacher, his Boy Scout leader, his basketball coach, his favorite French teacher, etc., for making those years so wonderful. Her voice quavered, but she didn't cry.

I was thinking that they had forgotten to mention that Ty was funny. I was remembering two years ago, around Christmastime. I teased him; I said Santa was going to bring him a stocking full of coal. I told him I hadn't decided yet if I was even going to get him a present.

I didn't mean it, of course. He knew I didn't mean it.

But then he said, and this I will never forget: "Well. I'm getting you a present."

"You are?"

"Yep," he said. "Just as soon as I can train the dog to poop into a box."

He was funny. Mom was up there talking about how kind-hearted he was, and I was in the front row staring at my shoes, trying not to laugh at a joke he'd told two years ago and trying not to cry at the fact that I would never hear him tell another joke.

Dad didn't speak at Ty's funeral. He sat two rows behind us with Megan. He stayed out of the way.

I didn't speak, either. Mom asked me to, but I was afraid that if I got up in front of everybody I would tell them about the promise I had made to Ty, that I would be there for him when he needed me, when he called. The promise I had broken.

Then it would have been me on trial.

Maybe I deserved that, but I couldn't face it.

At the end of Ty's funeral they played Elvis's version of "Take My Hand, Precious Lord." My mother's favorite church song.

Ty would have freaked. Elvis at his funeral.

But it didn't matter. Ty was dead. Mom was alive. In so many ways (the peach roses, the deep mahogany casket that matched our dining room table, the music, the scriptures, the food) she'd planned his funeral to be her own.

23.

AFTER PATRICK'S FUNERAL we drive to Wyuka Cemetery for the graveside part. It's sleeting, a miserable combination of rain and slush, and we stand under black umbrellas around the grave. His father and sister cry brokenheartedly when the men lower the coffin into the ground.

Mom cries, too.

I don't.

I didn't then, either. I was all cried out by the time we got to the cemetery.

The priest says a few final words, and then we move like a herd of sheep into a room inside the funeral home for the wake. Mom brings along the green bean casserole to be heated and served.

It's not as good as I remember.

They set up two poster-sized collages against the far wall. I slip away from Mom to look at them. It's not like Ty's collage, which was in a fancy frame. Patrick's collages are two pieces of poster board, the kind you can buy at the supermarket, the pictures stuck on with tape.

Patrick had a lot of friends, like Ty.

He was on the swim team. He was an athlete, like Ty.

He was an Eagle Scout. Ty never made it that far. But still, a Boy Scout, like Ty.

He played video games.

He was a good kid.

Like Ty.

This is the worst kind of déjà vu.

In the second collage, I find a picture I recognize, a copy of the same photo Ty used in his collage: Patrick from middle school with Ty and Damian, the three amigos, arms around one another because they hadn't learned yet it's not cool for boys to hug. First Patrick, then Ty, then Damian. Damian looks the same, I think, wearing his gray hoodie and pale denim jeans, lanky and uncombed. He holds his left hand up with his two fingers making a peace sign. The three of them smile mischievously into the camera like they know something I don't.

I swallow. I know something they don't, too.

Then the sound system over my head starts playing "Stairway to Heaven." I freeze. I look around and spot the funeral director—Jane, I remember—standing in a corner.

"Hey, Jane," I say as I approach her. "Why are you playing this song?"

"Hello, Alexis." She remembers me, too. "Patrick left a note requesting, among other things, a specific playlist to be played at the wake."

I close my eyes as Robert Plant starts singing, "There's a lady who's sure all that glitters is gold, and she's buying a stairway to heaven."

"Alexis?" Jane murmurs. "Are you all right?"

I open my eyes. "What about the collages?"

"What about them?"

"Did someone make them, or did he?"

She gives me a somber smile. "He made them."

He made them. Just like Ty. He planned all of this. Just like Ty.

Like he was using Ty's death as a template for his own.

Ty helped this happen. By showing Patrick that it was some kind of acceptable, maybe even cool, thing to do. He led by example.

This is Ty's fault.

All of a sudden, it becomes too much. I have to get out of here.

I search for Mom. It takes me awhile to locate her, and when I find her, I hold back, even though what I want to do is charge up to her and grab her by the hand and drag her out of here. But she's sitting in a folding chair next to Patrick's dad, looking into her lap as she talks. I can't hear what she's saying, but Patrick's dad is nodding, nodding, tears slipping down his face.

She could be awhile.

The song is building in intensity, the way it does, and as it builds I feel less and less in control of myself. The hole is opening in my chest. The room is closing in.

I stumble back and knock a chair over. It clatters loudly to the floor.

I see Damian, not wearing his gray hoodie but a black button-down dress shirt. He combed his hair. His eyes are red. He steps forward like he wants to say something to me. Like he wants to hug me.

I take another step back. I see Ashley Davenport standing by the collage. She's holding hands with Grayson, and they're both staring at me.

Everybody's staring.

I have to get out I have to get out I have to get out. I fight the urge to push people out of my way. I can't breathe I can't breathe.

A hand comes down on my shoulder.

Beaker. She meets my eyes and sees the panic, and her jaw sets determinedly. She whirls around.

"Hey, give us some room here," she says in a loud voice. "Let us by, please. Excuse me."

She weaves me through the crowd. Then we're outside. I sit down on the curb near the hearse and try to catch my breath. Beaker stands over me like she's keeping guard.

I've never been so glad to see Beaker. I could almost cry, I'm so glad.

"Are you okay?" she asks.

"Not really."

"Do you want something to drink? I think there's lemonade in there. It's the foul powdered stuff, but it's cold and it's liquid."

"No, thanks."

She drops down beside me and leans back, stretching her legs out in front of her. She's wearing a gray wool skirt and stripy socks.

Only Beaker would wear striped socks to a funeral.

"Well," she says after a minute. "That was like the worst thing ever."

I've missed Beaker.

"Where is El?" I ask.

"El doesn't do funerals."

"She was at Ty's," I point out.

Beaker looks at me gravely. "Yes. She went to Ty's. I thought I was going to have to get her a paper bag to breathe into—she almost lost it like ten times. Something about how she threw up at her great-aunt's funeral when she was seven."

"Oh." I feel dumb that I didn't know any of that. I wasn't paying attention to my friends at Ty's funeral. Apparently I assumed the world revolved around me and my pain. "If I'd known that, I wouldn't have asked her to—"

"She would have come anyway." Beaker yanks a blade of old brown grass out of the lawn and twists it around her finger. "She's your friend. She loves you. She wanted to be there for you. We both did."

"Thanks."

"We're still your friends, you know, El and me. And Steven, even though he can't really look at you without turning into a sad country love song."

"I know." I don't know what else to say. I know.

A shadow falls over us. It's Mom. She looks pale.

"Hello, Jill," she says faintly.

"Hello, Mama Riggs," Jill responds—the name my friends

always called my mother, like they were claiming her as their mother, too.

Normally Mom would make small talk in a situation like this, but I can tell she's exhausted. "Are you ready to head home?" she asks me.

I jump up. "Yes."

"I'll see you in the funny papers," Jill says as we walk away, her signature closing line.

Yeah, I think. Hopefully I'll see you there.

At home, Mom goes straight into her bedroom and closes the door.

I watch TV in the downstairs den. It's a risk, hanging out so close to Ty's room. One never knows when something mind-bending might happen there. But I need something to occupy my brain.

There's no sign of Ty, thankfully. No Brut. No reflections. No shadows.

For once, I feel completely alone.

I channel surf with the TV muted for a while, so I don't disturb Mom. I watch *TMZ*, which is pretty self-explanatory without the sound, and an episode of *Cops*. Then I land on the six o'clock news. I can tell instantly by the background that the story is about Patrick Murphy. The reporter is standing in the train yard. She's young and pretty, with that white-blond hair that almost looks silver in the sunshine, but her eyes are reluctant, like this isn't the kind of story she wants to be reporting on.

I turn up the sound.

". . . the second death in this small town this year, and the seventeenth teen suicide in the state of Nebraska in the last twelve months. As the community of Raymond gathers together today to mourn the loss of one of its brightest young stars, they are left with some haunting questions: What happened to this fun-loving, straight-A student and swim-team state champion to make him throw away the bright future that was ahead of him? What led him to this empty train yard? And how could this senseless tragedy have been prevented?"

I hear Mom stirring upstairs and mute the television again. As the reporter wraps up the story, they run a stock photo of Wyuka Cemetery, zooming in on a stone angel gazing stoically at the ground. I see an internet address, www.youthsuicideprevention.nebraska.edu, scroll across the bottom of the screen. Then Patrick's face.

Then the weather.

My heart is beating fast. My fists are clenched, my jaw tight. I shouldn't have been surprised by the story. I shouldn't get so worked up about it. But the weight of the day is crushing me.

Seventeen teen suicides. Seventeen.

I've flipped through Mom's books. I know that seventeen is not so many, when you consider that more than thirty thousand people die from suicide in the U.S. every year, the tenth leading cause of death, the third leading cause among teens. I could spout statistics, warning signs we should have heeded, factors that put Ty at risk. He lived in a house where there were guns present, which made him 5.4 times more likely to die by suicide. He came from what would be

out of the playhouse and he ran around yelling through the windows, "But I'm the mailman! You have to let in the mailman!"

So we told him we'd let him in if he brought us a letter or something. Therefore he went into the house and borrowed an envelope from Dad's office and on one side he addressed it, in crayon, to:

Sis.

Playhowse

R Backyd

And on the other side he wrote: *I the male Man. Let me in.*

We cracked up. And we let him in. I mean, how could you say no to the male Man?

I stifle a laugh. Mom thought it was so funny that she fashioned a little "mailbox" out of one of Dad's shoeboxes, with a slot on the top for Ty to slide the envelopes in. I locate the box on the little craft table in the corner. I sit down carefully in the undersized chair, and take a deep breath, in case this hurts, and then I remove the lid.

Inside the box there aren't any letters from kid Ty. Instead I find Mom's gleaming silver sewing shears, and under them, like a long-lost treasure trove, the missing photographs. I rifle through the stack: Dad and Ty playing chess. Dad and Ty standing by the grill together one Fourth of July. Dad and Ty at Carhenge one summer (which is a perfect replica of Stonehenge except it's made of spray-painted old cars), pretending to hold one of the cars up. Dad wearing Rollerblades at the parking lot. Dad giving two-year-old Ty his first haircut. Dad's college graduation photo. Dad and Ty watching TV. Dad with an electric knife showing Ty how to carve a Thanksgiving turkey. Mom and Dad at an H&R Block company picnic. Dad pointing to a sticker on his shirt that says I VOTED. Dad teaching six-year-old Ty how to ride a bike. Dad wiggling one of Ty's front teeth. Dad and Ty going hunting.

I let out the breath I was holding. Here's the mystery right here before me, but not quite solved. All these pictures, Ty collected them, but why?

I return to the top picture on the stack. Dad and Ty playing chess. It's different from the other pictures. It's smaller, for one thing. It's obviously been cut down from a six-by-four photo to a three-by-three square. It's a bit crooked, like he couldn't cut in a straight line. It has a jagged edge on one side.

Then I know the answer.

I get up. I go back to the house, down to the basement. To Ty's room.

I get Ty's collage from behind his door and lay it on the bed. I set the chess picture on the white space of the part that's empty.

It's a perfect fit. Three by three square.

Mom was right. This is where Dad's photo should have gone. Ty thought about it. He gathered up all these pictures as candidates. He decided on this one, cut it to size, but in the end, he didn't put it in the frame.

He wouldn't forgive Dad.

I become aware of the scent of my brother's cologne. It's all around me. I close my eyes.

"No," I say, because I've accepted this by this point, talking to nobody in case there's somebody actually there. "I won't do it."

Because I know what Ty would want now.

He'd want me to return the picture to this frame.

He'd want me to tell Dad.

To make it right.

I put the photo in my pocket and return the collage to its place behind the door. I turn the light off.

"No," I whisper to the empty room.

Upstairs, I go to my closet and get out my suitcase. And I start packing.

13 March

My dad left our family on a Tuesday morning in July. I was 15 that summer, and Ty was 13. It was 9 months before Ty would go on his little escapade with the 63 Advil and ask Dad to come home, 3 years ago now, although it feels like longer.

I was brushing my teeth when it happened.

Dad appeared in the mirror behind me, and he said, "Hi, Lexie. You and I need to have a talk."

My first thought was that he was going to lecture me about how little brain-work I'd been doing that summer. That's what he called it—not homework but "brain-work," stuff to keep my brain in shape during the months I was out of school. So I wouldn't lose anything, he always said. So I would stay sharp.

But it wasn't about brain-work.

It was about him moving out.

"Why?" I asked him, stunned, but I don't remember how he

answered. I just remember that he said he was going to live at a house in town. With a woman, he said. Who he'd fallen in love with.

I couldn't get my head around it.

"Everything is going to be okay, Peanut," he said.

That was the last time he ever called me that.

I said, "I love you, Daddy." Like maybe I could talk him out of it.

He said he loved me, too, and he took me by the hand and led me out to the living room, where Mom was sitting on the couch, crying so hard she was having trouble breathing. I sank down beside her.

Ty appeared in the doorway. He'd heard her crying from the basement. He looked scared, like he wanted to run away. Dad took him by the shoulders and walked him out to the back porch. I could see him through the window as Dad told him, his face folding in on itself as he tried to hold back his tears.

Dad brought him inside. Ty sat down on the other side of Mom. He took her hand. She stopped crying long enough to say, "Mark. Don't do this."

We looked up at Dad.

"I love you all," he said.

Then he turned and walked out the front door. We listened to his truck rumble to life. We listened to it crunch down the gravel driveway. We listened to the sound of his engine getting farther and farther away. And then he was gone.

Somewhere over the next few hours the details came out: Dad had been having an affair with the secretary. Mom had known about it for months.

I could see, in that hindsight-is-20/20 way, that both of my parents had been acting strangely for a while. Dad working late. Coming home smelling of cigarettes. Mom speaking to us more sharply than usual, trying to keep the house perfectly clean and organized, dinner on the table at precisely 6 p.m., running to reapply her lipstick when she heard him coming up the driveway. Like if everything was in place, if our home life was perfect enough, he would stop what he was doing.

There were signs. I was just too caught up in my own thing to catch on.

The only clue I'd noticed that summer was the dog. Our golden retriever, Sunny, had been lying around looking mournful. Whimpering. Not eating.

"What's wrong with Sunny?" I'd asked about a week before Dad steamrolled us with the news. "I think she's depressed. Can dogs get depressed?"

"I don't know," Mom had said. A lie.

"Do you think they make Prozac for dogs?" I'd joked. And she'd laughed. Which was also a lie. Mom knew that Sunny knew. The dog was there after everyone but Mom had gone to sleep. Sunny watched her cry.

At some point during that day, Mom's best friend, Gayle, showed up and tried to give my mom a pep talk. Gayle's husband had divorced her a few years earlier, and I remember that she kept saying, over and over, "You'll get through this, Joan. You'll be stronger for it."

But Mom just shook her head, wringing the tissue in her hands into smaller and smaller shreds.

We went out for pizza for dinner. Because Dad never let us go out for pizza. Because Dad was a tightwad. While we were eating, Ty, who'd been quiet for nearly the entire time, said, "I'm glad he's gone."

"Don't say that, honey," Mom said.

"No. I am. I'm glad," Ty said, his voice cracking on the word glad.

That night, after Mom went to bed, Ty woke me.

"Come on," he said, and I didn't ask questions; I slipped into some jeans and followed him outside. Under a full moon we walked to the park, to this rocky area behind the baseball field. Ty carried a cloth grocery bag and a metal baseball bat. He handed me the bag. It was full of bottles of Dad's old cologne.

"Put one right there," Ty directed. I set a bottle of Old Spice on the rocks in front of him.

Ty took a deep breath. He closed his eyes, like he was sending up a prayer or making a wish, then opened them again.

"He's a cheater," he said, and brought the bat down hard. The bottle shattered, and the smell of the cologne washed over us, so strong I felt nauseated.

"Now you." Ty handed me the bat.

I got out another bottle. Polo. My favorite on Dad. I'd given it to him for Father's Day one year.

"He's a liar," I said, and swung as hard as I could.

There was a certain relief in the breaking of the glass—the shattering of something other than our pathetic little family.

We went on breaking bottles. "He's a cheapskate."

"He's a phony."

"He's an asshole." Even then, though, I couldn't say the swear word with any conviction.

"He's a fraud."

"He's an adulterer."

We paused at this.

"I will never forgive him," Ty said, staring down at the reeking shards at our feet.

"I will never forgive him," I repeated, and it was as if we were making a vow.

In a way it felt like Dad had died. The man I knew, the quiet, gentle man who read Harry Potter out loud to me when I was 10, who helped me study for the 5th-grade spelling bee, who laughed over the funnies in the Sunday newspaper, that man was gone. All that was left was the cheater. The liar. The fraud.

In that moment, I knew it was true.

I will never forgive him. Not ever.

"Come on," Ty said, slinging the bat over his shoulder. He put his arm around me. The man of the house now. "Let's go home."

24.

WHEN MOM WAKES UP, I'M WAITING FOR HER.

"What's this?" she says as she comes into the kitchen and sees me standing at the stove in her blue gingham apron, scraping an only marginally burned portion of scrambled eggs onto a plate.

"Breakfast." She watches as I set both of our plates on the table. I take off the apron and put it back on its hook, pour us some juice, and sit down. "Bon appétit."

She glances at the oven clock. "This is wonderful, honey, but aren't you going to be late for school?"

"I'm not going to school today."

She stares at me. I never miss school. I have a perfect attendance record, as a matter of fact, because Ty died during Christmas break.

"We're going to take a trip," I announce.

"A trip?"

"You have three days off." I point to the work calendar she has posted to the refrigerator with magnets. "I will miss only one day of school."

She notices the far wall of the kitchen, where I've stacked everything we'll need: pillows and clean pillowcases and blankets to snuggle with in the car, anything resembling a snack that I could find in the pantry, a six-pack of Mom's lethal Diet Coke (which should get us through the drive there, at the very least), and finally our suitcases, both fully packed, which goes to show just how Valium-and/or-alcohol-induced my mother's sleep was last night, that I could move around her room opening and closing all her dresser drawers without her waking up.

"I have it all planned out," I say.

She sits down across from me. "You want to go on some kind of road trip?"

"Yes. A road trip."

"Where?"

"You'll see." On the table there's a stack of papers I've been reviewing—a hotel reservation and directions and other research—which I pull out of her reach. "Just say yes, Mom."

She pushes a clump of eggs with her fork. If she doesn't agree to this, what will come next is that she'll eat a bite or two, to placate me at least that much, and then she'll go back to bed.

"Please, Mom," I beg. "I need us to do this. I can't go back to school today, not with how people are going to be after Patrick. I can't do it."

Her lips purse for a few seconds, then relax. "All right," she says resignedly. "A road trip."

That's the spirit.

"Just you and me," I say. "Dave would call it quality mother-daughter bonding."

She laughs weakly, not her real laugh, but as good as I'm going to get. "Well, we have to do what Dave wants, don't we?"

"Hey, you hired him, Mom."

She smiles at me, a small but tender smile, and says, "All right. I think it will do us both good to get out of the house." Like the whole expedition was her idea.

It's raining in Memphis. We've had a long day's drive and a night in a cheap-but-fairly-clean Super 8 Motel on the edge of town, and now we've finally arrived at our final destination. The sky is a hard gray, an icy drizzle fracturing on the windshield as we pull into the parking lot. For a minute we sit in the car with the heater blowing in our faces and look up at the sign.

GRACELAND

My mom's always been an Elvis fan. He died on August 16, 1977, which just happened to be my mother's eighth birthday. She still remembered hearing the news about his death on the radio right after she blew out her birthday candles. From that point on she grew up feeling a connection between herself and the King of Rock and Roll. So Tyler and I grew up with Elvis, too. We heard "All Shook Up" when she was trying to make us laugh and "Blue Suede Shoes" when she was feeling sassy, and sometimes, on their anniversary or Valentine's Day, we'd catch her dancing to "Love

Me Tender" with Dad. The week after Dad left, I kept hearing Elvis's mournful croon muffled from behind her bedroom door as she played that song again and again.

Elvis was the soundtrack to her life and, by extension, mine.

"I've always wanted to come here," she says.

I know.

I put my hand on her shoulder. "Let's go in."

When we get inside, we're both shocked at the prices for the tour. There are three options: the basic mansion tour, which is thirty-three dollars; the "platinum" tour, where you can see Elvis's airplanes and cars and a few extra exhibits for thirty-seven dollars; and the Graceland Elvis Entourage VIP Tour, which is everything from the first two tours with an extra private tour, front-of-the-line access, an all-day pass to the grounds and mansion, and a special keepsake backstage pass.

Clearly we've got to do the VIP tour. We've come all this way.

It is seventy dollars.

Per person.

That's more than the hotel for the entire trip.

"Wow," Mom breathes as we stare up in horror at the board with the different packages on it. "That is pricey."

"Don't worry, Mom," I say quickly, whipping out my wallet. "I got it."

"With your MIT fund? I don't think so." She produces a gold credit card I've never seen before and ignores my raised eyebrows. I've never known my mother to buy anything on credit.

"The VIP tour, please," she says to the woman behind the

counter, and slides the gold card across the marble. "We want to see it all."

Graceland is what I expected it would be: a lot of sixties and seventies glitz, bright colors, shag carpet, gold-plated handles in the bathroom of the *Priscilla*—Elvis's private jet. Mom and I stand in front of a fake backdrop of the famous front gates and have our picture taken. We wander from room to room, Mom oohing and aahing over Elvis's jumpsuit collection, and chuckling over the one room with the zebra-striped walls and red velvet couches, and standing soberly in front of his grave, staring at his death date, which is also her birth date, where it's written in stone.

She's having a good time, I think, which was the point of this little adventure. I wanted to show her that it's possible to have a good time.

We haven't thought about Ty for the entire day.

"I needed this," she says later. We've just finished dinner at a Mexican restaurant in Memphis, and Mom is slurping down a giant margarita. I'm obviously going to have to drive us back to the hotel. "I really needed this."

"Me too," I say.

"Can we just . . . not go home?" she says with a sigh. "We could stay here. Visit Elvis every day."

I smile. I know she doesn't mean it. But this is my cue to tell her about my so-crazy-it-might-actually-work plan.

"You remember what Gayle said, about selling the house?"

Mom stirs her drink. "Gayle always has her strong opinions, doesn't she?"

"I think it's a great idea."

She stops. "You think we should move."

"I think you should move," I elaborate. "To Massachusetts. With me."

"You want me to move to MIT?" she says with a laugh. She thinks I'm joking. "I don't think I'd fit in your twin bed."

"Not my dorm room. An apartment or a little house or something. Freshmen are required to live on campus, but they make an exception if you're going to live with your parents." I reach into my backpack and pull out a sheaf of papers, which I set down on the table in front of her. "There are all kinds of places. This one is like a ten-minute walk to campus, two-bedroom, washer-and-dryer hookups, hardwood floors. Nice, see? And it's not unaffordable. Not when you factor in that I would have been paying around four hundred a month for student housing."

She stares down at the paper. "You've been giving this some thought, I see. And what would I do in Massachusetts?"

I rifle through the pages until I land on one with a large red brick building framed by leafy green trees. "This is Mount Auburn Hospital. It's listed as one of the best places in New England for medical professionals to work, in terms of both pay and environment. It's attached to Harvard Medical School." I sit back and let her look at the "About Us" page I printed. "It's less than two miles from MIT, approximately a nine-minute drive. There are currently sixteen job openings for registered nurses, one in the surgical wing like you're doing now, but that one's a night shift."

Mom hates night shifts.

"But"—I keep going before she can shoot me down—"you could always start nights and move to days once you're established. Or . . ." I bite my lip, then just come out and say it: "There are two positions open in the maternity ward. One in labor and delivery, and one in the nursery."

"I could work with the babies," Mom says.

"You love babies."

"I do love babies," she agrees, covering her mouth with her hand in a way that suggests she's considering it.

"So maybe Gayle is right, just this one time," I conclude.

"No." Mom shakes her head.

"No?"

"The babies would be worse, Lexie."

"How would babies be worse? Everyone's so happy around babies. It's the happiest part of the hospital."

"Babies die, too. Most of the time, yes, it would be wonderful to work in maternity. But every once in a while, more often than you might think, I'd have to watch some mother lose her baby. I don't think I could live with that." She picks up her drink, licks a piece of salt off the side of her glass. "Besides, those nurses in the nursery don't need to use their nursing skills. They change diapers and feed babies bottles and give baths all day. I want to do more than that. I want to learn. I want to be an excellent nurse. Not a babysitter."

"Okay, well, there are thirteen other RN positions open at Mount Auburn. I'm sure you could be an excellent nurse in one of those."

She finishes off her margarita, then sets the glass down and looks at me.

I can tell by her face that she's going to say no.

"What you've done here is very sweet, Lexie," she says. "But I can't go to Massachusetts with you. You need to live this next part of your life on your own. You deserve that. You deserve to live in the dorms so you can make all of the lifelong friends you're going to make in the dorms. You need to eat at the cafeteria and stay up all night cramming for finals and go to parties and have fun, without having to worry about anyone else. You need your own life."

"Yes, I need my own life. But so do you," I argue. It's been kicking around in my brain ever since Sadie asked me if I was bringing my mom to college. At first I was like, no way, who does that? But then I started to see the logic in the idea. The simple beauty of it. If Mom came to MIT with me, it wouldn't be the way I pictured it, with the late-night discussions in the dorm and strolling down the sidewalks with a group of friends. But it could be better. Because then Mom wouldn't be alone, and we could escape Nebraska and what happened in our garage. We would never have to go back. We could start fresh. Both of us.

"My life is over," Mom says again.

I exhale a frustrated breath. "Just think about it for a while, okay? It's a good plan. If you think about it—"

She sits up straighter. "No. My answer is no, honey. It's always going to be no. But I love you for the offer."

"Mom—"

"This discussion is over," she says in her official mother voice. She pulls out the gold credit card. "I'll get the check."

We don't have much to say to each other for the rest of the night. Or during breakfast the next morning. Or in the car on the way back to Nebraska, which is going to be about an eleven-hour drive. Mom drives for the first forty-eight minutes without saying more than "Looks like good weather today, doesn't it?" and that's when I decide I can't take it anymore.

"Pull over," I say.

"What?" She glances at me. "Do you have to go to the bathroom? You went before we left."

"No, just pull over, right here."

She brings the car to a stop at the side of the interstate. "What's the matter? Are you feeling sick?"

"Your life is not over. That's bullshit."

Her eyes flash. "Alexis. Watch your mouth."

"It's bullshit," I say again for emphasis, and this time I'm able to swear with conviction. Ty would be proud. "You're forty-four years old. The average life expectancy for a female in the United States is eighty-one. You're not overweight, and you don't smoke, and you're drinking a lot now, but I like to think that it's a phase and as soon as you stop feeling so fucking sorry for yourself you'll quit doing that, and you work on your feet for most of the day, and you like

265

vegetables, and you go to church, which studies have shown adds about seven-point-five years to a person's life, and you brush your teeth. If anyone's going to live to be a hundred, Mom, it's you. So stop saying your life is over. It's not even halfway over. And yes, your son died, and that's awful, and that hurts, but it's not your fault. And you know what? Everybody dies, and everybody loses people they love—everybody—and that is not an excuse for you to fucking die. I love you, and I need you to be my mother, and I need you to have a life. So get over yourself."

I take a much-needed breath.

We sit there. The turn signal is still on, blinking. Cars are blasting by us at seventy-five miles an hour. Mom looks straight ahead.

I just said the *f* word. Twice. To my mother.

I called her out on her drinking. I told her to get over herself.

"Mom, I—"

She holds a hand up.

"All right," she says, although I don't know if she means *All right, I've had enough, now get out of the car and walk, you ingrate* or *All right, you're grounded* or *All right, I'll stop saying that my life is over.*

"Mom?"

She sighs, then pulls the car back onto the highway.

"Would you look in my purse?" she says after we've gone about ten miles. "There's a book in there."

I forage through her purse until I find a small and yellowed paperback copy of *To Kill a Mockingbird.*

"This?" I hold it up, surprised.

She nods. "I was supposed to read it in eighth grade. I thought maybe you could read it to me now. To pass the time."

"Okay." It's odd, but at least she's not yelling at me. I flip to the first page.

"'When he was nearly thirteen, my brother Jem got his arm badly broken at the elbow,'" I begin.

Mom lets out a slow breath. "Yes. I knew this would be good."

So I continue reading. For the next seven-and-a-half hours, stopping for pee breaks and lunch and once because Mom feels the urgent need for a Diet Coke, I read. I read about Scout and Boo Radley and Mayella Violet Ewell. I read until my voice is hoarse.

When I'm done, Mom says, "I always wanted Atticus Finch to be my father. I used to imagine it, like I was secretly adopted and Gregory Peck was my biological father."

"I thought you said you hadn't read the book."

"I saw the movie," she says. "Have you seen it?"

"Yeah. In eighth grade, I think. You're right, Gregory Peck is, like, golden. So all this time I was reading, you knew how the story was going to end."

"I wanted to hear the words," she explains. "I knew how it ended, but I wanted to go slowly and see how it would all work itself out." She yawns against her hand.

"How about I drive for this last bit?" I offer.

She pulls over and we swap places.

We've gone about a mile, just outside Kansas City, when she starts to cry. I don't even notice at first, but at one point I lean over to adjust the radio and notice the wetness on her face, the trail of gleaming tears from the corner of her eye to the edge of her jaw.

I smell Ty's cologne.

I wonder if Mom smells it. If that's what's set off her crying.

"Are you okay?" I ask her gently. "We can stop."

She shakes her head and exhales in a shudder, then opens up her purse and starts to dig around for her pack of tissues. "I'm fine. It's just . . ."

SMELL ME, says Ty's cologne. *I DEMAND TO BE SMELLED. SMELL ME NOW.*

I glance in the rearview mirror, and then I see him, I see him clear as day, sitting in the backseat, his head against the window, like he always used to sit, looking out.

It's a miracle that I don't wreck the car.

Mom says, "It's just that, I don't know why we never did that before. Graceland. All these years we've been so close, a day's drive, and we've never gone. Why didn't we?"

Because Dad hates to travel, I think but do not say. Look up the word *homebody* in the dictionary, and there will be a picture of Dad.

"We should have gone," Mom whispers, wiping at her face.

"We've gone now," I answer shakily. "Graceland—check."

"Yes, but I wish . . . ," she says, and I know she wants to say we should have gone when Ty was alive.

But Ty hated Elvis. He didn't appreciate being subjected to Mom's obsession with the King. He said so many times.

My eyes flick back to the mirror.

Ty is still there. A chill runs through me like a trickle of ice water.

"Hey, uh, I think the lady in that red car behind us is texting," I say. "That's dangerous."

Mom turns to look. She gazes right through where Ty is curled in the backseat. She turns back to me. "You should let her pass you. It's always better to be behind the road hazard."

I let the red car pass. Mom gives a disapproving look to the driver, but the lady doesn't notice.

I try to keep my hands steady on the wheel.

Mom gets a tissue out of her purse and blows her nose. The tears keep coming, an endless river of grief. Ty stays with us too. All the way back to Nebraska.

25.

I WAIT. Until we're unpacked. Until we've eaten dinner. Until Mom is asleep. Then I slip down into Ty's room.

It's quiet.

I look at the mirror. The clock radio. The shadow in the corner cast by the closet door.

He's not here. But I want him to be.

"I want to talk to you," I say. "Ty."

Silence.

"Come on. We can't run away, right? That's what you were telling me today? That you're always going to be there, hanging out in the backseat. Your smell. Your shadow. Your memory. That's what you were trying to tell me, right? Well, I have things I want to say to you." I sit at his desk and turn on the desk lamp, which is like a spotlight in the dark. "Come on, Ty. I did what you wanted. I gave the letter to Ashley. Now do what I want, for once."

But there's nothing. No sound. No smell. No Ty.

Which pisses me off even more. And it's been a ranting kind of day.

I stand up. "You're selfish," I say into the darkness. "Do you know that? You're the most selfish person I know. You didn't even care, did you, about what this would do to Mom? Did you hear her saying her life is over? That's on you. That's on you, Ty. You're no better than Dad is, you know. You just do whatever you feel like doing and to hell with the rest of us, right?"

My eyes are drawn to the mirror. For a split second I think I see him, a dark shape moving, but then I realize it's my own reflection.

I stare at the Post-it.

Sorry Mom but I was below empty.

"What, you wanted to make some kind of grand romantic statement? You wanted to demonstrate to the world how much pain you were in?" The hole starts to crack open in my sternum but I push past it. "It's not romantic. You blew a chunk of your chest out and died in a puddle of your own blood—does that sound romantic to you? The people cleaned it up, yeah, all right, but they left a bunch of soaked bloody paper towels in the garbage outside for Mom to find when she emptied the trash the next week. Romantic, right? What an awesome statement. Oh, and your body loses control of its bowels when you die, and you shit yourself, how fucking romantic is that? And the little girl next door, Emma, you know, she came outside when the ambulance drove up and she was there when they opened the garage door and she saw you like that. She's six years old. Awesome statement you made there. Right this second you are

271

worm food, and people have forgotten you, they don't even remember you now, it's all Patrick Murphy now, but they'll forget him, too. They'll move on. That's what people do. You aren't Jim Morrison, Ty. You don't get to be some kind of tragic rock star who died young and everyone builds a shrine to. You get to be a stupid-ass kid. The only people who will remember your 'statement' are Mom and me, and that's just because we hurt too much to forget. Yeah, other people are in pain too, dipshit. Everybody feels pain. You asshole."

I tear the Post-it off the glass. The hole is an enormous chasm in my chest now, a swirling black hole, but I fight it. "I do not accept this shitty little note."

I crumple the Post-it. I drop it. It falls from my fingers and bounces on the floor and out of sight.

My vision goes dim around the edges. I can't breathe. Then I'm on my knees on the floor with my face pressed to the musty carpet fibers, and I see blue lights behind my eyes. Constellations of pain. But I don't see Ty.

"Where are you?" I wheeze into the floor. "Where did you go?"

The hole passes. I don't know how long it takes, but suddenly it's simply gone. I turn my face to the side and cough and lie there in the fetal position until I feel enough strength return to my body to sit up.

The first thing I do is get on my hands and knees next to the bed and search for the Post-it.

To smooth it out. To put it back. Because I can't stay angry at him.

Instead my fingers close on something hard and sharp. I jerk back, then reach underneath the bed carefully and pull the object out.

It's a tooth. A shark-tooth necklace, to be more precise. The necklace part consists of a row of tiny black beads on a rough string, with a single white and jagged tooth gleaming in the center. I sit up on my knees to inspect it, frowning. I bring it into the beam of light from the lamp. You don't encounter shark teeth every day in our part of Nebraska. Or any part of Nebraska. Landlocked state, if you recall. I don't remember this necklace. Ty wasn't the kind of guy who wore necklaces, period.

"What is this?" I ask to the empty air.

And then I remember where I've seen it before.

The picture of the three amigos: Ty, Patrick, and Damian making the peace sign.

I pull Ty's collage out from behind the door and find the picture in question. It was taken at the Henry Doorly Zoo in Omaha. Nebraska may not have too much in the way of snazzy tourist destinations, but we do have one of the best zoos in the country. I have always liked the gorilla exhibit, but Ty's favorite was the sharks. It's a huge blue tunnel where hammerheads and blacktips and grays and about ten other species of shark sweep through the water around you like they are performing a slow aquatic ballet.

Ty would sometimes stand in there watching the sharks for hours. I used to tease him about it. "Who loves sharks?" I'd asked him. "If you got tossed in there, I doubt they'd love you back. Two words: *feeding frenzy*."

"It's peaceful" was all he said in his defense. "I like it."

The three amigos photo was taken just outside the entrance to the shark tunnel. They must have been on a class field trip, because they are each wearing a fluorescent green badge. They are also each wearing a shark-tooth necklace from the gift shop. I stare at their hopeful faces. I close my hand around the shark tooth.

Ty.

Patrick.

Damian.

Three links in a chain.

The first time I thought there might be something wrong with Ty, the first time it occurred to me that he might be looking at the dying-young scenario a little too fondly, was when Samantha Sullivan, a girl from our church, died of pneumonia. Samantha was a sweet girl, the type who I always remembered smiling. She had braces, but they only seemed to accentuate her smile in a good way. When she got sick, nobody thought she would die. People we know don't die of pneumonia, not in this day and age, not 14-year-old violin players. She was in the hospital for a few days and scheduled to be discharged on a Monday.

On Sunday morning she developed a blood clot in her lung. On Sunday afternoon part of the clot broke free and traveled to her brain.

And then she was dead.

Samantha hadn't been super popular. She was quiet. She had a small group of close friends, like me. She didn't like to call attention to herself. But it seemed like every teenager in the city of Lincoln came to her funeral.

One of her friends made a playlist of all her favorite songs: Tay-
lor Swift, mostly, with some Carrie Underwood and the Pistol Annies
thrown in. Samantha liked country. The playlist looped all through
the viewing before the funeral. Samantha's mom bought several of
those collage frames and filled them with photos: Samantha as a baby,
Samantha canning tomatoes with her grandmother, Samantha on the
beach of Branched Oak Lake with a line of cousins, Samantha eating
ice cream with her friends, smiling her sparkly smile.

At the funeral, the people who got up to speak kept referring to
Samantha's gentle spirit and how she was a light that had gone out too
soon, but how she was home now. There was no sickness that could
touch her. She was safe. She had run her race. They tried to make it
sound like life completely blows, so thank goodness Samantha got out of
it when she did, while she was ahead, so to speak.

No tears in heaven.

I remember thinking, why? If God's so good, why take this girl
before she's even had a chance to live?

It didn't make sense.

It still doesn't.

Ty took Samantha's death hard. He spent the rest of the summer
playing Taylor Swift songs over and over. He had a picture of Saman-
tha, taken at a church potluck when they were both about 12, sitting
on a lawn chair with a paper plate balanced delicately across her knees,
about to dig into some potato salad. He tacked the picture up on his wall
next to his bed. It's still there.

What was weird was that he and Samantha hadn't been partic-
ularly close. Yes, they had known each other since they were kids, and

that much was upsetting in itself; nothing can remind you of your own fragile place in the universe so powerfully as someone your own age dying suddenly, here one minute, gone the next. But the level of emotion Ty showed over Samantha's death didn't correlate with what he'd felt for her in real life. He hated country music. He wasn't friends with any of her friends. So why did it settle into him so deeply?

In life, Samantha had been small and unassuming, a person who gravitated toward the background. But in death she was a shining star. Everyone spoke well of her. Everyone cried for her. They all cared.

I've wondered lately if that was what started Ty's fascination in his own death. He saw how everyone that one afternoon in the church, in the graveyard, loved Samantha Sullivan.

It was only a few weeks later that he took the Advil.

Maybe he didn't mean to die. I mean, he took the pills practically under Mom's nose. Who does that unless you want to get caught? To get saved? Maybe he was like everybody else. He just wanted to be loved. But then after he swallowed the pills he went down into his bedroom and went to sleep. Something must have changed in those moments after he took the Advil.

There were other factors, too. A few days after Samantha's death a football player at UNL killed himself in the empty locker room after a game, an overdose of some kind of over-the-counter drug. It was all over the news. That same summer a meth head died in what the press called "suicide by police." He pretended he had a gun, and they shot him.

There were all kinds of places where the idea might have taken root: that scene in the Twilight series when Edward tries to kill himself when he think he's lost Bella, because yes, that's a perfectly reasonable response if you can't be with the person you love: just die. Or the casual way people roll off the phrase I'm killing myself doing (fill in the blank). Or Dr. Kevorkian, or the death penalty, or the news, which is always spewing out some kind of terrible story about a crazy person with a gun and a death wish. Or _Romeo and Juliet_ in English class or _It's Kind of a Funny Story_ or a collection of poems by Sylvia Plath on Mom's bookshelf, from her college days, where she had underlined the lines:

> Dying
> Is an art, like everything else.
> I do it exceptionally well.
> I do it so it feels like hell.
> I do it so it feels real.

There's death all around us. Everywhere we look. 1.8 people kill themselves every second.

We just don't pay attention. Until we do.

26.

GOING BACK TO SCHOOL ON MONDAY IS ROUGH.

Even the bus ride is unbearable. Everybody wants to stare at the-girl-whose-brother-died, who must be extra fragile now because someone else is dead. It's how they treated me when I came back after Christmas break—like I've got a grief bomb strapped to my chest, liable to go off at any second. They either approach me carefully to attempt to defuse it, or they run for cover.

Plus, it's St. Patrick's Day, which makes the whole thing super awkward. Nobody's wearing green, I notice.

Fun times.

I look for Damian in the halls before class. I can't stop thinking about his voice when he was telling me that Patrick was dead. "He was my friend," he said. Now he's the only one of the three amigos left standing. But I don't spot him. Of course, he's easy to miss when he's trying not to be seen. Invisibility is his superpower, after all.

"If I disappeared one day, really disappeared and never came back, they wouldn't even notice." That's what he said to me that day in the gym.

And I said, "I see you."

That's what I have to do. He needs me to see him.

I cyberstalked Damian a bit over the weekend, to figure out how I might best do that—be his friend—and this is what I've gleaned from his internet activity so far:

He's into photography, especially black-and-white candids, photos taken when the subject didn't know there was a camera. I already knew that.

He likes to read. I already knew that, too.

What I didn't know is that Damian likes to read everything he can get his hands on: science fiction and fantasy and horror, but also books like *Marley & Me* and *The Kite Runner* and books about Descartes and Kant and Jung. He's really into philosophy. He describes himself as a "philosopher poet" on his various online profiles, and I don't know if this is simply an attempt to pick up girls, but that's the term he uses.

Philosopher.

Poet.

Which is great and all, except three days ago he posted this poem:

> *A white bone picked clean*
> *by the carrion few*
> *who will never know*
> *the pain that I do*

I worry that he could be the next domino to fall. He could be trembling on the brink of Ty's oblivion, about to step off into the abyss. I don't know. I don't know how to make things better for him.

But I'm going to try.

I find him at lunchtime. He's sitting at a table in the corner of the cafeteria, all alone, glumly picking at a pile of soggy french fries.

"So," I say, sliding into a chair across from him like it's what I do every day. "I want to talk about *Heart of Darkness*. I thought it was so interesting, the way Conrad explores how a person chooses between two different kinds of evil. So relevant, don't you think?"

Thank you, CliffsNotes.

Damian's face brightens, and he says, "I know. I think he was writing about the absurdity of it all. I mean, how can there be such a thing as insanity in a world that's already gone insane?"

"I know!" I agree enthusiastically. "So," I add, "I was wondering if you could give me some reading recommendations now that I'm done with Conrad. I really liked that one. What else could I try?"

His eyebrows come together thoughtfully, considering what I might like.

"Have you read Kafka?" he asks after a minute.

"Kafka." I jot the name down in my notebook.

"Classic existentialism. Start with *The Metamorphosis*. It's short, but it's brilliant."

Short is good, I think. Short is very good.

"I will check it out, literally," I say. I reach across the table and pop one of his french fries into my mouth. Damian smiles, a real, genuine smile, revealing a row of crooked teeth.

I'm so happy to see that smile.

In Honors Calculus Lab, when (after our initial ten minutes of homework) we pair up to play a blackjack tournament—winner gets cookies of their choice baked by none other than the multi-talented Miss Mahoney—Steven asks if he can challenge me in the first round.

I can't think of a good excuse not to. At least Steven's reaction to me is genuine. Even if it is awkward. "Okay."

I pull my desk to face his.

"Dealer or player?" he asks.

"Dealer."

He hands me the deck.

"Are you doing all right?" he asks as I shuffle.

Here we go. The bomb squad interrogation has officially begun.

"I'm fine."

"You missed school. You never miss school."

"Never say never," I joke, but he doesn't laugh.

"I tried to call you."

"I went on an impromptu road trip with my mom."

His eyebrows furrow. "A road trip. Where?"

"Tennessee."

More furrowing. "Tennessee."

"Yes. Are you ready?"

He nods. I lay a card faceup in front of him and one facedown in front of me. A nine for him. A two for me.

I lay down one more for him. A five. Then one more for me, face up. A jack.

"What's in Tennessee?" he asks.

I consider telling him that it's none of his business, but I know he's asking because he's worried. In spite of everything, he still cares about me. I shouldn't throw that back in his face.

"Graceland," I answer softly. "We went to Graceland."

His eyes light up with understanding. "Because your mom loves Elvis."

I can't help a smile. "Because my mom loves the King."

"Awesome." He smiles too, relaxes his shoulders. "That's great."

"So, the cards," I say, trying to get us back on track, because other pairs are finishing up now and ready to move to round two.

He glances at the cards. "Okay, hit me again."

I do. It's a six, which puts him at twenty. He passes, and I'm at twelve, so I draw one more for myself, a king. Twenty-two. Bust. It's over. He wins.

"Congratulations," I say. "Mahoney makes a killer chocolate chip. That's what I'd pick."

"Hey, let's not get ahead of ourselves," he replies. "I've merely won the battle, not the war."

But he goes on to win the next three hands. And he does pick the chocolate chip.

"I told you so," I say as we're leaving the classroom. Beaker and El fall into step behind us, but they hang back and let us talk, which feels weird, but what am I going to do about it, stop and insist that we walk all together?

"Yes, yes you did," he says. "How did you know?"

"Clairvoyant," I explain, tapping my temple like my brain is something magical.

"Ah."

For a minute things feel like they used to be. Before, I mean. When we were friends.

"So, I know you haven't felt like being involved in Math Club lately," he says as we round the corner into the commons. "But we're all going bowling tomorrow night. Parkway Lanes. Six p.m. Be there or be square."

"Well, you know I'm a square," I joke.

Steven shifts his backpack to the other shoulder and stops to squint at me. "I'd say you were more rectangular."

"You're so sweet," I say.

"So you'll come."

For once I really wish I could. "I can't," I tell him. "I have the stupid dinner with my dad."

Which is really the last place I want to be, considering. But that's the rule: I eat dinner with Dad on Tuesday nights. If I start breaking the rules now, who knows what could happen?

Steven tries to look like he's not disappointed. "Okay. Fair enough. Another time, then."

"Yeah," I murmur. "Another time."

17 March

This is going to sound trite, I suppose, but you never know when it's going to be the last time. That you hug someone. That you kiss. That you say goodbye.

I don't know what my last words were to Ty. Probably something like, <u>Smell you later,</u> as I went out the door that morning. I can't remember. It wasn't significant, is all I know. We were never one of those families that says "I love you" at the end of every conversation, just in case.

Steven's parents do that. When he calls to tell them he's going to be late or something, he always ends by saying "I love you, too." Even if he'll see them in 10 minutes.

I used to think that was the tiniest bit lame. If you say something that often, it loses its meaning, doesn't it? But now I understand. If the unthinkable happens—a car accident, a heart attack, whatever—at least you'll know your last words were something positive. There's a *security in that. A comfort.*

I broke up with Steven on New Year's Eve. There was a party at his house with his family—his 3 sisters and his parents and his aunts and uncles and cousins and half cousins once removed.

That night they treated me like a china doll, poor dear Alexis with the broken life.

Then we were counting down to New Year's, and I thought, This will be the first year without Ty in it in 3, 2, 1 . . .

Steven leaned in to kiss me and I flinched away.

"I'm sorry," I remember I said. "I can't."

"It's okay," he said. "I get it."

"No, you don't." I wished he would stop being so understanding with me, for once. "I don't mean this. I mean us. I can't do it anymore."

So many emotions crossed his face, but he swallowed them all down. "Okay," he said, his voice rough with the words he was holding back. "I know things are bad right now, so it makes sense that you need space. I can give you space."

"This isn't about Ty," I said. "I'd be doing this even if Ty hadn't died."

Hurt in his brown eyes then. A universe of hurt.

"Oh" was all he said.

"It was a good experiment, but . . ." I couldn't look at him. Out the window snow was falling in fat flakes, the kind of snowstorm that makes everything seem muted. "I've concluded that you and I aren't compatible. In the long run, I mean. I think you're a stellar guy, I do, but it was never going to work between us."

I sounded like a Vulcan. It was the lamest breakup speech ever, in the history of mankind.

All around us there was music and laughing, his little sister and cousins shrieking in a game of tag, drinks clinking and resolutions being made, a cacophony of noise, but all I could hear was the way Steven caught his breath.

"This is bad timing. I'm sorry. I should go," I said, and fled for the front door.

He found my jacket in the heap of coats on the guest-room bed, and held it out for me as I slipped my arms into the sleeves. Then he followed me outside to where the Lemon was parked down the street and helped me scrape the snow off my windshield. He said nothing the entire time. He didn't rage or argue or try to assign blame.

But when at last I met his eyes over the roof of my car, he held my gaze. There was snow in his hair, and his cheeks were red, the streetlight reflecting in his glasses.

"Why?" he asked.

"Why?"

"Why wouldn't it work between us?"

I didn't know the answer. I couldn't tell him about the text, so I floundered for some reasonable lie. "Do you know that there are different types of sperm?"

He stared at me. "You're breaking up with me because of my sperm? But you don't—we haven't—you have no basis for—"

"No. Not your sperm, specifically. Just . . . there are different types of sperm. I read about it. There are some sperm that are meant to swim as quickly as possible up the . . . well, you get the idea; they're meant to sprint for the finish line, so to speak. But there are also sperm that

are supposed to curl up along the way and die. Do you know why they would do that?"

"I have a feeling you're going to tell me."

"So they can block other sperm. They're like defensive-linemen sperm. Kamikaze sperm."

"Fascinating," Steven said wryly.

"So you know what that means?"

He thought for a minute before I saw the answer flare in his eyes. "It means that we're biologically engineered to be nonmonogamous. Females aren't designed to have one single mate. Not if our sperm is meant to compete."

"Exactly."

He ran a hand through his hair, dusting off snow. "That doesn't have anything to do with us, Lex. This isn't biology."

Then I told him the biggest lie of all.

"I didn't mean it. What I said that night. I got caught up for a minute, but . . . I don't believe in love. I believe in biology."

His eyes dropped from mine immediately. He started backing away toward the warm, welcoming light of his house and his family and his future.

"Drive safe, Lex," he murmured.

That was the last thing he said to me, as my boyfriend.

Drive safe.

27.

THIS WEEK WITH DAD IT'S THE OUTBACK. He's late. I sit at a table drinking strawberry lemonade for twenty minutes before I take out my phone, but I don't call him. I stare at the screen and think about calling him. I resent him for making me think about calling him.

Finally he shows up, jogging toward me in the darkened restaurant.

"Sorry," he says as he slides into the booth across from me. "Megan wanted—" He stops himself. He remembers I don't want to hear about Megan.

I suck down more lemonade as he takes off his coat and gloves and picks up the menu.

"How was your week?" he asks.

"Fantastic," I deadpan.

"I know things must have been difficult, what with the Murphy boy. It's such a shame."

I stare at him. Yes, a shame.

"You got into MIT, I hear," he says. "You're making plans."

He doesn't look thrilled. Why doesn't he look thrilled?

"How do you know that?"

"Your mother called me."

A swallow of lemonade goes down the wrong pipe, and I cough. "Mom *calls* you?"

"From time to time. She's worried about you, and she wants to discuss what to do with you."

I continue coughing. "What to do with me?"

"How to help you," he corrects himself, because obviously he phrased that badly.

"I'm not the one who needs help." This comes out without me meaning it to.

Dad looks away like he's embarrassed that I would be this rudely straightforward. Like he doesn't know me at all. The waitress comes for our order. Dad orders a huge steak and a Wallaby Darned, some kind of peach drink. I order a salad. Then we sit in awkward silence for a while, sawing off pieces of the dark rye bread that was served to us, chewing our thoughts.

"That's tremendous news, about MIT," Dad says finally.

"Yes. Tremendous."

"Do you have any idea how much . . ." He trails off, and that's when I understand what his hang-up is. He wants to know how much it costs. Of course he does. He has no money to send me to MIT.

"How much it will cost? Here." I fish the fat envelope out of my bag and hand it to him. He rifles through the pages until he lands on the financial-outlook sheet.

"So . . . you have a scholarship."

"A bunch of scholarships, yes. Which should cover tuition. But then I have to pay for housing, food, books, fees and other stuff, which I estimate will cost another fifteen thousand dollars a year. I can get a part-time job when I'm there; they have tutorships and stuff set up. And I have some savings."

"You have savings?" he asks, like the idea of me with money defies all logic.

"I have a little under twenty thousand," I admit.

His eyes widen. "Twenty thousand *dollars*?"

"No. Twenty thousand beaver pelts. Of course twenty thousand dollars."

"How did you manage that?"

"I saved every penny I made from my summer jobs for the past three years. You remember when I worked at the Jimmy John's downtown? That was eight dollars an hour, and a lot of sandwiches, so it was two birds, one stone that summer. I babysat for the Bueller triplets a bunch this year. I got birthday money from Grandma. It adds up. Specifically, it adds up to like $19,776.42. So, I can afford this. Without taking loans, I hope."

I watch the tension leak out of him.

"Lexie, this is . . . tremendous news," he says, and he means it this time. He breaks into a wide smile. "Congratulations, Peanut."

Peanut.

All it takes for me to become his little girl again is to pay my own way into a top-notch university.

"I'm so proud of you, honey." He points at the letter. "Did you read what it says here? You're one of the most talented and promising students they've had in the most competitive applicant pool they've had in years. You're one in a million."

"I'm one in eleven," I clarify. "There were 18,109 applicants and 1,620 students admitted, so that's one in eleven."

"Still." He refuses to let me take the wind out of his sails. "That's impressive. That's amazing. That's—"

"Can you stop?" I say.

He looks baffled. "Stop what?"

"Stop celebrating."

"Why? This is it, Lex. What we've dreamed about for you, all this time. The life we've wanted for you."

I can't hold it in. "Is it? This is the life you've always wanted for me?" I gesture around us, at all the happy people eating their happy steaks, celebrating anniversaries or birthdays or paychecks. "This?"

The waitress shows up with my salad and looks uncomfortable, because we're obviously having an argument.

"Hey, don't worry about it," I tell her. "Take it back. I'm not hungry anymore."

She sets the salad on the table anyway, then speed-walks away. I grab the MIT materials and return them to the envelope, then stuff it into my bag and start to gather up my coat.

"Peanut," Dad says.

"Don't call me that," I bark. "I am not your Peanut. You don't get to call me that anymore."

His expression hardens. "What is wrong with you? You're acting like a child."

"I am your child, technically speaking," I retort. "Or did you forget?"

He rears back like I slapped him. "Why are you so angry?"

Oh, let me count the ways:

Because this is not what I wanted my life to be. This is not the situation I pictured in my head when I told my dad I was going to MIT. We should be gathered around the kitchen table, Mom, Dad, Ty, and me. I would pass the letter around to them, and everyone would be smiling, and Ty would tease me about being an egghead, and I would fake-punch him, and we would laugh and celebrate my escape from Nebraska, but it wouldn't feel like an escape from anything bad. I shouldn't be telling Mom in order to get her through a crying jag and Dad at some crappy chain restaurant and Ty in the cold ground.

But that's my life.

And can I say any of this to him? Can I say, *You screwed up everything; it's all your fault,* the way I said it so easily to Steven last month? Can I tell him what I really think, call him a cheater? A liar? All the pieces of broken glass that night in the park with Ty after Dad left us?

Of course I can't. If I told him those things, I would lose him more than I already have. I would lose him for good.

I can't lose anyone else.

But I can't tell him about the photo, either. About Ty wanting that space in the collage for him. I can't.

He doesn't deserve that.

"I have to go," I say to Dad, my voice catching. "Enjoy your steak."

He stares after me as I storm out. I sit in the car for a few minutes, fogging up the windshield with my ragged breaths, trying to get myself together enough to drive.

"Please, Lemon," I plead, stroking the steering wheel. "You can do this."

I turn the key. She starts up with an unhealthy little sputter, but she starts.

"Thank you," I breathe, and then I put her in gear, and I refuse to look at Dad's face in the window as I make my getaway.

Sadie McIntyre is waiting on the front porch when I get back to the house, sitting on the steps smoking a cigarette. I don't know why I'm surprised.

"Don't you park in the garage?" she asks as I come up the sidewalk, then figures it out and answers her own question. "Oh, right. Of course you don't."

"Did you want something?" I'm ready to take Mom's approach and go to bed early so that this "tremendous" day will be over. Stick a fork in me; I'm done.

"I wanted to check up on you," she says. "I haven't, like, talked to you for a while. Not since . . ."

"Patrick," I fill in. I lumber down onto the steps beside her. "I didn't see you at the funeral."

"I had to work," she says with a sideways glance: yep, guilt. "But those things are hard for me. It takes me back to when . . ."

"Me too."

We sit for a minute, her smoking, me trying not to breathe it in.

"You know what I remember most, from my dad's?" she says after a while. "People kept saying, 'It's going to be all right.' That's what they told me, over and over and over, like *Don't you worry, little girl, it will all be okay,* because there's got to be some bullshit overall rule of the universe that no matter what happens, no matter how bad it gets, everything will be all right in the end."

"Yeah," I murmur.

"And you know what I kept thinking? I kept thinking, That is a fucking lie. It is *not* going to be all right. It will never be all right, ever, ever again. So stop fucking lying to me."

"You thought that? How old were you, fifteen, that you thought 'stop fucking lying'?"

Her blue eyes crinkle up in amusement. "I had an advanced vocabulary for my age."

"So I gather."

She laughs and smokes.

"I'm sorry I wasn't there for you," I say after a minute. "You came to Ty's funeral, but I didn't go to your dad's."

She shrugs. "I wasn't there for you when your dad checked out, either. Plus I wouldn't have been able to appreciate you being there at the time, anyway."

"And knowing me, I probably would have said something

stupid like 'It's going to be all right.'"

We both smirk.

"Well, you don't know until you know," she says. Then she's ready to change the subject. "So how's it going with the spirit situation? Have you seen him again?" she asks. "Since you gave the letter to Ashley? I want details."

I can't help but tense up. "I've seen him."

"A lot?"

"Yes. A lot." Like halfway through the state of Missouri in the backseat of the car a lot. "Anyway, there's something else now."

"Something else?" Sadie tries to sound like it's no big deal, but I can tell she's interested. She's able to see this Ty ghost thing as a simple mystery to be solved. Because it's not her house. Not her life.

"You remember the collage Ty made, for his own funeral? He put all of these pictures in a special frame?"

She looks appropriately somber. "Yes."

"And there was a blank space in the collage."

She nods.

I sigh. "That space was supposed to be for a picture of my dad. And I found the picture. And I feel like Ty wants . . . he would want me to give it to my dad."

"Oh. Okay. That sounds complicated."

"You're telling me." I lean my head back and wish there were stars to gaze up at, but the sky is muted by clouds, a dark, oppressive gray. It's March, but I can smell snow in the air. It feels like this winter is hanging on, that it's never going to end. I sigh. "I do not want to deal with my dad."

"I get that. Your dad's a douche," Sadie says.

I sit up. "What'd you say?"

"Your mom, she was—I mean, she *is* so great." Sadie puts her chin in her hand, her eyes lost in thought. "I always wished my mom could be more like your mom. My mom is so uptight about everything. Your mom was so laid-back and funny. She used to make pancakes shaped like teddy bears, with the chocolate chip eyes and the strawberry mouth, and she sewed you all these great costumes for Halloween, and you always got the best birthday cakes. My mom . . ." She shakes her head.

"Your mom was busy. She had a lot of kids to take care of," I say.

"I wish—" She stops herself.

It's not that hard to figure out what she was going to say. She wishes her dad were here.

Because her dad was the kind of dad all the kids wanted their dads to be. He was a fourth-grade teacher, but one of the cool ones, one of those who wore dress shirts rolled up at the sleeves, who could play Bruce Springsteen and Coldplay on his guitar, who didn't look dumb in sunglasses. He had this big booming voice that made you sit up and listen, but he was always in a good mood.

Sadie flicks ashes off her cigarette. "So. You think Ty wants you to make up with your dad."

I remember the way I kept finding the empty frame on the floor in the hallway. The light on in the playhouse. The cologne. I could explain all those things away, but they seem to add up to something. They seem to add up to Ty.

"I don't know," I say. "I wish there were some way I could figure it out definitively, one way or the other—I'm crazy or I'm haunted—I don't care. I just want to know."

"I get that," Sadie says. "I went to a medium once. Did I tell you?"

I shift on the step and stare at her. "No you didn't tell me. When was this?"

"Madam Penny." She takes a long drag, contorts her mouth to blow the smoke away from me. "About two years ago."

I reach over and take her cigarette out of her hand, chuck it in the snowbank.

"Hey. What the hell?"

"I'm doing your lungs a favor. Anyway, Madam Penny," I push on before she has time to get truly mad at me. "What was that like? I want details."

She snorts. "It cost me a hundred bucks for a half hour. I was so sure I was going to be able to talk to my dad. I had this gold watch that he used to wear all the time, because her website said she worked better if you brought in an item that you associated with the person you wanted to speak with."

I remember that watch. When Sadie's dad rolled up his sleeves to teach long division, we'd see it gleaming on his wrist. Sometimes during class he'd pick one of the students to hold his watch and keep track of time when he read out loud to us—because he'd get lost in a story, he used to say.

"So what happened?" I ask.

"I got in there, and she immediately said she could feel someone on the other side reaching out to me, an older male figure, she said. A wise man."

"Yeah? Your dad?"

"Nope." She picks at a hole in the knee of her jeans. "Gregory, she said his name was. He was a monk who died in the twelfth century."

I stare at her, completely baffled. "What?"

Sadie laughs at my expression. "Madam Penny said he was my spirit guide. He was there to direct me on my soul path. We each have an invisible helper in this life, she said, someone to lead us and help us along our way."

"If that's the case, then my spirit guide is fired," I say.

"I know, right?"

"So . . . did you get to talk to your dad?" I ask, but I can already see the answer coming.

She looks off down the street for a few seconds before she answers. "No. She went on about this Gregory person for twenty minutes, and then I tried to get her to look at the watch and she started telling me about my grandfather, who died when I was two so I wouldn't have known him from Adam, and then she babbled on about a great lover I had in a past life, a guy in a bomber jacket who fought in the Second World War, who loved me like the moon and stars, I remember she said. He wanted to send me a message of love and forgiveness, she kept saying. Love and forgiveness. Forgiveness and loooooove. And then my time was up."

It's quiet. Then Sadie finally says, "So it was a huge waste of money."

I try to keep it positive. "Hey, but it was entertaining."

"Right. It was a real barrel of laughs."

"I'm sorry. That sucks."

She shakes her head. "I was naive. God. A hundred dollars. It kills me to think about all the stuff I could have bought with a hundred dollars back then."

"It was an experiment," I say. "You went in with an open mind."

"I really thought my dad would talk to me," she says. "I thought I would get all the answers."

She sniffles, and that's when I realize she's crying. It's been two years and she's still so disappointed that she didn't get to speak to her dad that the thought brings her to tears.

I envy her for that.

I reach into my backpack to find a pack of tissues, which I carry around on the off chance that one of these days my tear ducts will start working again and then I'll cry a fricking river. I hand her one. "But you still watch *Long Island Medium*," I point out as she takes it and dabs at her eyes. "You're still a believer, right?"

"Yeah, well, I prefer to think that Madam Penny was flawed."

"Seriously, seriously flawed," I agree.

"I was so pissed. I egged her house later," Sadie confesses.

My mouth falls open. Then we both start snickering. Then outright laughing.

"You really are a delinquent," I observe when our laughter fades. "Wow. What did she look like? Was she all dark and mysterious and gypsy-like?"

Sadie thinks for a minute. "She looked like a cross between my

301

grandma and Betty White. I remember she was wearing a sweater with Christmas trees sewn on the front." She blows her nose. Sighs. "Shit. I came here to cheer you up, not the other way around."

"You did cheer me up," I say. Which is true.

She bumps her shoulder into mine. "You're a good friend, Lex."

No, I'm not, I think. "You're a good friend, too," I answer. "I'm glad you saw me running that night. I'm glad you took the time to figure out why."

"Hey, I was serious when I said we should start running together again," she says. "Just as soon as the weather warms up. You and me. Jogging."

"Don't push your luck," I say.

She smiles, the traces of tears still silver on her cheeks.

28.

IT'S FUNNY HOW SOMETIMES YOU DON'T SEE the obvious things coming. You think you know what life has in store for you. You think you're prepared. You think you can handle it. And then—*boom*, like a thunderclap—something comes at you out of nowhere and catches you off guard. Like on Wednesday, when Ashley Davenport ambushes me before first period.

She's there on the other side of my locker door when I close it. I jump a mile.

"Hi," she says.

She's dyed her hair again, a deep, glossy brown this time. It suits her, makes her face all about her huge blue eyes, which are focused on me like laser beams. Concerned. Determined.

"I've been hoping to catch you."

"Um—okay?"

"I saw you at Patrick's wake," she says, her voice hoarse like she has a cold.

She doesn't offer me any other explanation. She simply takes off her backpack and puts it on the floor and pulls out a familiar, tattered envelope.

For Ashley, it reads.

"I think you should read this," she says.

"Oh" is all I can think to say. I'm frozen. I don't really understand what's happening here. I thought that envelope was gone for good, that I'd never know what was in it, but here she is offering the letter, like what he had to tell her concerns me, somehow.

I swallow, hard. The text. The text.

"Do you want to go somewhere else? Like the library?" she asks.

"But don't you have class?"

The bell rings. She shrugs and smiles faintly. "I can be late."

We go to the library. No one bothers us as we make our way to the lonely corner behind the stack, where Ashley holds out the letter.

My hands tremble as I take it.

"I want it back. So I'll be over there." She tilts her head to indicate the study tables in the center of the library. "Take as much time as you want."

Then it's just me and the letter.

I slide it out of its envelope. The paper crackles as I unfold it.

It's dated December 10. Ten days before Ty died.

I take a shaky breath and slide myself down against the corner, draw my knees up to my chest, and I read.

Dear Ashley,

I wanted to write you this letter to explain why I broke it off with you.

First, I have to say I'm sorry for how I did it. I didn't know what to say to you or how to explain the truth about how I feel, so I went with the old cliché "this isn't working for me," which made it sound like the problem was you.

It's not you.

You're the most amazing girl I've ever known. You are ~~beautiful~~—but I think I should list smart first, because you are so crazy smart, and that's what I first noticed about you—that for such a gorgeous girl you sure had your head on straight, you're a girl who knows things, and you had all these ideas and these complex thoughts about life. You're beautiful, too. You know that. People always tell you that. Sometimes when I would look at you it used to make my chest hurt, how beautiful you were. And you're funny. Remember that time you made me laugh so hard I snorted chocolate milk up my nose? But you didn't make a big deal over it, and that's because you're nice, you're nice to everybody. You're always considering how other people feel. I think that's what I admire most about you, how sweet you are in this world that's full of crap.

Sorry.

So it's really not about you, Ash. Please believe me when I ~~say~~ write that. You are perfect.

This is <u>my</u> problem.

*The other night when I kind of freaked out on you—
sorry for that too btw—you were trying to get me to talk
about my dad, and I said I hated my dad, and you got this
surprised look, like you didn't know I was the type of person
who could hate someone. Who could hate my dad.*

But I am.

*That's when I saw how messed up I am. And I saw myself
so clearly right then, and it was like I could also see the future.*

*You're so perfect and you're so beautiful and you're so
kind and when I'm with you, I want to be those things, too, I
want to be the best person but the truth is, I can't.*

I'm messed up.

*I go through phases where I think everything's going to
be okay and the sky is blue and stuff and I can feel the sun
and the air going in and out of my lungs and I think, life is
good. But then every time, I also know deep down that the
darkness is coming. And it's going to keep coming. And when
I'm in the darkness I'm going to screw up everything. And if
you're with me that's when I'm going to screw you up, too.*

You deserve better than that.

*You've got good friends and awesome parents and this
amazing life ahead of you. You need to have a boyfriend who
will be part of that. Not me.*

*My sister has a boyfriend, and she's so into him and she's
freaked out that she's so into him, because that's how she
is, but when I see them together, I think, they work. Most
couples in high school you know aren't going to work out,*

and maybe that's how it should be. But with them, it's so obvious that they're right for each other. They make each other better, somehow. They fit.

You and me, Ash, we don't fit. You're like the sun and I'm like a big black cloud.

I'd always be darkening your skies.

I've tried, but I can't fix myself. I can't change it. So I did the right thing, letting you go. You'll see. It may take a little bit of time, but you'll understand.

I wish I had the guts to tell you this out loud, or even give you this letter, but I probably won't. Still, I'm glad I wrote it. Putting it into words, on paper, helped me understand some things. I get it, now.

Don't cry any more tears over me, Ash. I'm not worth it. But I want you to know, in case I ever do give you this letter and you read it first before you burn it or something, that for just a little while, you made me feel like I was really alive. Like I was special.

Thanks for that.

Thanks for picking me to be the one who got to stand in your sunshine for a while. I'll carry that around with me for the rest of my life—that you saw enough good in me that you wanted to hold my hand and kiss me and smile at me like I was the only guy.

Be happy.

Love,

Ty

My chest feels like it's in a vise, tightening, tightening. I brush my fingers over the words, Ty's words in Ty's messy print, and over the stains on the paper where Ashley's tears must have dropped when she read it. I read the letter again. And again. I try to memorize every word.

I sit there for a long time.

The bell for second period rings. The library stirs as if, up till now, time has been stopped, but it's going again. I find Ashley at the back table. When she looks up at me, her face wrinkles up like she's going to cry, but she contains it.

I hand her back the letter.

"Thank you for letting me read this."

"He was wrong, though." Her voice breaks. "I'm not perfect. I have dark days, too." She wipes a tear off her pale cheek. "I could have helped him, if he would have let me. If he'd just given me the letter himself."

"I'm sorry," I say.

She looks up with shining eyes. "No. Thank you, for giving it to me when you did."

I can't talk. I nod. She nods.

Then we both have to move on.

In the last photograph ever taken of Ty and Dad together, from back when we were still a family, they're playing chess.

June 24 is the date my mom scrawled on the back of the photo. The summer I was 14 and Ty was 12. The year before Dad traded us for Megan.

I remember that day.

There was a tornado—an F4 on the Fujita scale, and if you speak the tornado lingo, which pretty much everybody in Nebraska does, you'll know that's not the most powerful tornado (the F5 is), but it's still big enough to take out a town like Raymond. When the sirens started going off, the twister had formed 20 miles north of us. The sky turned green. Mom herded us all into the basement to wait out the storm.

We watched the news for a while on television, where a map of the area kept showing the tornado hovering above us, a swirling cartoon cyclone slowly moving in our direction.

Then Dad suggested a game of chess.

He'd been through his chess obsession a couple years before and hadn't played since. But there in the basement den was the beautiful mahogany board he'd purchased back then, and the marble pieces, and what else was there to do while we waited?

I played first. I lost. Spectacularly, if I remember correctly. In spite of my math affinity I'm not much good at chess. I'm shortsighted; I can't predict that far ahead, to the other player's choices and moves. I only see the pieces in front of me and react.

I wasn't surprised when I lost. I'd never won against Dad. He's not the type to let his kids win just so they'll feel good about themselves. In his chess phase I must have lost a hundred games to him, and every time he'd take my king, he'd say, "Well played, Lexie. You're getting better. One of these days you're going to beat me."

But I never did.

So on June 24, when I was 14 and stuck in the basement with my family and a chessboard, I played, and I lost. I stuck out my tongue at Dad, and he chuckled at me, and then he said, "Tyler. You're up."

Ty took his place on his side of the board with the look of an excited puppy.

Oh boy, I remember thinking. This is going to be quick.

But almost right away he made a move that surprised Dad.

"Where'd you learn that?" Dad asked, squinting down at the board.

Ty shrugged. "Is it a bad move?"

"No," Dad said distractedly. "No, that was an excellent move. There's a name for it, even, if I can just remember it."

Before long Ty made another excellent move. And another. And another.

Before long he was clearly winning the game.

Then we had to stop for a bit when the sky went black. The lights flicked out. We all went into the bathroom with candles, where the pipes would provide some extra protection if the wind ripped the top of the house away. Ty and I got into the empty bathtub with the emergency radio. Dad sat on the counter with his arm around Mom.

"The Caro-Kann Defense," he said after a minute. "That's it."

Yep, we were possibly about to die, and Dad was still marveling at Ty's chess moves.

I looked at Ty. He had a secret smile.

We didn't have to stay in the bathroom long.

The tornado skimmed by Raymond and carried on to the east, where it took out a whole string of farms before it dissipated, and we could come out of the bathroom.

Ty and Dad went right back to their game. Mom and I sat on either side of them, holding up candles to light the board, and watched it all go down, a rapt audience as Ty moved around the board like a pro. The whole time Dad looked so confused. I mean, Ty was 12 years old. When Dad had gone through his chess phase before, Ty had been like 10. He hadn't even really grasped the rules of chess.

"How are you doing this?" Dad asked finally when Ty took his queen.

"I've been playing a little on the computer," Ty confessed. He sat back. "Checkmate."

Mom and I crowed. "Oh, how the mighty have fallen," Mom said, *and I think she got a little too much satisfaction out of Ty winning, because she also had lost a hundred games to Dad.*

"I have to get a picture," she said. So that's when the photo happened.

In the picture, Ty has just won the game and he's practically glowing, he's so happy. Dad is looking down, beaten, but he is smiling, too.

He was proud.

"Well done, son," he said. He clapped his hand on Ty's shoulder and squeezed. "Want to go again?"

Ty shook his head. "I better quit while I'm ahead."

The power came back on. We all blinked in the sudden brightness of the room. Ty grinned over at Dad. "I have this new game on the Wii. Tennis. Do you want to try to beat me there? Loser buys McDonald's?"

"Sure," Dad said. "You bet."

Sucker.

It was a good day. A good memory.

I don't want to be the kind of person who hates my dad.

29.

THAT MORNING I WATCH THE SUN RISE, and then I
get in my car and drive. I know the way to Megan's house like I've
driven there a hundred times—straight down 27th Street to the
south part of town, where the houses are old but expensive and well
maintained. Wrought-iron fences and such.

Her house is a small tan-and-green one near the zoo. It has a
red door. Christmas lights are still strung along the edge of the roof.
A black-and-white cat stares at me from the window.

Dad's a dog person, by the way.

I tuck Ty's collage frame under my arm and make my way
carefully up the uneven sidewalk. I climb the steps onto the porch,
take a deep breath, and ring the bell.

It's warmer today, I realize. Water drips off the roof. The snow
is melting.

Megan answers the door. She is blond and bobbed and dressed

in a little navy blue suit dress. When she recognizes me her face becomes the quintessential picture of surprise, her burgundy-lipsticked mouth in a perfect O shape.

Behind her I see Dad, dressed for work, wearing a similar expression.

"Hi," I say, moving past Megan and into the house. "Do you have a minute? We need to talk."

The lie I told Dad:

The frame was behind the door.

There's an empty space in the frame, a picture missing.

By complete coincidence I discovered this photo of Dad and Ty (not in a frame) on the floor behind the door.

Therefore: it must have fallen out of its frame somehow.

Therefore: Ty meant to put that photo of Dad in the collage.

Therefore: Ty didn't leave Dad's picture out on purpose in order to hurt Dad.

Therefore: It's possible that Ty forgives Dad.

I don't know if he actually believed me, but it's a fiction I think we both can live with.

30.

"THAT," DAVE SAYS, "is what we in the business call a 'breakthrough.' Good job."

"It was no big deal." I fiddle with the edge of the rug. "I was only there for ten minutes."

"It's a very big deal, Lex." Dave smiles. "How long has your father been gone?"

"Three years."

"And in all that time, you've never gone to his house?"

"Megan's house," I correct him. "No. I've never been there."

"Why?"

"Because . . ." I don't know how to explain my reasons so that they seem rational. Perhaps they aren't rational.

"Why yesterday, I mean," Dave says. "Why go to Megan's house now?"

I shrug. "I finally had something I wanted to say to him."

"And what was that?"

"I wanted him to know that his picture belonged in Ty's frame. That's all."

"How did he react when you told him?"

He cried. I'd never seen Dad cry before, not even at Ty's funeral, so it shocked me. He didn't make a big show of it; he put his hand to his eyes for a few minutes while his chest heaved and his shoulders shook, and then finally he dropped his hand.

Then he said, "I'm so sorry, Lexie. I know what I did hurt you and your brother, and I am sorry for that."

I wanted to hold on to my anger when he said that. I could have answered that his sorry wasn't good enough. His sorry can't bring Ty back. Which is true.

But my anger was a slippery thing, like a fish I was trying to keep hold of, and it wiggled out of my grasp.

I looked at Dad, and he looked at me with his hazel eyes, Ty's and my eyes, and he said, "I would have stayed. If it could have stopped Tyler from doing this. I would have come back."

I shook my head. It's too confusing, too hard to think about the what-ifs. I have my own personal list of what-ifs, without having to deal with Dad's.

He whispered again that he was sorry, and cried some more, so I laid my hand over his on Megan's kitchen table. He put his other hand over mine and squeezed, and we stayed that way for a few minutes, until I slid my hand away and told him I had to get going to school.

"Thank you for coming," he told me as he walked me down

the driveway. "For telling me about the picture. It means a lot."

It didn't matter that almost everything I'd told him about the photo and the collage was a total fabrication on my part.

"You're welcome." I got into the car.

Dad knocked on my window and leaned down to say, "Maybe . . . maybe you could come to dinner here next week. We could talk about MIT."

"Maybe," I said, because MIT was still feeling pretty far away, and I didn't know—I still don't know—if I was ready to make Megan's house a regular thing. "I have to go." I put the Lemon in gear. "Take care, Dad."

"Take care, Lexie," he said.

I could see him in the rearview mirror, standing on the sidewalk in his suit and tie, his hand lifted in a wave as I drove away.

"Alexis, are you still with me?" Dave prompts, because I'm just sitting there, not answering. "Are you all right? Would you like some water?"

I cough. "Sure."

He opens the minifridge under his desk and gets me a Dasani. I drink.

"He said he was sorry," I say when I'm ready to talk again. "For the divorce. For the way it hurt Ty and me."

Dave nods.

"Aren't you going to write that down?" I ask him. "It seems important. A breakthrough, like you said."

He doesn't write it down. "Do you accept his apology?" he asks.

"Sort of. Maybe. Probably not."

"Do you feel like you've started to forgive him?"

"I don't know," I say. "I don't think he should get off that easy. But it was nice to hear him say he's sorry. I didn't think I'd ever hear him say that."

Dave strokes his beard, which is what he does when he's about to say something terribly profound. "Forgiveness is tricky, Alexis, because in the end it's more about you than it is about the person who's being forgiven."

"Like that old saying about how holding a grudge is like drinking poison and then waiting for the other person to die."

"Exactly." Dave sits back, puts his feet up on the coffee table. "I'm proud of you. To go to that house, to face him, to give him that small kindness with the picture, that took courage. It was a step in the right direction."

"The direction to what, though?" I ask. "Where am I headed?"

"Acceptance. Which is the path to healing. Growth. Contentment."

I mull this over. "I will never be happy again," Mom said. She said it like it's her duty now, her motherly obligation, to consider her life ruined because she lost Ty. I don't view things the way Mom does, but it's difficult to imagine being truly happy again.

I don't know what my duty is.

"How did you feel when you were done talking to your father?" Dave asks.

"I felt . . . slightly better," I tell Dave.

This he feels compelled to write down in his yellow legal pad. He underlines the words.

"Slightly better is good," he says.

I agree. Slightly better is good. But I don't know what I'm supposed to do now.

"Lex?" Dave says. "Are you okay?"

"Sometimes I think I see Ty." I don't know where this comes from, this sudden confession, but suddenly it's out there. I glance at Dave quickly. "Sometimes I feel like he's there. In the house. And I feel like he wants something from me."

I brace myself to be sent off to the funny farm.

Dave nods. "That's very common, actually."

I stare at him. "Common?"

"It's common for people to continue to see loved ones who have passed. When he was alive, your brother took up a certain space in your life, a physical space and an emotional one. Now that he's gone, the brain naturally tries to fill in that empty space."

"So it doesn't mean I'm going crazy," I venture.

Dave lets out a bark of laughter. "No, Lex. You're certainly not crazy."

And it doesn't mean that Ty is a ghost, either. For some reason this revelation brings on the ache in my chest.

It turns out there's a logical explanation, after all.

So why don't I want to believe it?

31.

SADIE'S RUNNING OUTFIT IS HOT PINK. It's impossible
to miss her at the end of my driveway, hopping from foot to foot,
warming up. She says the pink makes her feel like an atom bomb:
like a nuclear explosion is her exact phrasing, pronouncing it "nuke-
cue-ler," the way George W. Bush used to say it even though he
knew it was wrong, just to piss people off.

How Sadie and I are friends, I still don't know.

"Come on," she hollers at me. "Let's get moving already."

We run. Spring seems to have finally arrived, so we've been
running. Today is our second attempt this week in the couch-to-5K
plan. I'm wearing yoga pants and a MATHLETE T-shirt, and I do not
feel anything like a nuclear explosion. I hate running as much as
ever. It's a horrible thing to do to yourself. Waterboarding, really,
would be kinder.

There's an upside, though. I do like the quiet of the early

morning jogs around our neighborhood, the only sound our footfalls on the asphalt and our labored breathing in the spring air. I like the stillness in the air just before the sun rises. I like the colors that gather in the sky. The way everything, for just those few moments, seems fresh and unsullied.

Sadie's watch beeps. "Okay, walk," she says.

We slow to a brisk walk. This is the early part of the jog—before I feel like I am going to die—so I am able to answer Sadie when she asks me if I've seen the ghost.

"I haven't seen him. Not since I told the big whopper to my dad about the collage. How about you?" For some reason I can't bring myself to tell her about what Dave said, that seeing Ty is a common occurrence, my brain filling in the spaces my brother used to occupy.

"Me?" She looks over at me quizzically.

"How's Gregory, the spirit guide?"

I grin. She grins back.

"Oh, right. Gregory is fabulous. He's got my life all planned out."

Her watch beeps. "Run!" she orders, and off we go.

"Actually," she says when we're at the next walking interval, "I'm thinking about going to college. Not the Massachusetts Institute of Technology or anything," she says with proper dramatic flair, "but I've looked into a few community colleges, and then if I liked that I could transfer to UNL."

"Good for you!" I beam at her, as much as I am capable of beaming in this jogging situation. "I told you. You're smart. You should do something with that."

"I'm thinking psychology or counseling. Get paid the big bucks for people to tell me all of their problems."

We pass by one of our neighbors, old Mrs. Wilson, who is watering her flowers. She looks at us suspiciously. Sadie waves. Mrs. Wilson scowls and goes back in the house.

"What about MIT?" Sadie asks me. "What's going on with that?"

"Not much. I'm supposed to be getting a call from one of the students this week, and next month I'm going to visit the campus."

"You don't sound very excited."

"I am, though."

"You're scared," Sadie teases.

"No. I'm just anticipating this huge change. And I've never been great with change."

I've been thinking about MIT a lot. Just six months away. I know better than anyone how much can change in six months.

Sadie's watch beeps. "Run!" she yells, and we run, and I stop thinking for a while and focus on survival.

Walk.

Run.

Walk.

Run.

I'm out of breath. I have a stitch in my side. I'm pretty sure I hate Sadie. For each step of the routine, the run parts seem longer and the walk parts seem shorter. After six of these, I feel like I'm going to die.

"Walk," she says finally. "Last leg."

Thank God. If I believed in God.

"How's your mom?" Sadie asks between pants as we cool down. "I saw her at the grocery store yesterday, and she looked—"

"Slightly better," I fill in.

"Yeah. She looked better."

"She's doing okay. She laid off the wine and the pills, and she's going to church again, which seems to give her some energy, so yes. She's doing better."

Mom and I haven't talked about my little speech in the car on the way home from Graceland, but I feel like she heard me. That's something.

"It's such a cliché, the whole 'time heals all wounds' thing, but it's true. Clichés are clichés for a reason, I guess," Sadie says as we drag ourselves into her front yard. "Hey, do you want a ride to school later?"

I check my watch. "You mean in like fifteen minutes later? Sure."

It would rock to not ride the bus.

"Okay, so shower, do something with that hair—I'm just saying—or whatever you need to do, and meet me back here in fifteen minutes."

Fourteen minutes later I'm back at the McIntyre house. Sadie comes out, hair still wet but eyeliner perfectly in place, and unlocks the doors to her old Jeep Grand Cherokee with its peeling red paint.

I'm still thinking about MIT.

"Are you okay?" she asks me.

"Fine. I'm just jealous that you have a car that actually works." I glance at the dashboard. "You're almost out of gas, by the way."

She shrugs. "Gas is expensive."

"The light is on. Do you even have enough for us to make it to school?"

She rolls her eyes, annoyed that I have to be so darned practical, and turns the car off. Then she unbuckles her seat belt. "Wait here."

She leaves the door open and the keys-in-the-ignition alarm ringing, goes into the garage, and reappears a few minutes later lugging a big red gasoline can.

"Seth always keeps extra for his motorcycle." She reaches under the seat to pop the gas door.

As if on cue, Seth and said motorcycle pull into the driveway. He sputters to a stop next to the Jeep and removes his helmet. His spiky hair is smashed, and he runs his hand over it as he watches Sadie struggle to pour the gas into the tank.

"Um, may I ask what the hell you're doing?" he asks.

"I'll fill it up for you after school."

"You be sure to do that." He looks like he wants to say more, but he's noticed me sitting there. He smiles. I roll down my window as he walks around to my side of the car.

"Hey, Lex," he says. "Still hanging out with this loser?"

This is the most awake I've ever seen him look.

"Yes." I try but can't think of a clever quip. "Did you just get off work?"

"Yep. Time for the party to begin." He smiles again.

Sadie scoffs and says something I don't catch but is undoubtedly

325

an insult, which seems doubly rude since she is stealing his gasoline.

He leans against the window.

"So," he says casually. "Seen any ghosts lately?"

I stare at him, frozen, until I remember the ghost story he told us. "Uh, yeah," I try to counter. "I saw one just last month, as a matter of fact."

"Cool," he says.

Sadie slams the gas compartment shut and sets the empty gas can on the floor behind her seat. "All right, Sethy, we have to go now," she says in a singsong voice. "We don't want to be late for school."

Seth ignores her. "I could still give you that ride."

I stare at him. "What, now?"

"How about it, Lex? You, me, Georgia, the wind in your hair . . ."

Sadie jumps in and starts the Jeep. "Not today, Seth. She's covered, ride-wise," Sadie says. "Bye. Have a nice sleep."

Seth looks at me like he's still waiting for an answer. I cough.

"Not today," I say as the car starts to move. "Thanks."

"Someday, though," he says.

"Sure."

"I'm going to hold you to that," he calls after us as Sadie and I back out of the driveway.

I'm sure he will.

We blast down the road toward school. Sadie is a definite lead foot.

"Hey, about Seth," I venture.

"Yeah?"

"Was he . . . flirting with me? I'm terrible at interpreting these things. But he keeps trying to get me to ride his motorcycle."

Sadie snorts. "Don't take this the wrong way, Lex, but no. Seth doesn't know how to talk to women without flirting. But when he really likes a girl, he gets all tongue-tied."

I don't know whether to be insulted or relieved. "Good to know."

She frowns and taps at the gas gauge, which is still moving toward empty.

"You know, if you're planning on going to college," I can't help but inform her, "it might be wise to start riding the bus more regularly. There are"—I do a quick calculation in my head—"sixty-three days of school left. That's a hundred ninety-three dollars and forty-one cents. That could buy your books next semester."

She looks at me like I've lost my mind.

I take eighth period off, which is starting to become a bad habit of mine. Instead, I sit in the gym and watch the cheerleaders practice. So I'm present for that one moment that Ashley Davenport looks up and sees me, and waves, and I wave back, and my wave says, *Thank you.*

I shouldn't be surprised when Damian comes to find me.

"Hey," he says, appearing at the top of the bleachers. "I have some pictures for you."

I flip through them. They're mostly in black and white, stills of Ty about to make a shot on the basketball court, one where he is lifting a water bottle to his lips, sweat gleaming off his brow. One where he is smiling at a very particular cheerleader.

And then, at the bottom of the pile, a picture of Damian, a selfie, shot at a strange, lopsided angle so I can see his torso and his face but the top of his head is chopped off.

In the picture he's wearing the shark tooth necklace.

My chest gets tight. "This is nice," I murmur. "You're talented."

He clears his throat. "Thanks."

"I read *The Metamorphosis*," I report. "You were right. It's an amazing book. Talk about absurdity, right?"

"You read it already?"

"I did." I stayed up all night with it a couple nights ago, no CliffsNotes this time. It was actually pretty cool.

Damian shoves his hands in his pockets and beams at me. "I love that we never get an explanation of why one day he wakes up as a bug. He simply is."

"It's brilliant how he shows us the way our bodies can become disconnected from our minds," I add. "Gregor's a bug, but he always manages to keep a part of his humanity, even when being a bug makes everyone hate him. He's still human, inside."

"But he's alone," Damian says softly. "He's always going to be a bug on the outside. Until they decide to get rid of him."

I clear my throat. "Anyway, I was thinking, we should meet up sometime and talk about this stuff. Books, I mean. You seem to know so much about literature, and I'm going to MIT next year— and I am really intimidated by the English requirement. I feel like every time I open my mouth I'm going to end up saying something completely stupid."

"You won't," he says. "You're so smart, Lex. Come on."

"I'm not smart about books," I argue. "Not like you. So, can you help me?"

He brushes his long hair out of his eyes, but it falls right back in his face. Then he straightens up his hunched shoulders and says slowly, "We could meet at Barnes and Noble. I could show you some more books you might like."

"That sounds perfect," I say. "How about tomorrow night?"

He looks startled. "Saturday night?"

"Yeah. After dinner, maybe. Seven?"

He gives a little laugh. "Okay. The SouthPointe Barnes and Noble, that's the one I always go to."

I'd prefer to avoid that particular B&N, for reasons I don't want to explain to him, but it is what it is. "Okay. Do you need a ride? My car's always a bit of a gamble, but I think I could get us there."

He shakes his head quickly. "I can drive myself. I live in the boonies, and I wouldn't want to make you go all the way out there. I'll meet you at seven at the bookstore."

"Tomorrow. Seven. We'll talk bugs," I say.

"And books."

"And books."

"Right now I have to go catch my bus, unfortunately."

"Right. Bye. Have a good night."

He stands a little straighter as he walks off.

32.

ON SATURDAY MORNING I get a phone call from a junior at MIT.

"My name is Amala Daval," she tells me. "I'm a math major."

"Great," I stammer after an awkward pause. "How are you?"

"I'm studying theoretical mathematics at MIT," she says, dead serious by the sound of it. "How do you think I am?"

"So . . . good, right?"

"For the right kind of people," she says, like she hasn't made up her mind yet that I am the right kind of person. "It is amazing."

"Who's that?" Mom asks me from across the breakfast table.

MIT, I mouth, and her eyes widen. She takes her coffee cup and disappears into the living room.

"So it looks like you haven't RSVP'd to the campus visit next month," Amala continues.

"Oh no, I am planning on coming to that," I tell her. "I've just had a lot on my plate lately, so I haven't gotten around to—"

"Are you considering another school?" she asks me, point-blank.

"No!" I blurt. "No. It's MIT for me. It's always been MIT."

"Because I will just tell you, and not because it's my job to tell you this at this point, but if you love math, you should come to MIT. It'd be stupid to go anywhere else."

"I completely agree," I say. "That's why—"

"Not just because the professors are phenomenal and you'll be challenged and you'll be working on things you've never dreamed about, but because you're allowed to be yourself here. You're not expected to mold yourself into something else. You're celebrated for your own particular intellect. And that's something I don't think you can find anywhere else. Okay?"

"Okay."

"So sign up for the campus visit. I'll show you around."

"Okay."

"And keep those grades up, all right? They were serious about that. Because yes, they will accept you for who you are here, but they will also expect nothing less than your very best work. Got it?"

"Yes," I say, finding myself nodding even though she can't see me. "I understand."

"I'll see you in a few weeks, then," she says.

"Yeah. I'll see you then."

The minute I hang up the phone Mom comes charging back

into the kitchen. I wonder if she was just outside the door listening, although I'm sure she couldn't have gotten much from my series of okays.

"Everything all right?" she asks.

Excitement flutters in my stomach.

"I'm really going to MIT," I say, and it finally feels true. I have to write that stupid essay for English class, if Mrs. Blackburn will accept it more than a month late. I have to go to Miss Mahoney and see if I can improve upon my tragic midterm score. I have to show them my best.

Mom smiles, too. "You're really going to MIT."

I'm still in a bit of a daze from the MIT call when I meet Damian in the café at the SouthPointe Barnes & Noble. He looks freshly showered and he's wearing a black polo and clean jeans and not his standard gray hoodie.

I order a green tea latte.

"Are those good?" he asks when I pick it up from the end of the counter. "They're so green. They look like blended grass."

"They grow on you," I answer.

He orders a salted caramel mocha. We sit at a table for a while and discuss Kafka. Damian gives me a few other titles to try: Dostoyevsky's *Crime and Punishment* and James Joyce's *Dubliners* and Herman Melville's *Moby-Dick*. I'm going to be busy reading for a while.

Then the conversation stalls.

"So," I say after a few minutes of awkward silence. "This is going to sound silly, but I've become interested in poetry lately."

"What's silly about poetry?" he asks, shifting in his chair.

"Nothing! There's nothing silly about poetry, but I've been wanting to write some, and I'm finding out that I'm not any good at it. Do you read poetry?"

"Yeah. I read poetry," he says lightly. "I write some, too."

"Maybe you could give me some suggestions for poets I could read, and then I could imitate them or use them for inspiration or you could tutor me—"

"Lex," he interrupts. "Stop."

I stop my babbling. "What?"

"You don't have to . . ." He smiles. "You don't have to come up with ways to get my attention."

He reaches across the table and puts his hand over mine.

"I get it," he says. "I know what you're doing."

Heat rushes to my face. "You do?"

"When did you figure it out?" he asks.

I stare at him, then at his hand. "Figure it out," I repeat.

He laughs. "I knew it. On Wednesday, when you came up to me and wanted to talk about *Heart of Darkness*, I thought, She knows."

Naturally I have no idea what he's talking about. There's something off about the way he's looking at me. A warmth in his gray eyes. An expectation.

He's been interpreting this all wrong.

I am stupid.

I am smart, sure, but oh boy, in the romance department, I am a moron.

"Damian . . ." I don't know how to back out of this.

He lets go of my hand to reach down to unzip his backpack. "I brought you something."

He pulls out a rose made of paper.

It's made of red paper, this time. There are words on this one, too, an entire poem I can only read part of:

> *Loving in truth, and fain in verse my love to show*
> *That the dear She might take some pleasure of my pain*
> *Pleasure might cause her read, reading might make her*
> *know*

"It was you," I breathe.

"Guilty," he says.

"Last year, too. Valentine's Day. It was you."

"I found a pattern for a paper daisy in one of my mom's old magazines," he says. "And I thought of you. I'm glad you figured it out. I've wanted to tell you for such a long time."

"Why didn't you just write your name on it?" I ask, stricken.

"Too chicken, I guess. It was more romantic that way, right? And then you had a boyfriend, and you seemed happy with him, so I didn't want to—" He puts his hand over mine again. "But then you broke up with your boyfriend, and you and I started to talk more, and I thought . . . Lex?"

I've closed my eyes.

Steven didn't give me the flowers. He didn't write those words to me.

The disappointment of this revelation is like a knife in my chest—a hard pain, sharp and penetrating.

This is our place, too. This bookstore. Where Steven asked me. Right over there.

Where I said yes, and part of the reason I said yes was the paper flower.

It's not fair, I think. On top of everything else that gets taken away.

I want Steven to be the one who made me that flower.

"Lex?" Damian tries to console me for all the wrong reasons. "Hey. It's okay that you didn't figure it out earlier. You figured it out now. We can make up for lost time, right?"

I open my eyes just as he's leaning across the table to touch my cheek. I flinch and pull away, my hand sliding out from under his. "No."

His smile fades.

"I'm sorry," I gasp. "This isn't . . . I didn't mean to lead you on. . . . I didn't know."

He sits back. "You didn't know I made the flowers."

I shake my head, horrified at my own stupidity.

"But then why have you been . . . talking to me? You've been acting interested. You were acting like you liked me."

This is a train wreck. "Damian, I do like you," I begin. "But I don't feel like—it's not a romantic kind of thing. That's not what this is about for me."

His gray eyes are like cool stone now. Unreachable.

"You were buttering me up," he says in a low voice. "You were using me."

"No."

"Did you even read *The Metamorphosis*? Or was all of this some kind of bribe? So you could prep for MIT?"

"Yes! I mean, no, it wasn't a bribe. I did read the book. I liked it. I swear."

"What is this, then? What do you want?"

He's talking so loud that people are starting to glance over.

"Nothing," I say quietly. "I thought you seemed lonely, is all. I thought you could use a friend."

Wrong answer.

Damian draws himself up. "Oh. How altruistic of you, Lex. Since you're such a friendly girl yourself."

"Hey," I object. "Let's not forget that you had ulterior motives here, too. You were using the book thing to seduce me, right? You weren't just helping me out of the goodness of your heart."

He snorts. "*Seduce* is a strong word. And I was only doing it because I thought that's what you were doing. I thought you liked me," he accuses, spitting out the *t* on *thought*. "I really thought you liked me." For a moment his expression is tragic, like he might cry. Then he hardens himself. "I was wrong."

He's so upset that his hands shake as he gathers up his books.

"Damian, please. I'm so sorry."

"Don't," he says sharply. "I don't need your pity. You don't get to use me as your charity case because you feel bad that your brother died. I'm fine."

Then he's gone. The people around me stare for a minute and then go back to their previous conversations. I swallow.

I have to live with the fact that, in spite of my good intentions, I have just made everything worse.

30 March

The last time I saw my brother—in real life, I mean—it was the morning of December 20. The morning of the day he died. It started like any other morning. Mom cooked breakfast. We all sat around the table together, Mom with her cup of coffee and her toast, looking through a nursing scrubs catalog and me daydreaming about MIT, which I had just sent in my application for, and Ty doing what he always did at breakfast time: eating enough food to sustain a small African village.

I probably made some comment about it, the way he always ate like he was never going to get another meal.

He probably made his usual comment that he was a growing boy.

I don't remember that part. What I do remember is that sometime during that meal, Ty cleared his throat and said, "I was thinking about maybe getting my own car."

Mom stopped perusing uniforms, and I stopped imagining the tree-lined walkways at MIT, and we both looked at him. This comment was a little out of the blue, I thought. He hadn't even mentioned the idea of his own car around his sixteenth birthday.

"Okay," Mom said thoughtfully. "So how are you planning to acquire this car?"

His face fell. "I was thinking that maybe, between you and Dad, you might be able to—" He swallowed hard. "It wouldn't have to be a very nice car."

Mom was already shaking her head. "We don't have that kind of cash right now, honey. I'm sorry."

Because of the divorce, I thought and didn't say.

Ty turned to me for support. I lifted my hands in surrender. "Hey, don't look at me. I worked after school for three years to buy the Lemon. And it's the Lemon."

"Yes, that's what you'll have to do, honey," Mom said. "You'll have to save up."

Ty nodded, but it was a resigned kind of nod. He knew there was no way for him to get a real job with all his extracurricular activities— basketball being the big one.

I tried to soften the blow. "But come on, what would you do with a car, really?"

His eyes flashed. "I'd drive to school. I have my license. I'd take girls out on dates. I'd take road trips, get out of the state of Nebraska for once in my stupid life."

Mom and I exchanged worried glances.

Ty closed his eyes and sighed. "Anyway, it's fine. I just thought I'd ask."

And he went back to shoveling in his food.

I was thinking, as I finished up my own breakfast, that I could give him the Lemon. Once I got to MIT, of course. I wouldn't need a car there.

It was the Lemon, but still. It was a car. Maybe Ty could do what I had never bothered to attempt: he could fix the Lemon up.

But I didn't say any of that. I didn't tell him.

Mom finished her coffee. "It's off to work I go," she said cheerily. She paused as she got up from the table to smooth down a tuft of Ty's hair that was sticking up in back. "Have a good day, my beautiful children."

I probably rolled my eyes. Ty and I finished eating, and I left him to wash the dishes. Because it was his turn. I was nearly out the front door when I stopped to call out something like, "Hey, you better get with it or you'll miss the bus."

Ty appeared in the doorway. "I've got a ride with one of my buddies," he said.

A lie.

I didn't know that it was a lie. So I said whatever it was that I said, and I left the house.

That was the last time I saw him alive.

The last time.

But in the past few months I've found a way to reconstruct the rest of December 20. I can put the pieces together. I can figure out what happened from there.

First, Ty finished the dishes and ran the dishwasher. Because it was his turn.

Then he waited for the school to call the house to inquire about his

absence. He told the secretary that he was home sick, the stomach flu,
he said, couldn't keep anything down, he said, and that Mom forgot to
phone it in but he'd get her to call from work later.

Then he walked 7 miles in the ice and snow to the nearest city bus
stop.

He rode a bus into Lincoln and disembarked at the Westfield Gate-
way Mall.

This, according to a wad of receipts I found in his back jeans pocket
in his clothes hamper, was what his next few hours looked like:

11:17 a.m. Foot Locker, Nike LeBron XI basketball shoes, $199.99

11:33 a.m. Lids, Trailblazers T-shirt, $24.00

11:49 a.m. Sunglass Hut, Ray-Ban polarized sunglasses, $149.95

12:14 p.m. Panda Express. Shanghai Angus Steak bowl, $7.95

12:36 p.m. MasterCuts, shampoo and cut, $25.00

1:02 p.m. American Eagle, Slim Straight jean, dark tinted indigo,
$49.95

1:25 p.m. Precision Time, Toxic Area 51 men's watch, $189.00

2:18 p.m. J.C. Penney

>*Hanes 4-pack boxer shorts, $40.00*
>
>*Gold Toe 3-pack crew socks, $17.00*
>
>*Levi's reversible belt, $30.00*
>
>*Dockers trifold wallet, $28.00*
>
>*Dockers faux-leather black bomber jacket, $140.00*
>
>*Brighton collage picture frame $60.00*

All total, he spent $960.84, which we discovered later he stole from
a jar that Mom had hidden in the back of her closet for emergencies.
Almost exactly a thousand dollars, once you include the sales tax.

He could have almost bought a car for that.

Then he rode the bus back and walked the 7 miles so he could arrive home around 3:40 p.m., just in time to pick up the phone when Mom called to check on him, which she always did when he got home from school. He told her he had a good day.

Then, as far as I can figure, he spent the next 2 hours putting together the pictures in the collage out in the playhouse.

At 6:07 p.m., he ordered a pizza: Canadian bacon with pineapple, his favorite.

If it took the normal amount of time to be delivered, the pizza would have arrived by 6:45.

He ate three pieces, then wrapped the rest and stuck it in the fridge to save for Mom and me.

He put his plate in the dishwasher.

He spent some time doing regular stuff on the internet. He clicked on 3 fairly random links.

He set his new clothes—basketball shoes, socks, underwear, jeans, belt, wallet, Trailblazers T-shirt, bomber jacket, sunglasses—in a neat pile on top of his bed, for him to be buried in, we could only assume.

He made 2 phone calls, both to numbers that I don't know and I haven't had the guts to call to find out.

He sent 1 text.

He wrote 1 note.

Then, at 7:49 p.m., just as Mom was getting ready to get off her 12-hour shift, he went into the garage.

He loaded the gun. He took the safety off.

He called 911.

He pulled the trigger.

The bullet struck him in the chest, severing his subclavian artery.

It took him 30–60 seconds to bleed out.

And then he died.

33.

IN THIS DREAM, TY AND I are rock climbing, something we never did in real life. Okay, not rock climbing for fun, I surmise from our apparent lack of ropes and harnesses.

Cliff climbing.

On an at-least-five-hundred-foot cliff.

Fun times.

We don't talk in this dream. We focus on making our way up the rock face. It reminds me of the Cliffs of Insanity from *The Princess Bride*, the blue endless sky above us, the blue crashing ocean below us. Only there's no Andre the Giant to take us up. No rope to climb. We just have to make it on our own.

About twenty feet from the top, the ledge I put my weight on crumbles from under me.

I start to fall. I open my mouth to scream, like screaming is all you can do when you're about to plummet to your death, but before the sound leaves me Ty catches my hand. He pulls me to a safer spot.

"Thanks," I breathe.

"You really messed up," he says.

"I know."

"No, with Damian. That was a disaster."

"Yes. Yes, it was."

"You should apologize."

"I plan on it."

"You should work it out beforehand," he advises. "You're not very good on the spot."

"Oh, thank you, Ty. Thank you very much."

"No problem."

"How are we going to do this?" I ask him, craning my neck to look up the cliff.

"I don't know. Be more careful," he says.

The words have just left his mouth when he falls. It's not like it was with me a few seconds ago, all slow motion where I have time to scream and he has time to grab me. He reaches up, grabs a rock. He makes a distressed sound, like *whoops*. Then he's gone.

I look down just in time to see his body hit the rocks before a wave crashes over him.

34.

MONDAY MORNING.

I have a speech. An apology. A plan.

That's the funny thing about plans.

The first thing that goes wrong is that I wanted to drive to school today, in order to get to school early, in order to have plenty of time to seek out Damian, but then the Lemon doesn't start, and I spend so much time trying to get it to turn over that I miss the bus. I call Sadie hoping to get a ride, and—get this—she informs me primly that she took the bus herself. To save money. For her college books, she tells me.

Right.

I do finally get the Lemon started, but I don't get to school until after the first bell rings, so there's no time to head to room 121B with the crudely crafted paper flower I made for him yesterday, which says *I'm sorry* on every petal.

It's lame. It's pathetic. But I'm hoping it will work.

Then we have an impromptu danger drill at lunchtime, where we all have to pretend that there's a shooter on campus and get under the tables and lock all the doors, so I don't see Damian then, either.

But I can track him down during eighth period, I rationalize.

During sixth period, as everyone's getting set up for gin rummy, the game of the hour, I ask Miss Mahoney if we can talk.

"Absolutely," she says. "What's up?"

"I wonder if there's some extra credit I can do, to make up for my lousy midterm."

"Of course. Or you can still retake the test, if you'd like," Miss Mahoney says without hesitating, which is funny because there is no "of course" about it. "Will Friday work for you? Lunch hour?"

"Friday will work."

"Excellent. Friday it is."

I turn to head back to the card table, but she stops me. "Can I ask why you changed your mind?" she asks. "I mean, your original grade isn't great, but it's not that important in the grand scheme of things. You don't have anything to prove to me, Lex. I know you know your stuff. So you don't have to—"

"I got into MIT," I say.

The whole room goes quiet. Miss Mahoney's mouth falls open.

"As in the Massachusetts Institute of Technology. As in the best mathematics program in the country," she says. "That MIT."

"Yes. That MIT."

"Lex, that's amazing!" she says when she's recovered enough

347

to speak, and what's great is that I know she means it. Her face has gone pink, she's so pleased for me. "That's wonderful!"

"There's a part of the acceptance letter that warns that their offer is contingent on me passing the rest of the school year with flying colors," I say.

"I see. That makes sense."

"So I intend to give them flying colors."

She looks like she's about to start dancing. "I have no doubt that you will, Lex. Wow. MIT. Congratulations."

"Thank you." I allow myself to smile about it then, for the first time. I let myself feel it.

Back at the card table my friends are all staring at me with a quiet awe.

"Very impressive," Eleanor says as I take a seat next to her. "You deserve it."

This is big coming from her, because I know she applied to MIT herself, and this must mean she didn't get in or hasn't heard yet.

"Thanks, El."

Beaker, on the other hand, looks pissed.

"You didn't tell me you got into MIT," she accuses, shuffling the cards like she's punishing them.

Uh-oh. I'm in trouble. "I didn't know how to tell everybody," I try to explain. "I think I wanted some time for the news to sink in before I went public."

She still looks pissed. Clearly this excuse isn't good enough for her. She's my best friend. She should have been the first person I called.

"What about you? Have you heard back from any place yet?" I backpedal.

"Williams College. Sarah Lawrence. Amherst. But I'm still waiting for Wellesley."

"I'm sure you'll get in," I tell her. Beaker's been fantasizing about Wellesley for a while, something about it being all women and one of the best liberal arts colleges and Beaker wanting to explore career options, since in addition to math and science Beaker loves theater and plays a killer flute solo, and she doesn't know what she wants to be when she grows up.

She nods, but her expression says she doesn't forgive me.

We settle into playing rummy. A few minutes into the game I notice that Steven is smiling. Like he can't stop smiling. A secret kind of smile.

"What?" I ask finally. "What's going on with you?"

His smile widens. "Nothing. It's just that I'm happy for you. Truly."

He picks up a seven of hearts from the discard pile and sets down three pairs of sevens.

Eleanor snorts. "Right. You're happy for you, too."

"El," he warns. "Don't."

Don't what?

She ignores him and turns to me like this is something that needs to be said and she has appointed herself the messenger. "He's going to Harvard."

I glance quickly at Steven, who's blushing. "You got into Harvard?" I gasp.

"I got into Harvard," he admits.

This is huge. I feel the urge to hug him, to celebrate, but that would be decidedly awkward. "You got into Harvard! Why wouldn't you want her to tell me that?"

He scratches at the back of his neck. "It felt like we should be celebrating your moment, that's all."

Eleanor smirks. "Right."

I still don't get what she's being so cat-ate-the-canary about. "What's wrong with you?"

She fixes me with a no-nonsense stare, like she doesn't understand why I haven't already figured this out. "MIT and Harvard are both in Cambridge, Massachusetts. Did you know that?" she asks.

"I think I did know that, yes," I say, and I understand immediately where she's going with it.

"I visited both campuses last year. They're two miles apart." She pulls out her phone (which we are not supposed to do in class but Miss Mahoney generally allows because she's not supposed to be watching YouTube, either) and does a quick search. "Yes. It's one-point-nine-six miles from MIT to Harvard. Nine minutes, by car. You and Steven will be one-point-nine-six miles away from each other for the next four years. Now do you see why he's so ridiculously happy?"

"El, come on," Steven says, and he's really blushing now.

My face is red, too. I turn to Steven, who's meticulously studying his cards. "So you're going, of course. To Harvard. Not to Yale or Dartmouth or any of the others?"

He doesn't smile this time, but it's in his eyes. "That's the plan."

"I bet your family is thrilled."

"They're over the moon. I'm the first Blake male who's not going to be a farmer, and they could not be happier."

"And how about you, is it what you wanted?" I know it is. We didn't discuss it much when we were applying. We didn't want to pressure each other. But it was the best-case scenario: me at MIT, Steven at Harvard.

It meant the possibility of more.

But that was before.

His warm brown eyes meet mine.

"Well, you know," he murmurs. "I hear Harvard's a pretty good place to study chemistry."

I instantly have butterflies in my stomach, and I try to squash them. I wet my lips and attempt to breathe properly. How does he keep making me feel this way, even with all that's happened? I should not feel this way.

I think about what Ty wrote in his letter, how it's so obvious that Steven and I are right for each other. That we fit.

Beaker and Eleanor have been looking back and forth from me to Steven gleefully, like they'd like a bowl of popcorn. Then Beaker throws me a lifeline.

"Hey, are we playing cards here or what?" she asks, rearranging the cards in her hand. "Time is candy, you know."

We go back to playing, but Steven is still smiling.

I have a hard time concentrating on the game.

* * *

I'm so befuddled by the exchange with Steven, the idea of Steven at Harvard, that I forget to ditch eighth period. So I don't remember about delivering the paper daisy to Damian until the bell rings at the end of the day.

I check his locker. He's not there. I try his cell phone, but it goes straight to voice mail.

I bump into El in the commons, where everybody is milling around.

"Lex, are you feeling all right? You look scared," she observes.

I am scared, for a reason I can't quite put my finger on. Damian should be here. Why isn't he here? A bad feeling is boiling up from the pit of my stomach. "Can you help me find Damian Whittaker?" I ask El.

"Sure. Who's Damian Whittaker?"

I fish the photo of the three amigos out of my backpack. "This one." I point to Damian.

"Oh, Gray Hoodie," she says. "I know him."

We check the library. The gym. We start walking down the halls, poking our head into random classrooms, hoping to find him. Somewhere along the way we pick up Beaker, then Steven, who checks the guys' bathrooms and locker room.

No Damian.

Back in the commons, El hacks the school's computer system to check the attendance record. "He's marked absent today. No explanation as to why. It's an unexcused absence," she says from behind her laptop. "Which means his parents didn't call him in sick."

That's when the terrible thought occurs to me.

I grab El's laptop and turn it toward me. I check a few of Damian's social media websites before I stumble across a new poem on one of them:

> *She makes the stars go out.*
> *She makes the rain.*
> *I give her my heart*
> *as a rose made of paper*
> *but she lets it fall*
> *on the dirty floor.*
> *She gives me a cup*
> *full of pity and pain*
> *to drown myself in.*

And this is when the terrible thought becomes even more terrible.

"What does that even mean?" El asks from over my shoulder, reading the screen.

The poem was posted an hour ago. I try to ignore the panicked clenching in my stomach and take out my phone to call Damian's cell. I get his voice mail again.

"Hi, you've reached Damian. You know what to do," he says.

I hang up. I don't think he'd want to hear my voice right now. But I have to see if he's home.

"Get me his home number," I say to El. "The landline."

She finesses the school's records system again, and produces a number.

It rings and rings and rings. No answer. No machine.

"Lex, who is this guy?" Steven asks.

"Gray Hoodie," El fills in helpfully.

I jump up. "I have to go. What's his address?"

She clicks some keys. "2585 West Mill Road."

I'm already running for the school's front door. For the parking lot. For my car.

El, Beaker, and Steven fall in behind me.

"2585 West Mill Road," I repeat to myself. "That's not far, right?"

"It's about ten minutes, I think," Steven calculates.

But the Lemon doesn't start.

I turn to my friends, panting a little. "Tell me one of you drove."

El doesn't have a car, and Beaker looks guilty. "No," she says. "I got a ride with Antonio."

I turn to Steven. He shakes his head. "Sarah has the car today."

I try the Lemon again, but it's no use.

Why? I think. Why will the universe not give me a freaking break?

"Lex," Steven starts nervously. "What's going on? Do you think that Damian is . . . Why do you think that Damian's going to—"

I shake my head. "Be quiet for a second, okay? I need to think."

So I think as hard as I've ever thought. I strain every neuron. And I see the answer.

I dial and lift the phone to my ear.

"Come on," I whisper. "Come on. Be awake."

"Hello?" says a sleepy voice. "What's up?"

354

"Seth," I breathe in relief. "This is Lex. I need a favor."

"Sure, Lex," he says. "Your wish is my command, yo."

"Thanks." I meet Steven's eyes. "Seth, I'm going to need that ride."

35.

TWELVE MINUTES LATER I'M FLYING UP North 27th Street headed out of town, my teeth chattering, my hair tucked into Seth's helmet, holding Seth tight around the ribs.

It's warmer out now, but still chilly. Over our heads white cirrostratus clouds are stretched in rows across the sky, cut by the sharp trail of a plane descending into the Lincoln airport.

"Are you all right back there?" Seth yells.

"Can we go any faster?" I yell back.

We're going so fast already, but Seth pushes the engine harder, making the telephone poles start whipping by us at an increased rate.

I'm so cold I can't feel my face.

We turn on West Mill Road and head out into the deep farm country, cornfields and more cornfields. The snow has melted, leaving the muddy brown fields stubbled with the dead cornstalks from last year. The farmers will plow it all under soon and plant again. The air smells like cow manure and fresh water and growing things.

It smells like spring.

I hope we're not too late.

Seth asks for the number again, and I yell, "2585," and he slows way down and yells, "I think this is it up here."

We pull off onto a long driveway and drive up to a gray two-story house.

I recognize Damian's car parked out front. "Yes, this is it."

Seth takes us right up to the front step. I clutch at him as he leans to put his foot down.

"You'll have to get off first," he says. "Just swing your leg around."

I dismount in the most awkward way possible and take off the helmet. I hand it back to Seth. We both step back to get a look at the house.

"Whoa," Seth says. "Gothic. I bet this place is haunted."

Ramshackle is the word I would use. It's your basic two-story farmhouse with the windows that look like eyes and the door like a mouth. It needs a new paint job and maybe a new roof, and it does look like something out of an old black-and-white horror movie, but it has good bones, as Beaker would say.

I climb the porch steps and knock on the door.

Nobody answers.

I knock again, harder. I find a doorbell, but when I press it I don't hear any sound.

"I don't think he's home," Seth says.

"No, he's home. That's his car." I point. I bang on the door with the flat of my hand. "Damian! Open up! It's Lex!"

No answer.

He's mad at me. Maybe I shouldn't scream "it's Lex" quite so loudly.

I try his cell again. I try the home number. We listen to it ringing inside the house.

I feel more desperate with each ring. "Damian!" I scream. "Come on!"

Seth looks worried. "Lexie, what's this about? Why are you so . . . freaked?"

"Damian was Ty's friend. Ty's and Patrick's." I bang again. "Damian!"

"Yeah, so. . ."

"So he's depressed right now. And I did something on Saturday that upset him, and he didn't show up to school today, and he posted this poem on the internet, and . . ." I call the house number again. "Come on, pick up, Damian."

It rings and rings.

Seth looks at the house with a new awareness. "So you think he might off himself?" He glances at me, cringes. "Sorry. You think he would . . ."

"I think he would. I have to get in there."

Seth pounds on the door. "Damian! Come on out, dude!"

I go around the side of the house, checking the windows. They're all locked. I try the back door. Locked. I try the other side of the house.

On that side I suddenly become aware of music floating down from a second-story window. Acoustic guitar. Then a lone male voice.

Robert Plant's voice. From "Stairway to Heaven."

"Damian!" I holler up at the window.

No answer. No movement. Nothing.

Seth comes up beside me. He squints at the house. "Hey, there's a light on," he says.

"I'd bet money that's Damian's room." I glance around wildly. There's no way to get up there, no convenient, helpful tree or gutter to climb. I cry out in frustration and head back to the front door, Seth trailing me.

"Are you going to call the cops?" he asks warily, like he gets why I would need to do that, but he's not too fond of the police.

"No. It would take too long. I need to get in there now," I say, my mind going a mile a minute. I turn to face him. "Pick the lock."

"What."

"He's in there. He could be dead already. He could be dying. Right now. Do it, Seth."

Seth glances toward the bedroom window. "You think he's killing himself right now."

"I think there's a strong possibility. If we're lucky, he didn't do it fifteen minutes ago. I know he was alive an hour ago. But now I don't know."

He rubs a hand over the back of his head. "Man."

"Pick the lock, Seth."

"Hey. I don't know how to pick a lock. What, did you think that just because I smoke and ride a motorcycle and I have some tattoos, it must mean I'm a criminal? Hey, what are you doing now?"

I don't look up from my phone. "Googling how to pick a lock."

"You're—"

I dump my backpack out onto the grass and sort through what comes out until I find two large paper clips. I get to work shaping them into lockpicks.

Sometimes it pays to be a nerd and carry around a large assortment of office supplies as a general habit.

"Whoa," Seth says. "I don't know if I like this. It's illegal, right, breaking and entering?"

I'm on the porch by this point, crouching in front of the door.

"You're making me, like, an accessory," Seth says.

I push the straightened pin into the lock. "You're free to go."

He doesn't go, though. He watches me as I try and fail and try and fail again.

"Okay, so, you can't pick the lock, so what are you going to do n—"

"Here." I hand my phone to him. "Read it out loud to me—the part with the raking. It says the squiggly paper clip is the rake, and the straight one is the tension wrench, but then what does it say?"

He stares at me. "Lexie."

"Help or go, Seth. Help or go."

He sighs and clears his throat lightly. "'First, slip your tension wrench into the bottom of the keyhole and use gentle pressure in the direction you want to turn the lock. Then, take your rake and

360

quickly slide it back and forth to jostle the pins into place.'"

"Go on." I swipe at my forehead with my sleeve. "What next?"

"'After raking back and forth through the lock, quickly jerk the rake out of the keyhole while attempting to turn the tension wrench. If everything has gone just right—'"

There's a loud click. I turn the knob. The door swings open.

"I can't believe that worked," Seth murmurs.

I'm already taking the stairs two at a time. I'm sprinting down the upstairs hall. "Damian!"

I follow the music to the last door on the left. The song is in the hard rock part of it by this time, loud and wailing. I try the door. It's locked.

I left the paper clips downstairs.

I imagine Damian behind this door, his body sprawled on the carpet, his wrists cut and bleeding, his eyes open but unseeing.

"Whoa, Lex, wait!" Seth's coming up behind me as I raise my foot and kick at the door hard. It crashes open on the first try, the cheap particle board door splintering, and I push into the room, Damian's name on my lips.

He's there.

He's sitting at his desk in his boxers, staring at me, his mouth fallen open. The music is so loud around us I can't hear anything else. I stand there, chest heaving, staring.

Slowly he reaches up and turns off the speakers.

I feel like I've gone deaf. "Damian," I manage to get out. "You're alive."

"Uh," Seth pipes up from behind me. "I'll be outside, 'kay?"

Damian closes his eyes and opens then again slowly, like he must be hallucinating the sight of me.

I'm so happy to see him alive that I can't help but smile.

"So," I say after a minute. "This is awkward."

He scratches at the side of his neck. "Can you turn around or close your eyes or something so I can put my pants on?"

"Sure." I clap a hand over my eyes.

"Not that I haven't fantasized about a situation like this," he says. I hear the whisper of denim, the zip of a fly. "Okay."

I lower my hand. He sits down on the end of his bed and puts on a T-shirt and socks. He motions for me to sit in the desk chair where he was sitting a minute ago.

I sit.

"Okay," he says. "Let's start with, what are you doing here, Lex?"

"You weren't at school today."

"I was sick," he explains.

"You don't look sick."

His face is turning red. "I was embarrassed. I didn't want to see you. Okay?"

I nod. "I was worried about you."

"Why?"

"I read your poem."

His eyes brighten. "You read my poem." He tries to keep his voice steady, casual. "What did you think?"

"I thought you might . . . I thought you were feeling so bad that you . . ."

Finally he understands. "You thought I'd be like Ty. And Patrick."

I let out a breath. "Yes."

His watery eyes meet mine. He brushes his hair out of his eyes and leans forward, settling his weight onto his knees. "I'm not like Ty and Patrick," he says very slowly, like he wants to be sure I understand every word. "I don't want to die. Things can get bleak sometimes, at school. There are bullies, right?"

"The carrion few," I supply.

He glances away, laughs weakly. "Right. But I don't have it in me to . . . It's just high school, man. Those guys are just high school guys, and in ten years they're going to be working for people like me. I know that. I have to make it through two more years, and then I'll be home free. I swear, I couldn't ever do what Ty did. I would *never*."

He takes a deep breath and lets it out. "I'm sorry if my poems made you think I would."

"I'm sorry that I inspired one of those poems," I reply.

I feel something sharp in my pocket, poking into my hip. I remember what it is and pull it out.

Ty's shark necklace.

I hold it out to Damian. "Here. I found this."

He takes it and fingers the edge of the tooth gently. Suddenly there are tears in his eyes.

"I should have told you," he says. "I've been working up to it, but I didn't know how."

"Told me what?"

He swallows. "Ty called me, the night he died."

It feels like my heart's stopped beating, but I know it hasn't. If my heart stopped beating I would die. But here I sit, alive. Breathing. Listening.

Damian's voice wavers as he keeps talking. "I knew that Ty sometimes thought about . . . what he did. Two years ago, the first time he tried, with the pills, he told me afterwards."

"He told you?" I never knew that Ty told anyone.

"We were playing this song by the Doors—'The End'—and he told me. I said, you know, we can talk about how things suck and how our parents are assholes and how the future isn't exactly super bright, but I still think life's worth living, don't you? And he said, yeah, he knew that. And I said that if he ever felt that way again, like ending it, that he should call me. And he said he would."

"And he called you," I whisper. "You talked to him."

Damian nods. "But he didn't say anything that night about wanting to die. It wasn't that unusual for him to call me, actually, not so unusual that I thought anything was up. We've kept in touch, even though we don't hang out much at school. He calls—he called me sometimes and we'd talk about how life blows and people are morons and how most people don't understand what it's like when your life just goes to crap and there's nothing you can do about it. He read my poems sometimes, too. So that's what we talked about that night. The same old stuff."

He shakes his head. "I should have known something was wrong. He'd just broken up with Ashley, and he was low; he seemed like he was stuck in his own head, and I should have figured out that something was off." He snuffles. "I've thought about it so many times since then, been over the entire conversation back and forth, looking for clues that I should have picked up, but . . . sometimes I think he just called me to say goodbye."

He clutches the shark tooth in his hand and starts full-out crying. I move to sit on the bed next to him and try to hug him, and he lets me for a little while. Then he pulls away and drags his hand through his hair and sighs.

"I'm sorry I didn't save him," he says. "I would have tried."

My heart aches for him, because those words are my words, and those thoughts are my thoughts, and I finally understand why they don't matter.

"You couldn't have saved him," I answer. "Nobody could have saved Ty but Ty. And you're probably right. He wasn't calling so that he would be talked out of it. He was calling to say goodbye."

Damian nods miserably.

I squeeze his shoulder. "You were a good friend to him. And to me. Thank you for that."

We sit for a minute not speaking. Then I ask him, "Are you okay? Do you need to write a poem to get it all cleaned out?"

He laughs. "I'll back off the black-hearted poetry."

I shrug one shoulder. "I'm not a book critic or anything, but I like your poems, Damian. Although I wouldn't give you a cup full of pity and pain to drown yourself in. I'm all out of pity."

I stand up and go to the window. Outside, the sun is setting over the cornfields, a marvelous haze of fire orange and royal purple. I watch a vee of large birds—sandhill cranes, I think—riding the air.

Migrating home.

There is so much inside me in that moment, I feel like I'll burst. So much I understand now that I didn't yesterday. So much to say.

"Lex?" Damian asks from behind me. "What are you going to do now?"

I turn. "Actually, do you mind if I borrow a pen?"

I need to tell you about that night. I know you already know the details. You were there. But I need you to see it from my perspective, so you will understand why I did what I did.

That night we had dinner at the Imperial Palace. You had lemon chicken, like you always do, and I ordered kung pao chicken. Over dinner we were talking about MIT and Harvard and Beaker maybe going to Wellesley and how we had at least 70 days left before we heard anything, and how hard it was to wait. March felt like eons away, that night.

After dinner you took me to the natural history museum at UNL. It was closed for the night, but because your sister works there, she let us in. I knew you were planning something spectacular by the look on Sarah's face, the way she kept smiling at me. You left me in the elephant hall, staring at the giant fossilized bones of prehistoric mammoths and camels and rhinos that used to roam the grassy plains that once stretched across the middle of the country hundreds of thousands of years ago, while you and Sarah disappeared for a while to set things up.

Then you came and got me. You blindfolded me, but I could tell you were leading me to the planetarium. How many shows had we seen there, Steven, really? You sat me down on a soft blanket. I could smell candle wax and your aftershave. There was music playing—Mozart, I think; you'll have to tell me sometime, what, exactly it was—a soft serenade of piano and violin.

You took off the blindfold.

We were sitting on a red plaid blanket, like we were having a picnic in the woods, with two short white candles burning in the center, and a bottle of sparkling cider in a bucket of ice, and two plastic champagne glasses. On the planetarium ceiling, thousands of tiny blue lights shone down on us: not stars or constellations, but particles.

"It's from the show on dark matter," you said.

I craned my neck to gaze up. "I thought dark matter was invisible."

You leaned back and put your arm around me, pulling me to your chest, and I relaxed into the heat of your body.

"It is invisible," you said. "Well, theoretically, it is. Scientists have never been able to prove that dark matter exists, you know."

I did know.

"We can only truly conceive of the fact that it's there because of the way the galaxies behave as they move through the universe, and how the light will always bend around it." You shifted your body closer to mine. You looked down at my lips. I knew you were going to kiss me. Your breath, which smelled like lemons, bathed my face. You looked into my eyes.

"Anyway," you murmured. "It's pretty."

You kissed me. I curled my hand around the back of your head, your hair soft under my fingers, and kissed you back. Blue lights spun over our heads. You kissed the corner of my mouth. My cheek. My ear.

I smiled. "So. This is romantic."

"Yes. I wanted to be romantic." You laced your fingers with mine. "It's December twentieth," you announced.

"Yes?"

You tucked a strand of my hair behind my ear. "On June twentieth, six months ago today, we started this little experiment. In a bookstore, which was not the most romantic place, but the best I could do at the moment. I didn't think I'd be able to get you in here back then. And on June twentieth, I kissed you for the very first time."

"It was a good kiss."

"Spectacular," you remembered.

"So happy six months," I said.

"Happy six months. Which is precisely 183 days." You consulted your watch. "Which is 4,392 hours. Which is 263,520 minutes. Which have been some of the best minutes of my life. So far."

God, you were sexy.

Irresistible.

I pulled your head down to kiss you again, but my phone suddenly buzzed.

I took it out and looked at it.

It was a text.

I never told you who it was from. I never said, "It's my brother." I never told you what it said.

All this time, and I've never told anyone.

But I'll tell you now.

It said, Hey sis can you talk?

This is the part where reality unravels for me, the part where I turned the phone off, and slid it away from me, and we went back to kissing.

But there's an alternate version of what happened that night. There always will be, for me. In the alternate version of reality I get the text and I tell you, "Hold that thought," and I kiss you quick, once, on the mouth, but then I get up and take the phone to the hallway and I call Ty. In that reality—which I know isn't a reality but a fantasy, wishful thinking, a prayer that goes unanswered—Ty tells me what I need to know. That he is sad. That he's stuck in the present. He can't get perspective. He's lost the future.

Then I tell him that he's strong enough to get through the sadness.

I tell him I don't want to go through this messed-up world without him, and I tell him that I need him.

I tell him Mom needs him.

I tell him even Dad needs him—he may not see that right now, but he will see it, sometime.

I tell him that in 5 more days it will be Christmas, and I remind him that Christmas is his favorite holiday, and we'll wake up early and bounce up and down on Mom's bed like we did when we were little, and we'll belt out "Silver Bells" as we scurry downstairs to the Christmas tree and unwrap our presents, and I got him something good this year, and doesn't he want to find out what it is?

I tell him that we have a minimum of 63 Christmases left to share with each other, and I don't want to miss even one of those. Not one.

I tell him I love him.

And me telling him those things is enough to slay his demons.

And he lives through the night.

He lives.

But instead, I turned my phone off, and I kissed you. We stretched out under the dark matter, that invisible, improvable stuff that binds the universe, and I looked up at you, all framed in blue lights, and I said that I loved you.

Your eyes flashed with surprise. You didn't expect me to say it. You thought I didn't believe in love.

But you didn't hesitate to answer.

"I love you, too," you said. "So much."

"It's impractical, how much," I whispered.

You nodded. "Totally impractical."

We drank the cider and talked about dark matter and talked about how we are all made of the stuff of stars, that wonderful quote from Carl Sagan. We are each part of the universe.

Then somehow the conversation shifted to the subject of sandhill cranes.

How every year, in March if the weather holds, 80% of the world's population of sandhill cranes pass through this one part of Nebraska, millions of birds all at once, and how it's supposed to be this incredible sight to behold, and how we'd both lived in Nebraska for our entire lives and we'd never seen the cranes. We would go, we decided. Before we went off to Massachusetts or wherever fate was going to take us, we would go see the sandhill cranes. Together.

We kissed then, and time bent around us. Time went away.

But somewhere in those missing seconds, my brother was walking into the dark cocoon of the garage with Dad's old hunting rifle and a bullet I must have overlooked.

To ruin everything, I think sometimes.

To die.

We only came back to ourselves when Sarah burst into the planetarium, and I knew the second I saw the look on her face that something was terribly, terribly wrong, and that something involved me.

I remember she said, "She's right here," before she handed me her phone.

I remember it was my dad's voice I heard then, sharp, like I was in trouble for something, like he was grounding me. "It's Ty," the sharp voice said.

I don't remember what else.

I was looking at you. He was telling me. My hand started to shake—not tremble, not waver, but shake, violently, like I was having a seizure. I couldn't control it.

You reached up and put your hand on mine. You held me steady.

After I hung up, you guided me down the hall toward the parking lot. You put your coat around my shoulders. You knelt beside me when I suddenly veered off and bent and vomited my kung pao chicken onto the snowy sidewalk next to the giant mammoth statue in front of the museum. You helped me stand up. You smoothed the hair away from my face. You reached over me to buckle my seat belt, once you got me in the car.

There were Christmas lights all along the way to the mortuary, red and green and white, strung through the trees.

The whole time, your eyes were wide and incredulous, like this couldn't really be happening.

At the mortuary, you waited in the hall while the funeral director took me and Mom and Dad into her office and played us a recording. Ty had called 911, seconds before he pulled the trigger. It took me a few days to piece together why he would do this, but it was a kindness, I've concluded, so Mom or I wouldn't come home and find him when we opened the garage.

We listened to his voice and confirmed that it was Ty.

He said, "There's a dead person in the garage in the green house on the corner of Nickols and Second Street. He killed himself."

That was it. He hung up. It was 12 minutes before the ambulance got there, they told us, but he was already gone.

He didn't sound scared, in the recording. He didn't sound sad. He was perfectly matter-of-fact about it.

They took us into a back room, where Ty's body was lying on a steel table with a sheet covering him up to his neck. We stood for a minute in a tight semicircle just looking at him—Dad in his suit and tie, then me, then Mom in her scrubs—the last time we were truly a family together.

Then Mom stepped forward and laid shaking hands on Ty's chest, like maybe she could wake him, and when he didn't stir, she tipped her head back and a sound came out of her that was sheer pain—a mix of howl and wail that didn't even sound like her voice anymore, that didn't sound exactly human. I'm sure you heard it, from where you were.

Dad put his hand over his mouth and closed his eyes and stumbled back to a chair against the wall.

The sound kept coming out of Mom, and it was unbearable in the way it filled my ears and my head and solidified everything.

My brother was dead.

Mom's knees gave out. I caught her before she hit the floor and dragged her to the chair next to Dad's, and she stopped howling and cried in breathless, ragged bursts.

There was nowhere for me to sit next to them. All I could do was stand and stare at Ty.

He looked like he was made of wax. One of his eyes was coming open. He had beautiful eyelashes—thick and dark and curved just right—and between the seam of lashes there was a sliver of pale gray, like dirty snow. His lips were almost black. This was before you saw him, before the makeup and the formal clothes and the stiff folded hands. There was a smear of blood on his neck, disappearing under the sheet. I was struck with the urge to pull back the sheet and see the wound that killed him, something that would explain this terrible mystery of him being this empty thing when I'd just seen him twelve hours earlier, at the breakfast table, and he was fine.

I would have looked, but Mom and Dad were there. I backed away and stood by Mom and held her hand and cried with her until we both ran dry.

I can't cry anymore. I think that part of myself is broken.

When it came time to leave, Mom didn't want to go. She would have stayed with Ty all night, all day, until we buried him. But they made her go back into Jane's office to sign some papers and talk about the next steps in the process of losing her child.

You were still waiting in the hall. You stood up when I opened the

374

door. Your eyes said you believed it now.

That's when I remembered the text.

I took the phone out of my pocket and checked, and it was still there.

Hey sis can you talk?

Ice washed over me. Dread. Numbness. I shoved the phone back into my pocket. I looked up at you. I thought, This is your fault.

If you hadn't kissed me.

If you hadn't distracted me.

If I hadn't been so tangled up in the emotions I felt for you, the impractical emotions, I would have answered the text.

I would have stopped this.

I didn't stop this.

And I thought again, It's your fault.

I thought, I wish time travel was a viable option. If I could make a time machine, I would go back to that moment, and I would answer that text.

I'd save him.

I understand now that nobody could have saved Ty but Ty. There's no one else to blame. Not you. Not me. Ty was holding all the cards.

I understand this now, with my head.

My heart still wishes for the time machine. I will have to make my heart forgive us for that night.

I can forgive you so much more easily than I can forgive myself.

And there's so much I would ask you to forgive me for:

For shutting you out.

For the way I stopped talking to you.

For the absolutely stupid reason I gave as to why I wanted to break up.

I didn't break up with you because of your sperm. Or because it wasn't working between us, because it was working. It worked.

You deserve the truth.

Whether you choose to forgive me or not, you deserve to know that I meant it. What I said that night.

I love you.

I tried really hard not to. You have no idea how hard I tried.

Or maybe you do have some idea.

But I love you.

If you don't know what to do with this information, that's okay.

I just want to tell you everything, if you want to hear it. If you want to know.

I'll start with this.

36.

WHEN I COME OUT OF DAMIAN'S HOUSE, Seth is sitting on the porch steps smoking a cigarette.

"Is everything all right with the kid?" he asks.

"Yeah. He's going to be okay."

"Good," he says with genuine relief. "I was about to come in and get you. I have to go. I'm late for work."

"You should go," I tell him.

"You going to need a ride anywhere?"

I clutch my backpack to my chest. "I can get a ride. Thank you, Seth. Really. Thank you."

"No sweat." He takes a long drag. "I'll call you if I ever need to pick a lock. Damn."

I laugh and take the cigarette out of his mouth and step on it.

"What the hell?"

"I'm trying to keep everyone from killing themselves today," I explain.

He snorts and gives me a half-irritated smirk. Then he gets on the motorcycle, puts his helmet on, and starts up Georgia with a roar. I wave as he speeds away.

I can't believe I rode that thing.

I get out my cell. Mom won't be off work for another hour. I take a deep breath and dial another number.

"Hey, Dad," I say when he answers. "Can you come get me? Everything's okay—I'm fine, but I need a ride."

Dad pulls up to Steven's house and puts the car in park. We both peer out from the windshield for a minute. The Blakes' house is a white two-story farmhouse with a big wraparound porch, like a well-maintained and well-loved version of Damian's house. All the lights are on. The windows are bright, and the house looks warm.

Steven is lucky to live in that house, with his mom and his dad and his sisters, all under that roof.

I try very hard not to resent him for that.

I ring the bell. Sarah answers. I can tell by the look on her face that she's not sure what she thinks of me being here right now.

"Is Steven home?" I ask.

She pushes the door open and steps aside to allow me to come in. "Steven!" she yells as she stalks off. "Someone to see you."

My heart starts going fast when he appears at the end of the hall. For roughly 2.5 seconds I almost chicken out.

"Hi," he says softly. "How's Damian? I've been so worried all day. But I figured you would have called if . . ."

"Damian's all right. False alarm."

Steven lets out a breath. "Good. Whew. Good." He tilts his head to one side, confused now as to why I'm here, and looks at me hard, before seeming to decide something. "Do you want to have dinner with us? We just sat down."

"Oh, thanks, but no. My dad's waiting for me in the car."

"Your dad?"

"I just stopped by to give you this."

I hand him the journal.

He looks at me blankly. "Should I know what—"

"No. It's an experiment, of sorts. It started out as an assignment from my therapist." I find that I can't look directly at him when he's holding the journal. "I want you to read it. I mean, if you want to read it. You don't have to. Dave—my therapist—he said that I needed a recipient for my writing, like an audience. And tonight I figured out—I've concluded—that my recipient is you. If you want to read it. If you don't, I get that, and I can take it—"

"I'll read it," he says, taking a step back like I might make a grab for it.

I think, Oh dear God, what have I done?

"Good," I say, backing toward the door. "Have a nice night."

Dad drives me home. He doesn't ask questions, which I appreciate. When I get to the front door, Mom comes out to meet me. She looks a little bit freaked out. She watches Dad drive off without comment.

"Do I want to know?" she asks.

"No. Is there anything to eat? I'm starved."

She finds us a box of macaroni and cheese, which she makes on the stove and then cuts some hot dogs into. I feel about five years old when I'm eating it, but I wolf it down. Mom watches me until I finish.

"Are you all right, Lexie?" She reaches across the table and grabs my hand. "Do you want to talk about it? I'm here for you, sweetie. I know things have been hard, but I'm here for you. I will always be here for you."

I squeeze her hand. "I know. I know you are." I take a deep breath. "I was at Damian's house this afternoon. He was one of Ty's friends."

"Yes, I know Damian," she says. "Did you know, he put the most beautiful paper rose into your brother's coffin? I've never seen anything quite like it."

Wow, the things I did not know that would have been so helpful. "Anyway, I thought that Damian might be feeling like Ty and Patrick, and that he might need my help. But then it turned out that he helped me."

She nods. "Funny how that works."

"I'm sorry for how I've been."

She blinks at me, startled. "How you've been? There's nothing wrong with how you've been. You've been getting by the best you can."

"Well, I'm sorry for how I acted in the car on the way home from Graceland. That was not okay."

"You said what I needed to hear," she says. "I'm glad you did. It woke me up to what I was doing to you, while I was paying so much more attention to myself."

"Mom . . ."

"I kept feeling your brother near me," she says with a sigh, looking down into her lap. "Sometimes I would smell him, or I would hear his footsteps on the stairs, and I was trying to drink it away, Lex, and I'm sorry for that. I won't do it again."

"Okay."

"About a week ago, I was driving back from work," she says, "and I felt this presence with me, in the car."

Uh-oh. Ghost in the car. Never a good thing.

"I was crying, the way I . . . do sometimes, and then I just felt it so strongly, that someone was there with me."

She shakes her head like she still can't believe it.

"And then what?" I prompt.

"Then I heard the voice."

I stare at her. "And what did Ty say?"

She glances up at me, startled. "It wasn't Tyler, sweetie."

"It wasn't?" I'm confused now.

"It was another voice. And it said, 'Will you put your son in my hands?'"

I swallow, hard. "Mom . . ."

"And I said yes," she murmurs. She lowers her head again, but she's not crying. "I said yes." She takes a deep breath, the kind of breath you take when a weight has suddenly been lifted from your shoulders.

"I haven't felt Ty since then," she tells me.

I put my hand over hers.

It has been one crazy day.

The doorbell rings. Mom and I glance at each other.

"I'll get it," I say.

I go to the door and open it. On the other side is Steven, the journal in his hand. He looks thrashed, red-eyed and bleary, and his hair in the front is all poufed up like he's been tugging on it.

Steven's a fast reader. I'd forgotten that.

"Hi," I whisper.

He's crying. He lunges through the door and folds me into his arms, crying.

"I'm sorry. I'm sorry. I'm sorry," he says, and sobs into my hair.

Something inside me fractures. Breaks.

"I'm sorry, too," I say, and I'm crying then, finally, like the floodgates have opened, and we're clinging to each other, weeping, as the water pours down and down.

37.

IN THE DREAM, THIS LAST DREAM, I'm playing solitaire in a dark room. It's like an interrogation scene from a movie, a small card table and two chairs, a dim overhanging light. I am comfortable here. I turn the cards over one by one, not making sense of them. Sometimes I see them as little yellow Post-its. I keep turning the cards over: a king of hearts, an ace of spades, and then the note to my mother. *Sorry Mom but I was below empty.*

I lay this card in the discard pile.

Then Ty is there, on the outside edge of the light.

"How did you get in here?" I ask.

"I don't know. It's your dream. You tell me."

He sits in the chair across from me. He doesn't look like a ghost. He seems real. He even looks taller to me, and older, like he's aged during the time he's been gone. He is not quite the Ty I knew.

"Do you remember how to play war?" he asks.

I give him a look like, *Oh, please.*

"You always cheated," he says.

"Did not."

"Did."

I hand him the cards. I watch his long fingers shuffle them easily. He divides the deck into two even piles and gives one to me. Then we begin to lay cards down in threes to fight each other. Higher numbers beat lower. Jack of spades beats nine of diamonds. Five of hearts beats two of spades. Aces beat all. The goal to win the entire deck.

"What do I get if I win?" he asks suddenly. He has just taken three of my cards.

"What do you want?"

"I think," he says without emotion, "that if I win you have to stop watching me die. It's a little morbid."

He takes three more of my cards.

"So what do you want?" he asks. "If you win."

I stare into his hazel eyes. I want to answer that text in time, I think. I want to save you. But underneath it all is: "I want to have a chance to say goodbye. I never got to say goodbye. You didn't give me that."

He exhales a laugh. "Okay. Deal. If you win you can say goodbye."

This seems unlikely. He's winning the game. He has most of the deck. I know it will be over soon, and I am terrified to wake up and never see him again, never be able to talk to him.

"Ty . . ."

"The people we love are never truly gone," he says. "Haven't you learned that?"

"Oh, don't tell me you listen to Dave."

He looks at me steadily and takes another set of my cards. "You did say goodbye to me, you know. Don't you remember?"

"What?"

"That morning. You said come on, I was going to miss the bus. I said one of my friends was going to give me a ride."

"Which was a lie," I add.

"Yes, it was," he admits. "But then you said, 'Okay, see you later,' and I said, 'Love you, sis.' And you said, 'Love you, too, bro. Bye.'"

"I said that?"

"You said that."

I remember. I remember.

And as I sit there, remembering that small single moment in time, I'm suddenly flooded with other memories of Ty.

Good memories.

So many good memories. Building my first snowman in that front yard with Ty. Helping Mom in the garden. Ty trying to eat corn on the cob without the benefit of his two front teeth. Raking leaves with Ty. Teaching him how to drive. Clinging to his arm when we secretly rented *Jurassic Park* when I was twelve. The funny way he laughed. The time he tried to cut his own hair. The male Man. The time when I was four and I dressed him up in my old clothes and put a wig on him and walked him around the neighborhood introducing him as my new sister, Vikki. The way every year

385

on the first day of school Mom had us stand in the same spot on the front porch and she took our picture together, holding hands, year after year after year.

My first day of kindergarten, when he clung to my hand and wouldn't let go when I tried to go off to school without him.

"Take me with you," he begged.

"I can't. You have to stay," I said. "But I promise I'll come back. And then we'll play."

"See?" he says now.

I say, "I miss you. I will always miss you."

"I miss you, too," he says. "For what it's worth."

I lay down a king of clubs, which he takes with an ace, and a ten of diamonds, which he beats with his jack of hearts. I only have one card left.

"Bye, Ty," I whisper.

He smiles and turns his card over.

From the Author

My brother killed himself in 1999. He was seventeen years old and a junior in high school; I was twenty and a junior in college. I miss him every day. Those are the facts.

Having said that, I want to clarify that this novel is a work of fiction. My facts are not the ones that occur in these pages. Ty isn't my brother, and I'm not Lex. I am not a math genius—that much should be obvious. My mom didn't respond to my brother's death by taking up drinking (which would have been a disaster, since my mom is a complete lightweight), my father is not a bored accountant (and he's never graced the deck of a sailboat as far as I know), and my stepmom is not, as Lex phrases it, a walking cliché (my stepmom's actually a book geek, which has served us well over the years). I'd also like to say that, unlike some of Ty's friends in the book, my brother had amazing, thoughtful friends. I've always been thankful for the way our community of friends and neighbors tried to take care of our family in the days after he died, and the way they've continued to show us their love and support in the years since.

So. With the disclaimer out of the way, I have a lot of people to thank for making this book possible:

Erica Sussman. Thank you for laughing at Lex's jokes and crying at Lex's tears and always making sure I had a thorough understanding of what you loved about this story, even when the editing road for this book was long and difficult. You are the most brilliant of editors.

The always-finding-new-ways-to-amaze team at HarperTeen: Stephanie Stein, Christina Colangelo, Kara Brammer, Ray Shappell, Melinda Weigel, Alison Donalty, and Karen Sherman. You make me look good as a writer when most of my real job involves messy hair and yoga pants.

Katherine Fausset. I say this every book, but it continues to be true. You are the best agent a writer could hope for. I'd be adrift in an ocean of doubt without you. Thank you.

My friends:

Amy Yowell. Wow, I have so much in the way of thanks for you I don't even know where to start. For being on my speed dial for math stuff. For your unwavering support of the book and your time reading it and your honest opinion, even though I know it was particularly hard for you to go there. For being the embodiment of a true friend. For driving me home that day.

My Spring ladies: Anna Carey, Veronica Rossi, and Tahereh Mafi. I don't know if this book would exist if not for a late night in Miami when the three of you read my first fifty pages on your phones and had a fierce discussion of what it needed. You made me think and you made me laugh and you rock.

Brodi Ashton. For being there one rainy day in Idaho, even though I didn't know you, and there again one rainy day in Texas thirteen years later, when I did, and there so many days after that. If I have to pick a person to be beside me on a roller coaster in the dark, I'll always pick you.

Jodi Meadows. Thanks for being such a quiet fountain of encouragement. And for taking such excellent notes when I dragged you off to research my session with Miss Penny. I'm so happy to call you my friend.

And finally, my oldest and dearest bestie, Sarah McFarland. The one who takes me to Jamba Juice in the middle of a crisis. The one who's just there, no matter what, no matter how many miles separate us.

My family:

My mom, Carol Ware. Thank you for letting me talk through this time in our lives more this year, even though it hurt. You're always the first person I want to talk to whenever something wonderful or terrible happens, and I'm glad we have that. I love you. I also want to thank Jack Ware, for being very real proof that happy endings are possible even in the saddest of stories.

My dad, Rod Hand. You always tell me that I can do anything, and then you stand back to let me do it. I'm so grateful for that, and I love you.

John. You helped me to understand that, in spite of how

impossible it seemed, I really did have the strength within me to write this novel.

Maddie. Thanks for always wanting me to be the one who sings you to sleep, and for how quickly you learned to say, "I love you too, Mom." I needed that.

Will. My little boy. When you heard I had a brother who died, you went and made a headstone for him out of cardboard in the backyard and put flowers on it. The neighbors might have thought it was a bit morbid. I thought it was the sweetest act of empathy I could imagine, and I love you so much, and it breaks my heart that my brother isn't here to get to know you.

READ EVERY NOVEL
IN THE CAPTIVATING
UNEARTHLY SERIES
by CYNTHIA HAND

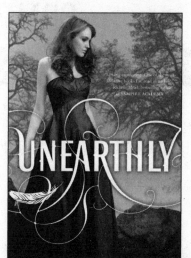

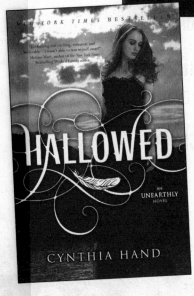

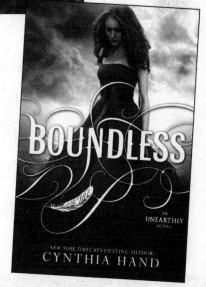